One Last Question

One Last Question

Mike Pattenden

Red Door

Published by RedDoor
www.reddoorpress.co.uk

The author and publisher gratefully acknowledge permissions granted to
reproduce the copyright material in this book

p 69 "I Love It When You Call" Words and Music by Ciaran Jeremiah, Daniel
Sells, Kevin Jeremiah, Paul Stewart and Richard Jones
© 2006 Reproduced by permission of Sony Music Publishing Ltd, London
W1T 3LP

p 78 "All My Friends" Words and Music by James Murphy
© 2007 Guy With Head And Arms Music
All Rights Administered by Kobalt Music Publishing America, Inc
All Rights Reserved Reproduced by permission of Hal Leonard Europe Ltd.

p 178 "Citrus" Words and music by Craig Finn (ASCAP), Tad Jason Kubler
(ASCAP)
© 2006 Reproduced by permission of Reservoir Media Music (ASCAP) obo
itself, Muy Interesante Music (ASCAP) and Key Hits (ASCAP)

p60, p167, p175 p238 Extracts taken from 'The Love Song Of J Alfred Prufrock',
© the Estate of T S Eliot. Poem first appeared in the collection Prufrock And
Other Observations, 1917. Reproduced by permission of Faber & Faber Ltd.

ISBN 978-1-913062-68-2

A CIP catalogue record for this book is available from the British Library

Cover design: Patrick Knowles
www.patrickknowlesdesign.com

Typesetting: Jen Parker, Fuzzy Flamingo
www.fuzzyflamingo.co.uk

Printed and bound in Denmark by Nørhaven

For All My Friends

'I am Lazarus, come from the dead, Come back to tell you all, I shall tell you all.'

T S Eliot

'A sudden bold and unexpected question doth many times surprise a man and lay him open.'

Francis Bacon, 1597

Prologue

Bad Place for a Good Time

The distress flare arrowed through the upstairs bedroom window with an almighty crash, showering sparks everywhere. In the tense silence that gripped the house it sounded like an HGV jackknifing through a greenhouse.

The projectile hit the back wall and dropped smouldering onto the floor, leaking red smoke and hissing furiously. Within seconds the carpet began to take. Jack raced upstairs and flung open the door. Not for the first time tonight he felt a wave of panic. The holiday let was moments away from going up in flames. He stood there dumb-struck; shock had him by the throat and was throttling any rational response out of him.

Offshore, Karen trod water vigorously as she attempted to support Matt and stop him from going under. Meanwhile, Thom was trying to locate them in the freezing seawater, which sparkled like anthracite beneath the star shell. Back on the beach, Damon stood before the crashing surf with the flare gun dangling in one hand while his black mastiff barked into the void.

There had been a few messy moments on previous Boys' Weekends. Five years ago they all went down with food poisoning, prompting synchronised all-night vomiting. Then there was the time a bath overflowed, leaked through a downstairs light fitting, blowing the fuses of the entire house.

The owner could not be contacted, so they spent the rest of the weekend without power. But this was on a different scale. This was a meltdown of epic proportions.

It would have been tempting to blame Will. It was usually Will. Will's dodgy molluscs were the source of the food poisoning and it was Will who left the taps running and passed out on his bed. But this time it seemed unreasonable to hold him to account, not least because he was dead.

Will, who had never had a day off sick in his life and did triathlons. A man who had never smoked a single cigarette but somehow contrived to die at fifty-two. His death had reduced the Boys from six to five. Now that figure looked like it might be cut to four, possibly even three.

Actually no. Will had to take some responsibility because things would likely never have unravelled as spectacularly had they not all had to suffer one final Brainmelter.

Chapter One

The Weekenders

'Looks like you've done us proud again, Will,' said Matt, staring over the steering wheel at an architecturally striking, white-rendered new-build towards the far end of a row of beachfront properties. A hand-painted wooden plate attached to the wall by the front door bore the name 'Ilium'.

'My old dad would have been proud to have knocked this up,' he said picking up a laptop bag from the front seat of a vintage white VW Scirocco Scala. He stepped out of the car, stretched briefly, swung the bag over his shoulder then took a box and a holdall from the boot. He set them on the step, fished out the holiday rental company's set of keys from his pocket and let himself in. The sharp aroma of cleaning fluids hung in the air.

'So, who lives in a house like this?' he said aloud. 'A well-off London family that can afford a second-home status symbol, I'd say.'

Retrieving the box and the holdall, he walked past a hall stand with an anaemic-looking spider plant spilling listlessly out of its pot and stepped into a large, bright kitchen-diner. The front featured cream cabinets and a black quartz kitchen island, the centre was dominated by a large oak table, while comfy chairs filled the rear. Floor to ceiling windows led out to a small garden with a table and chairs. Beyond a low picket

1

gate set into a garden wall lay the beach. The tide was in and the roar of the surf was just audible through the double-glazing. A fresh wind whipped up the waves so they sparkled in the sunlight.

Setting the bags on the island, Matt emptied the box into the fridge, setting a bottle of craft ale to one side. He rummaged through a drawer, extracted a bottle opener, popped the lid and made his way up the stairs carrying his bags.

'Let's grab the best room before it's too late, mate,' he said. 'You don't want to be sharing with any of that lot. They've got nasty habits.'

He glanced around the front of the second floor which had two bedrooms; one a small double, the other two singles. The back had two further large doubles, with en suites, facing onto the beach. Matt chose one, set his bags down and hauled a shutter up. Sunlight flooded the room.

'Not a bad view to wake up to, is it?' he said, gazing at the golden sand that stretched from the back wall to the water's edge.

He swigged greedily from the bottle and took in the view. Below, the beach shelved away gently. Weathered groynes stepped into the water up along the section of coast. Out to sea, a container ship inched across the horizon. A few seagulls wheeled around, framed in an azure sky, their cries piercing the air.

He went to the toilet, took a leak and washed his hands. Peering into the mirror he ran a damp hand through hair shaped in a feather cut concealing ears that stuck out a little too far. Sapphire blue eyes stared back, the skin to their sides cross-hatched with crow's feet.

He inserted a finger into one nostril and examined it. There was dried blood inside. He dampened a finger, ran it around the cavity then rinsed it off, cleared both nostrils into the sink and let the tap run for a moment before exiting the room.

In the bedroom he extracted the laptop from its bag, kicked off his trainers and sprawled onto a double bed covered with a vast duvet that threatened to swallow him up. Lying on one side he flipped up the computer's lid. To his surprise it flickered straight into life. He could have sworn he'd shut it down after checking the video was still there for what must have been the tenth time last night.

Will's face stared back, as if waiting for Matt to say something. He was sitting behind the desk in his study with a small pile of prompt cards in front of him: The Brainmelter, a quiz that was the climax of Saturday night's scheduled entertainment and a ritual part of every Boys' Weekend.

'Hello mate. Just checking you're still there. Yes, I did bag the best room.'

Will stared back, sphinx-like.

'Never seen you so quiet. Most unlike you. Are you sure you're OK? Oh, sorry, you're bloody well dead, aren't you? You selfish bastard! Who said you could do that?'

This was the tenth Boys' Weekend and the first without Will, their chief architect. He chose the location and booked the accommodation. He was invariably first to arrive too, beating everyone to the best room. Instead here they were, paying him posthumous tribute. And doing his infuriating quiz.

***

Shortly after Will's fifty-first birthday he had gone down with a nasty dose of flu. Two months later he was still struggling with it. He suffered from nausea and horrendous night sweats. His normally supercharged energy levels plunged to rock bottom. Finally, his wife, Annie, persuaded him to see a doctor. He was told he was run down. Annie sought a second opinion. Will was diagnosed with acute myeloid leukaemia.

The prognosis was unclear but treatment initially proved effective and he went into remission, but it returned aggressively. Another round of chemo and radiotherapy made him sick but not better. Stem cell therapy failed. When it infiltrated his lymph nodes he was on borrowed time. It was a bitter twist for a man who had literally been yards away from Ground Zero on 9/11 on a business trip. He had queued with thousands to be evacuated by boat as the Twin Towers came down.

Matt had visited his home in Wandsworth a week before Christmas. He looked tired and pale, sitting sipping chugs from a small plastic cup of pink methadone. An end-of-life care nurse hovered in and out before Will waved her away. Matt sat down in a threadbare armchair, sweeping off a few crumbs first. The room was very warm. Sweat began to prick his pores almost instantly.

'Nice to see someone looking worse than me,' said Will acidly.

'At least I've still got a full head of hair,' sneered Matt.

'I checked out a few syrups but couldn't find one that suited me, so I settled for a hat,' said Will tipping a flat, checked cap at a jaunty angle. His voice was croaky, aged before its time.

'Good to see you haven't lost your sense of humour.'

'Good to see you still haven't discovered one. Actually it's a relief to wield it. Annie hates me talking like this. It upsets her, so I've stopped, but it's fucking tiresome. I mean, let's pretend everything's going to be fine, eh?'

'It's impossibly hard for her, Will. She's just trying to shield the kids and soldier on,' said Matt. 'How are you coping?'

'I just... soldier on. I've stopped raging now. It's a waste of energy and it solves nothing. I enjoy the day if I can. Small things. I used to be a complete zen-aphobe, now I'm pure zen. Jazzed. Maybe it's the drugs. You could probably help me there.'

'It's definitely the drugs,' agreed Matt. 'They sound great. Any going spare?'

'You have no shame. Anyway I've been trying to be practical, settle my affairs, that sort of crap. And I've put together a funeral playlist. Choosing the songs you go out to is surely the only good bit about being given due notice. It's a musical last testament. You should do it, you never know when Thanatos plc will text you, notifying you of the delivery of a small lethal package.'

'What's on it?' asked Matt, refusing to be knocked off his stride. 'No, let me have a guess. Robbie's "Angels"? James Blunt's "You're Beautiful"?'

'I'm not using one of your playlists, thanks. You'll have to wait and see.'

'Give me one at least, so I can sing along. "I Should Be So Lucky"?'

Will's chest heaved. 'Don't make me laugh, you bastard!'

'One, just one. So I can nod along and smile knowingly.'

'I thought about Radiohead's "Exit Music" but it's a bit umm, downbeat.'

'To say the least.'

'"Atlantic City". The Hold Steady version.'

'Mmmm, good choice. Out Springsteen's Springsteen. Big, heroic, valedictory.'

'Rousing. Not a dry eye in the house.'

Matt looked away.

'You better not. No one cries. None of my mates, anyway.'

'How are the kids?' Matt asked, changing tack swiftly.

'They're OK. They know, but I'm not sure they've quite

5

grasped it. I wasn't sure I did but it's going to be a relief. I'm out of fight.'

'I'm sorry, Will.'

'You've said that. Nothing to be sorry about. It's just the way the cards fell, the cookie crumbled, the corpuscles divided...'

Will had always had a fatalistic streak in him. Years earlier they had assembled in a pub following news of the death of an old classmate, killed as he walked down the street by a loose roof slate, of all things. He was just twenty-six. They were no longer in touch with him but it was a huge shock, as much because of the random nature of the event than anything else.

'Statistically in a class of thirty, one will be dead by the age of twenty-nine, and two by fifty, after that it's game on for the grim reaper,' Will had casually observed, downing his pint.

And now here they were, six minus one. Reduced. Diminished. Less than the sum of their original parts.

One night they were sitting around playing with the idea of who might be the first to go. Paul topped the list because he could be shockingly clumsy. Co-ordination eluded him frequently so a hedge-trimming accident had to be a possibility. Thom was also in the mix, simply because he rode a motorbike. No one had got on the back with him for three decades because of the speed he drove it. Jack was also in with a chance, Will suggested. He was so profoundly annoying that someone, a random stranger, could easily be tempted to throttle him.

Lately, Matt had to acknowledge, he was making progress up the list. A good-time, party lifestyle had given way to something darker. A nest of viperous thoughts swarmed at him the moment he woke up some days. He had begun taking the black dog for more frequent walks.

On the surface he had a successful career as a food photographer but a passion for taking pictures of quinoa was not the reason he had picked up a camera. The eighteen-year-old Matt would have sneered at his middle-aged, sell-out self. What happened to those much vaunted ambitions to be the next Don McCullin?

Two failed marriages hardly boosted the self-esteem. One could happen to anyone; two made you question your character.

The first, to a redhead from Manchester he'd met at a photoshoot, lasted just over five years. It was blighted by their inability to have a child and resulted in her leaving him for another man. A year after they separated she had had a baby, leaving Matt feeling like a failed reproductive system.

The second marriage was an error of judgement. She was a half-Japanese girl he'd met at a party in a pub in Dulwich. They had both mistaken clubbing and great sex as grounds for a long-term relationship. Once they settled into married life, and she decided to cut back on drink and drugs, they found they had little in common beyond a decent record collection. Eighteen months after they were married she had been headhunted for a marketing job in Manchester, which made the decision easier for her. She accepted the offer while Matt remained in London. He gave it a month before taking the train up to see her for a long weekend. They fell into bed that night, argued the next morning, and agreed to separate over lunch. He came home a day early.

He used to think that a shared passion for music and good taste was the bedrock of a great relationship but it turned out it wasn't enough. Now there was an on-off girlfriend in Putney, a jewellery maker whom Matt liked but definitely did not love. He no longer trusted his judgement. He no longer trusted himself.

The drinking had scaled up and he had gone back to drugs; a habit he'd kicked a decade earlier when he had begun to mess up jobs. Christmas was the perfect time of year to cane it. The whole city was pissed for a month. However he'd had a scare and sworn off the stuff in January. One moment he'd hailed a taxi, the next he was in A&E. Apparently he'd fainted and hit his head on the cab on his way down. When his lips turned blue the cabbie drove him straight to hospital. They patched him up and released him following a stern ticking off about 'life choices'.

Will's passing put an end to abstinence. The day Annie rang him with the news he unscrewed the top from a bottle of Grey Goose languishing in the freezer. The next night they'd all met up. Tears flowed. Drink flowed. And it hadn't stopped since.

It still felt like a choice, something he could step back from. And he would, soon. Probably as soon as the Boys' Weekend was over. No chance of that being restrained. He was usually tempted to add his name to a list of those in need of a liver donation when they were over.

Will was the last person anyone would have identified as a candidate for an early demise. He was fit. He played football for decades and had taken to triathlons in his forties.

It was Will who brought up the next Boys' Weekend the last evening they were together. Matt shrugged, said it was hardly likely to go ahead in the circumstances, but Will wouldn't hear of it. He was determined they should continue in his absence. He said he'd found a place in Camber and booked it for mid-May. All they had to do was turn up. He also announced he had made a video of The Brainmelter, in lieu of his traditional role as quizmaster on the day. Four rounds as per usual: music, film, current affairs and 'Our Life and Times', a segment that focused on moments from their past, events at school, ex-girlfriends, embarrassing moments, that sort of thing.

The Brainmelter had been an integral part of every Boys' Weekend since they'd begun going on them a decade ago. It was Will's idea, a way of providing some evening entertainment, some light relief from baiting each other, trading insults and generally drinking themselves comatose.

'I've burnt it onto disc. Bit old school I know but I'm an old school kinda guy.'

He handed Matt a jewel box with a sticker that read, 'Brainmelter'.

'Put it in your pocket, so you don't forget it.'

Matt did as ordered. He'd copied the video on to his MacBook hard drive the following day just to check it worked, ignoring the temptation to fast-forward through to the answers. He usually came bottom when they did The Brainmelter.

'Have you been partying too hard again?' Will asked, eyeing him. 'I was only half-joking about you looking worse than me.'

'It's Christmas, festive invitations, you know?'

'Not any more. Amazing how quickly you get crossed off the list, and it's very difficult to get a good glass of methadone at parties these days. What's that under your cap, looks like a cut.'

'This?' said Matt touching the cut. The stitches had dissolved. 'Nothing to worry about, just a bit of a fracas.'

'Matt the party animal! That party was over ten years ago, mate. A fracas? Do me a favour! Wake up and take care of yourself,' Will admonished him angrily.

The lecture ended as the nurse entered the room. Will was tiring rapidly. They parted with a weak high five. Matt closed the door gently and headed for the stairs. Now, he was sitting on the bed, looking at the image on the laptop, trying to gauge Will's expression. It was an odd mix of tiredness and determination. The face, nevertheless, of someone in charge, the man who had all the answers, even if they were only for trivia questions. Poor Will. Poor Annie.

His eyes glanced up at the top of the screen. The battery was showing forty-eight per cent. He'd left it on standby overnight. He slid off the bed and rummaged through his bag for the power cable. He began to turn his clothes over agitatedly. Then he emptied the contents on the floor. No power cable. He'd left it at home.

'Oh, you useless pisshead, Matt,' he muttered, kicking a pair of balled-up socks at the wall.

He turned the laptop off, picked up his phone and messaged in the hope a few hadn't left yet.

Urgent: Bring MacBook charger!

He tossed the mobile to one side. If the machine died before they reached the answers it would be such a let-down.

Finishing the beer in one glug, he kicked his trousers off, crawled under the covers and swiftly fell asleep.

Chapter Two

Boys Keep Swinging

The BMW M3 slowed to a crawl as Ed negotiated a large pothole full of muddy water left by a recent deluge. He pulled up just beyond the crater outside a large white house, glanced at a piece of paper on the dash and, satisfied he had the right address, eased the car into the drive, next to the Scirocco. Just a glance at the pristine, architect-designed white-rendered concrete and glass structure was enough to confirm that Will had excelled himself.

He climbed out holding his backpack, extracted a Louis Vuitton holdall from the boot, and made for the door. Heavy-set, bald, with dark-framed spectacles sitting on a saturnine face, Ed was more well-heeled Bob Hoskins than Ray Winstone, but possessed the menace of neither.

A set of keys dangled from the front door lock. Matt was inside, already ensconced in the best bedroom, no doubt. Bastard. Lovely guy, too, obviously. Bit of a lush, but hey. Funny too, but they all were in their own way. No opportunity for a joke was passed up when they were together, however off-colour, and nothing was so mundane that it didn't require a punchline or a bad pun at the very least.

He let himself into the house and put his bag in the hall, then went back to the car, retrieved a box of food and drink from the boot and put it in the fridge. A row of bottles already lay inside, chilling, but it was otherwise devoid of food. He considered opening a beer but thought better of it, instead opening a bag of crisps and stuffing a large fistful into his mouth. He picked up his bag and made for the stairs.

'Hello? Hello? Hands off cocks, on with socks!'

On the first floor he headed for the back of the house and opened the first door abruptly. Matt was lying in bed, spark out.

'Wake up, you tosser! The house is on fire!'

Matt sat up abruptly. 'Sorry, must have dozed off.'

'Pissed already?' Ed picked up the empty bottle and waggled it, accusingly. 'I suppose you nabbed the nicest room?'

'I do apologise, I know you're used to the best. I'll get my bags and move now. As it happens, next door is identical. Lovely view, too. You can almost smell the ozone.'

'I thought it smelt like skunk.'

'Got a bit in my bag. Can you smell it?'

'It's like opening the loft hatch of a Camberwell bedsit.'

'Did you see my text?'

'No, what did it say? "Bring more booze, I've drunk mine already," or "Where do they keep the hash pipe?".'

'I need a power supply for the MacBook. Forgot it.'

'I switched to PCs, better for gaming. What's wrong with your phone?'

'Nothing, but it's not much use for showing Will's video.'

'Oh, that. Are we really going to go ahead with that ghoulish charade?'

'It's not charades, it's a quiz. And of course we are. He put a lot of energy into it. It would be a crime not to. Now if you'll excuse me while I use my en suite,' Matt disappeared through the door.

Ed left to commandeer the room next door. There he sat heavily on the bed and began to check his mobile for messages. Nothing, besides the one from Matt which he'd ignored while he was driving. He resisted the temptation to ring Amber, his wife and the finance director of their mobile games company. He was determined to try and switch off for a couple of days.

He went to the bathroom and began to urinate. His eyes widened in horror.

'Jesus H!'

The water had turned pink. He could feel panic rising. Blood. Cancer. Was he next? His mind raced for a diagnosis and came up with a solution. He breathed an audible sigh of relief. Beetroot. Amber had brought a carton of beetroot juice on a health whim. He'd had some at breakfast that morning. Never again. Will's passing had sprinkled intimations of mortality everywhere. Reassured, he zipped up, flushed and wandered back next door. Matt had climbed back into bed.

'Where is it then?'

'What?'

'The video. Let's see what it looks like.'

'You can't. There's less than half the battery left. It has to wait till everyone's here before we run it now.'

'I just want to see what he looks like,' said Ed flipping up the lid.

'Don't, we may need every bit of juice if no one brings a charger.'

'It's going to feel very, very fucking weird watching it.'

'Some things you just have to do. Like going to the funeral. Which you didn't.'

'You know full well I couldn't. I didn't want to miss it, it was a horrible choice but I had to go to the States. I wouldn't have gone if it wasn't vital.'

'Of course not. LA couldn't possibly be more important than saying goodbye to a mate.'

'Look,' said Ed, his irritation rising. 'You work in an artsy business where you can do what the fuck you like. I have people who rely on me for their jobs.'

'Yeah, well, it was a shame and don't pretend you haven't been avoiding us since. Solidarity helped everyone through what was a very difficult day. Your absence was noted by Annie, too. We made your excuses.'

'I sent her my apologies personally, thanks,' said Ed, walking out and slamming the door.

The church had been rammed for the funeral. Not just with family but lots of people the Boys didn't recognise, work friends and colleagues. They were forced to share Will with people who didn't know him. Not enough to really, really care. What did staff and ad agency people know about Will?

The four of them had a pew to themselves just as they used to at school. They shared a couple of sheets titled 'Disorder of Service' and sang the hymns too loudly, prompting other mourners to turn round and stare.

Will's brother, John, gave the eulogy. He told sibling stories about Will always breaking windows playing games in the garden, putting a dead mouse in the microwave, and a family holiday when he'd been sick into the hotel swimming pool after helping himself to a jug of sangria. His aged mother sat ashen-faced in the front row next to Annie and the children.

Matt agreed, after some pressure, to do a reading. He took the lectern, trying not to fix on anyone, and began to read Dylan Thomas's 'Do not go gentle into that good night'. It was Will's favourite poem. Matt would ring sometimes and ask idly what he'd been doing and Will would say, 'Raging, mate, raging against the dying of the light.'

He had every right to be furious now.

When the funeral playlist began to play, tears flowed despite Will's insistence that none be shed. He slid off to

Smog's "Dress Sexy At My Funeral", a typically mordant twist that appalled older members of the congregation, then, when it was all done and dust they left to the strains of Springsteen's "I'm On Fire", surely Will's darkest joke ever. And that from a man who changed his employer to 'Death' on LinkedIn knowing people would receive reminders on his work anniversary. Few in the room knew how to deal with it. Matt wiped an eye and smiled at the ground.

The Boys went to Will's house after the service for the sake of face. Annie was running around keeping herself busy, but making polite conversation with Will's family and other friends was too much effort, so they'd removed to a nearby pub as quickly as possible. They didn't want to share stories about Will with anyone else. Their world was hermetically sealed and their stories were theirs alone.

'Do you remember that party in Kensington?' asked Matt downing a chaser with his pint. In a moment of perfect symbiosis the pub jukebox dropped Thin Lizzy's "The Boys Are Back In Town".

'Who could forget,' said Paul. 'No?'

'I remember,' said Thom. 'I thought we were going to spend the night in the cells.'

They had been at some rather posh girl's party on the top floor of a big townhouse in Kensington when Will had suddenly tipped a bucket of water out of the window onto a policeman who had arrived to deal with a complaint about the noise. It was another classic Will moment. Spontaneous and reckless, something none of the others would have dared do. They had made a hasty escape down the fire exit at the back of the house before the party was broken up and sang Pogues songs all the way home on the night bus, encouraging other passengers to join in.

Incidents like this formed part of their personal folklore

and they guarded it jealously. Naturally each had his own social circle but they rarely mixed them together. When someone from outside the group appeared – a work colleague or old uni friend – it unbalanced the evening. They were too tight-knit. Exclusive.

One night Ed brought along a workmate from the software company where he was head of production before he launched his own business. The chap seemed pleasant enough at first but after a few drinks he began making off-colour remarks about 'slags' and 'poofs', secure he was on a boys' night out. It was the height of laddism, so he may have been trying to blend in, but Will shut him down brutally.

'Mate, if you hate women and you don't like queers, what's left? A lifetime's onanism, I'd wager?'

Ed looked a little embarrassed. His friend wasn't entirely sure what Will meant but he had enough sense to know he was being insulted. He glanced at his watch and realised he had a train to catch.

It wasn't as if none of the Boys ever made a politically incorrect remark, far from it. But different rules applied. They all knew where they stood.

People were always surprised to find that six men who had met at primary school had stuck together for over forty years but it was completely unremarkable to them. Wives and girlfriends had to put up with the gang ethic and the in-jokes. And, despite their political correctness, it was hard to pretend there was not a whiff of the 'gentleman's club' about them. When they went out, the women were rarely invited and when they did attend without prior notice it was regarded as something of an intrusion. WAGs nights had to be sanctioned and usually received clearance for special occasions like birthdays and Christmas.

It was less about sexism than collective narcissism, a sense of superiority born not of snobbery but self-satisfaction. Each validated the other, in turn. Together they were wittier, cooler and smarter than anyone. They were the Boys, a gang of over-confident permateens; a rock band with no back catalogue. It was no coincidence that they'd spent their teens and twenties posing in leather jackets and long overcoats as if they were shooting an album cover. There was an entire portfolio of moody, pouty black and white images of earnest young men lolling against brick walls or gazing existentially out to sea, much of it taken by Matt with his first camera.

* * *

The sun had warmed the bedroom. Matt pulled on a pair of navy shorts and wandered downstairs to the kitchen where the kettle was boiling.

'Enough in there for two cups?'

'Only if you put those away,' said Ed, nodding at his bare legs.

'Just because you came straight from the golf club. How's your swing?'

'I don't play golf. I don't have time for golf. And those legs look like two bits of uncooked pastry hanging out of your shorts.'

Ed handed Matt a mug of tea and sat at the kitchen counter with a sleek, matt black laptop. He clicked a few keys and an electric piano struck up a lazy groove before it was joined by drums. A saxophone stepped in with a breezy five note melody.

'Sounds exotic,' noted Matt.

'Cannonball Adderley. "Mercy, Mercy, Mercy". I've entered my jazz phase.'

'You groovy old bastard.'

'The way I see it, pop music is programmed shite these days and rock music is a spent force. This may not be new but it sounds new to me,' said Ed, sipping from the cup. 'Those bop era musicians were taking jazz to new places, they were pushing the envelope and they were cool.'

'And smackheads to a man. I wonder what it was that sent them to heroin?' pondered Matt, blowing his tea. 'I s'pose it was the drug of choice then but free jazz was totally up its own arse. Smack would be mutually compatible with that.'

'I'm not trying to get to grips with the out-there modal stuff yet. I haven't got a clue whether it's any good but you can't argue that those guys could play. It's like unlearning all the rules. Painters used to compose accurate portraits of women then Picasso came along and painted 2D tits. It's the gamechangers that make everyone reconsider their viewpoint. Anyway what's not to like about this?'

'Absolutely nothing.'

Matt fished a pack of Bourbons from a cupboard and bit into one, carefully testing its freshness, before handing the pack to Ed.

'No thanks. Despite, actually because of, what I look like, I've cut back on the sugar massively,' said Ed switching the track to some Mingus. 'Sugar is the new smack, you know? Haven't you read about all those contemporary jazz artists and their chronic sugar habit? They actually buy it in lumps and drop it into their tea. The problem is so widespread, they're selling it in packets on street corners.'

Matt wandered round the kitchen opening cupboards with a critical eye.

'It's pretty well kitted out for a holiday home.'

'The artwork is a bit crap. The sort of thing you get from a warehouse chain.'

'Not everyone can afford a Damien Hirst like you, Ed.

Why not leave them a bad review on Tripadvisor: "To our utter dismay the house was full of cheap chain store prints that totally detracted from its magnificent beachside setting".'

'Good idea,' agreed Ed, tapping the keyboard cartoonishly. '"I was disappointed by the lack of thought that had gone into finishing the property. It showed little regard for aesthetic taste or delight in the finer things in life. On top of that the selection of DVDs contained not a single subtitled foreign language movie. One star".'

'Not to mention the total absence of 2D tits,' added Matt.

'Anyone in?' sang a voice from the hall.

Jack stood in the doorway holding a vintage suitcase, like an extra from *Brief Encounter*. With his slender frame, high cheekbones and short, sandy hair he looked a good ten years younger than his age. He was wearing a red checked, short-sleeve shirt, slim cut navy chinos and grey canvas trainers. He had casual-stylish nailed but was one of those men who managed to look like he had merely pulled on the first things that came to hand.

'Is this the rest home for middle-aged beatniks?'

'No, this is the local crack den mate,' said Ed, rapidly flicking from Mingus to Biggie Smalls.

'Excellent! Let's fire up a pipe and get the weekend going in style!' boomed Jack in a big, plummy voice.

'Smoking isn't it? Ed's entered his boho phase,' said Matt.

'Good for him. What a fabulous place. He's done us proud again, hasn't he? Great view of the sea! Anyone fancy a dip?'

Matt put down his cup. 'You're not serious, are you? The sun may be out but it's not Barbados, despite the golden sand and complete absence of black faces out there. You'll freeze.'

'Bah! Just a brisk dip. Good for the soul.'

'Yeah, so were cold showers and buggery at one time, apparently.'

'I'm going to put on my cossie. Anyone who wants to join me is welcome.'

Matt shook his head. 'I think on balance I'd prefer not to get hypothermia.'

Jack ran upstairs, reappearing a few minutes later in shorts and T-shirt. A towel hung round his neck.

'Come on then, you pair of absolute ponces.'

Matt and Ed looked at each other, shrugged and followed him through the back of the house, out of the garden gate and down the beach towards the sea. A couple walked past followed by an old, overweight mongrel with silver chops. Bits of seaweed blew up the beach, a Styrofoam cup flew up as if thrown by an unseen hand. They reached the water's edge and Jack handed Matt the towel and began to strip off. Underneath his clothes he was wearing a stripy one-piece, prompting gales of laughter from the other two. He adopted a strongman pose.

'Right! No one else then? Not up to it? Very well!'

He marched into the water. 'Christ on a bike!'

Matt and Ed laughed louder. Jack began to run, whooping before plunging into the water with a howl. He then began to thrash about, performing a variety of frantic swimming strokes in four feet of water.

'It's lovely once you're in! You should try it. Really. Oh mother! Dear God, please help me!'

He began to scream comically.

Ed picked up a large pebble and lobbed it in his direction. It dropped into the water with a loud plop rather closer than he'd intended.

'Oi! I'd rather not get brained by a rock, thanks,' said Jack coming to a halt.

'If I wanted to hit you, I would have,' said Ed stepping further away. He looked carefully in the sand, fished out a flat stone and skimmed it across the water. Matt joined him. Their stones skipped off whipped crests of water.

There was another strangled howl. This time Jack was hopping up and down in the water making noises of genuine distress.

'That was nowhere near you,' said Ed indignantly.

'No, I think something bit me!' Jack began hobbling towards the shore.

'They get weever fish here, I read about it,' observed Matt helpfully.

'Maybe it was a great white?' suggested Ed.

'Skinny white in his case.'

Jack limped out of the water and slumped to the ground. He grabbed his foot and attempted to examine the damage.

'Look, it's bleeding,' he said holding his foot aloft. 'I can feel it swelling up, too. I think I feel sick.'

'Let's have a proper look before we call out the air ambulance, eh?' suggested Ed.

Jack held his foot up.

'Can't see a thing, your feet are all sandy. We need to clean it up indoors and have a proper look.'

'I can't very well walk back, can I?' protested Jack.

Matt and Ed looked at each other, and with a collective sigh made a chair with their arms.

'Get on, you big girl,' said Ed.

Jack slumped pathetically between them. Ed and Matt did a swift 180 and staggered up the beach to the house, with Jack whining in their ears.

Chapter Three

The Boy with the Thorn in His Side

Damon watched the three-ring circus stagger back to the house with sour amusement. His upper body appeared to be constructed from breeze-blocks of muscle stacked against each other. Tube-like veins snaked down the sides of his shaven head into his neck and threaded like industrial wiring into biceps and pectorals. His skin was a relief map of muscular hills and meat valleys, overlaid with purple tributaries.

A black-coated mastiff cross, sitting obediently by his feet, barked at the farcical scene as if offended. It appeared almost as hypertrophied as its owner.

'I know mate, I know. Complete and utter shambles.'

His eyes followed the trio as they reached the garden, whereupon Jack dismounted and hopped through the gate, followed by Matt and Ed.

With the beach now empty, Damon trebucheted a tennis ball into the stratosphere with a snap of his hand. It instantly became a tiny dot against a blue background before dropping back to the beach not far from where Jack had required medical support.

'Fetch.'

The dog gave him a bemused look, as if to say, 'Throw it, then!'

'Fetch, you daft animal!' urged Damon, incredulously.

The dog stared back at him blankly.

'There!'

Damon stabbed a finger down the beach in exasperation.

The dog trotted a few feet in the direction of his pistol finger but the ball had merged into a sand-hole.

'Drogba. You're fucking useless, mate. But at least you're loyal and you do what you're told, which is more than can be said for most people,' he said, ruffling its head. 'Let me show you how it's done.'

He strode towards the spot and rapidly located it.

'Watch and learn, Drogs,' he said, leaning down to pick the day-glo ball up in his teeth. The dog darted forward.

'No you don't. My ball,' said Damon grabbing it with his hand and waving it about. The dog made a lunge for the ball. Damon seized the dog by the collar and man and beast fell to the ground in a wrestling match before he finally let the ball go. The dog darted off with it clamped triumphantly in his jaws and did circles.

'You win, then,' said Damon, dusting himself off. 'Hello, what's this?'

He bent down and picked up a black leather wallet lying in the sand just a few feet away. It was swollen, bulging with bank cards, receipts and a sizeable wad of cash.

'Woah there's some wedge in here, Drogba,' he muttered. He skimmed through the cards and extracted a driving licence. Ed's bespectacled features stared out.

'Looks like one of those useless tossers. Come on, let's see if matey wants his money back. Maybe he doesn't need it.'

They walked up the beach to the back gate of the house. Damon opened it, strolled through the patio garden and up to large double doors which stood open.

'Hello? Hello? Anyone in?' He tapped a gold ring on double-glazed glass and peered in.

Jack lay contorted on the couch examining his foot. Ed was watching him with amusement. Matt had run upstairs to search the bathroom.

'Lost something?' asked Damon, waving the wallet into the room.

Ed span round. Jack put his foot down, self-consciously.

'Oh, hang on,' said Ed, feeling in his back pocket. 'Shit, maybe. Yes, yes. Where was it?

'On the beach where you were fannying about,' said Damon. 'What's yer name?'

'Ed Simmons.'

'Then it is yours. Looks like your boat on the driving licence, too. You wanna be a bit more careful with all that cash in there; not everyone round here is honest,' said Damon tossing him the wallet.

Ed fumbled it, retrieved it hastily and opened it to examine the contents.

'It's all there, you don't have to fucking check,' snapped Damon.

'Of course, I didn't mean to imply it wasn't,' said Ed, shamed. 'Can I give you something for your trouble?'

'No mate, on the house. And very nice it is, too. Actually, tell you what, make a donation to Help for Heroes.'

'I will. Definitely.'

'Safe. Right, must be off. Enjoy your stay, gentlemen,' Damon ducked out before Ed could say any more, walked back through the garden and turned left for home.

Less than a hundred yards up he stepped through a gap in the beach wall and crossed over to his house, letting the garden gate swing shut behind him. Where many properties on this stretch of gravel road behind the beach had been extended or rebuilt as second homes or holiday lets, Damon's abode held little kerb appeal. Its brown window frames were

24

peeling. Paint flaked away from its filthy cream walls leaving large, eczemad patches. No work had been done on it since his mum's death three years ago. The house now belonged to him and his younger sister, Karen. She didn't have the time to do it up, he didn't have the inclination. He preferred it to look shabby. It attracted less attention.

Across the main road, a vast holiday camp lined with rows of static white caravans resembled the cells of an insect colony, a huge leisure superorganism. Damon used to play hide and seek among them in the off-season when he was a kid. As a teenager he had a holiday job there working with the maintenance team. He lost his virginity under one with a girl from Streatham. Happy days.

He strode up the front path, past a small shed, and breezed through the front door into the kitchen. Drogba galloped after him.

He paused to down a glass of water before going through to the living room where Karen was sitting in front of the TV in her dressing gown doing a crossword.

'Clueless,' she said without looking up. 'Two and four letters.'

The dog padded to a large bed by the fireplace and flopped down, exhausted. A large Ragdoll cat called Ossie, curled up on the sofa next to Karen, slept on oblivious.

'No idea,' he strode past her and up the stairs.

Priceless. She smiled quietly to herself.

Damon made his way to the spare room at the back of the house that he referred to as the Roid Room in his head. A workbench ran round three walls. One side was arranged as a mini production line featuring scales, jars of powder, mixing tubs, hotplate and a stamping machine. The opposite bench contained a computer, printer, racks of easy assemble cardboard boxes and jiffy bags. Either side of the window stood a couple of large glass tanks. On the left, the bigger of the two contained three dwarf hamsters huddled among heaps of straw. On the right a more expensive terrarium contained a large Brazilian giant whiteknee tarantula, squatting by a small log.

'Alright JT, how you doing?' said Damon putting his face to the glass. The arachnid remained motionless. Its inertness gave the impression it was fake but it had a bite like a pair of pliers. Damon sniffed loudly and turned to the packing bench where he went to work, inserting phials and pill bottles into small boxes, which then went into Jiffy bags bearing printed address labels, ticking off names from a list as he went. Each phial or pill bore the Ironman logo, the brand he had settled on for the DIY steroid business that had replaced the carpet-laying trade he'd embarked upon following his discharge from the army.

He'd joined The Rifles at eighteen in 2005, after a couple of years knocking around Camber working for various local builders and maintenance companies doing up houses in Rye. His timekeeping was poor, he lacked commitment and often did not turn up for work. Bosses let him go. His uncle Terry, his mother's brother, a former corporal with the Royal Fusiliers ventured down from Nottingham at her behest to give him the talk about joining up. Damon was non-committal, but signed papers a few months later. It may have had something to do with a dispute with a local scaffolder over a parking space that turned nasty. Blows had been exchanged, leading to threats of revenge.

Two years later he found himself stationed in Basra Palace, Iraq. Things had been calm in the early stages of the conflict with local people happy to have the British there, but those days were long gone by the time Damon's posting arrived.

The men in his regiment were a solid enough bunch.

Damon was particularly close to an older, more experienced squaddie, Colin 'Treggers' Treggarick, a Cornishman. Treggers had been a fitness trainer before joining up. He'd seen service in Sarajevo, knew the drill, and kept an eye out for Damon who was both naive and gung ho. They spent their downtime packing muscle, discussing their dreams and making each other laugh. Meanwhile, the 'liberation' was rapidly turning sour. The Allies were now the oppressors and a boiling resentment had broken out between sectarian militias.

Soon the building was under siege from insurgents, night and day. Mortars and rockets regularly fell into its grounds. Armoured patrols were subjected to incessant fire the moment they left the gates. IEDs were triggered at repeated intervals. Every local was soon treated as a potential suicide bomber.

One Sunday morning, Damon was part of an APV patrol that broke down a couple of miles from base. It immediately drew fire from every hostile in the vicinity. Another APV was sent to tow them back to base but was hit by a rocket the moment it arrived. In a frantic rescue effort several more vehicles were mobilised to pull both vehicles out as the insurgents closed in. One was towed back, the other had to be left behind in a fierce firefight in which British firepower was just enough to see off the opposition.

Later that night, Damon revelled in the action but, in truth, he had been half terrified. A couple of days later he was due to join a night patrol but mid-afternoon he began to feel dizzy and sick. Viruses circulated the camp as easily as the flies. He lay in his bunk-bed shivering and was soon vomiting. When he was discovered missing, Treggers was sent to locate him.

'I'm throwing up, mate,' he gasped. 'Got a fever.'

'Get yourself to sickbay then, Damo. Cover yer arse, boy, I'll take your seat,' he said tapping him on the arm.

The evening patrol was hit by an IED buried in rubbish less than a hundred yards from the palace. One man died instantly, two more were badly injured. One was Treggers whose legs took the force of the blast. The casualties were flown out by helicopter as Damon slept the fever off. Sergeant Vickers walked into sickbay in the middle of the night and woke him with a shove. 'Your mate's legs are in bits. They've flown him out and he probably won't survive. You dodged that bullet, didn't you, son?' He turned around and left without another word.

For the rest of the night Damon was tortured by nightmares in which he tried to gaffer-tape Treggers' bloody limbs back on to his butchered torso. A few days later he was informed his friend had pulled through but would never walk again. Double amputation.

His command abandoned the palace a month later, not before more casualties. Damon witnessed another member of his squad virtually eviscerated by shrapnel. The retreat was inevitable. His regiment was stationed at a new base in Basra airport, which was more secure and less exposed. Nevertheless, he watched a Lynx helicopter downed by a ground-to-air missile just a few hundred metres from base in his first week there. The handful of guerrillas responsible were long gone by the time they arrived at the location. Three months later his tour came to a welcome end.

Back home, on leave, he went out and drank himself paralytic. The next night he met a couple of other squaddies from the Queen's Lancashire Regiment, also recently returned from Iraq. They shared war stories and laughed at the sheer madness of it all. Damon didn't bring up Treggers. Later, they went clubbing and he took ecstasy for the first time. It was like someone had pulled him into a big, warm hug. It filled the bottomless hole that had opened up in Basra. He sought more. Two months later he failed a drugs test. Ecstasy was discovered concealed in his washbag and his discharge was almost instant. One minute he was in barracks, the next he was on civvy street. No one bothered to ask why he had taken to drugs and he offered no defence.

Damon returned to Camber but kept the truth from his mum and polished up his war stories in the bars around town where everyone was ready, at least initially, to buy him a drink.

After a few months he began to feel better about himself. He imagined he'd put the army and the carnage behind him and moved out to a flat in Pinner where he joined a carpet-laying business owned by Lee, a former member of his regiment. His life settled into a comforting routine. They won a good contract with a local carpet warehouse and Damon spent much of his downtime in the gym. His body became an obsession and sculpting it took up hours of his time. The army had turned him into a gym rat but dysmorphic dreams took him towards obsession.

He graduated to bodybuilding and discovered steroids. He knew about them and had never considered them necessary, but he was looking for more and more bulk. He was pushing himself towards human perfection, a state his friend would never enjoy. He dreamed of running his own fitness centre. Eventually he parted ways with Lee following an argument about timekeeping.

At a loose end, he plucked up the courage to visit Treggers who now lived with his parents in a specially adapted house on an estate just outside Truro. It was an awkward encounter, although his comrade appeared to bear him no ill will, despite his circumstances. He had spent six months in hospital and twelve in a rehab unit. More operations would be necessary.

Damon looked at the ramps outside the house and nearly went home. Instead he knocked. Treggers flung open the door with a smile and they had an awkward hug. They sat down with a cuppa and some cake Treggers' mum had baked and talked about anything but that day. Damon could see his disappointment at the discharge but there was no condemnation. He managed to stay half-an-hour before excusing himself. Treggers understood. He wheeled to the door in his wake. As Damon opened it, he turned round and hesitated.

'I'm so, so sorry mate,' he said with a sigh that sounded like a sob.

'It wasn't you that did it, son, was it?' Treggers shrugged. 'Some naughty Arab boys did it and ran away.'

'I know, but I feel like I deserted you.'

'Bollocks, you were sick. Did you want your legs blown off, too?'

'No, but...'

'Well be grateful, son. I'm here like this and it's just the way it is. I'm lucky to be alive, apparently. And there's always the Paralympics, eh?'

Damon smiled mirthlessly, gave him a salute and closed the door behind him. He walked back to the station in a daze, bought a half-bottle of Scotch in a tiny off-licence en route, drank it before the train arrived and slept the whole way back to London.

Not long after, a Pole called Andrezj who ran a no-frills gym Damon used to frequent under railway arches in Deptford, beckoned him into an office that had its windows taped over with newspapers. They had a tentative discussion about the pros and cons of steroids, then Andrezj showed Damon how to make T-Up pills using powdered testosterone purchased online from China. He demonstrated how to mix it with soya oil, then how to add benzyl benzoate and benzyl alcohol to sterilise the batch and heat the formula on a hotplate. The science was basic but demand was high and Andrezj was looking to take on an assistant.

'You don't need GCSE in chemistry to make this stuff,' he explained. Though a GCSE in science was one of only three Damon possessed. He proved to be a master apprentice, even making little refinements with herbs and spices.

But Andrezj was careless. He sold a batch to an undercover police officer and was sent down for two years. Duly schooled in the art of steroid manufacture, Damon moved back to Camber to live with his ailing mother, Carol. The spare room became his lab. The Roid Room.

Damon traded online only, through a closed Facebook account. All payments from the bodybuilders and martial artists who made up the bulk of his customers were channelled through an offshore account. Any cash, which some people insisted on sending regardless, was squirreled away in a safe box under the shed outside. On the last day of every month he sent Treggers an envelope containing £200 in cash with no accompanying note.

In the three years since its launch, Ironman had proved lucrative. Social media was the gift that kept on giving. He lived comfortably. He had bought a black Mercedes X-Class truck and a share in a holiday apartment in Marbella. One day, sooner rather than later, he'd retire out there.

Trade was ticking over nicely but Damon was sweating on the delivery of a new batch of chemicals. If they didn't arrive by midweek at the latest he was going to run out. He popped a pill, washing it down with the rest of the water. He was cycling again, packing muscle onto muscle.

'Hell yeah!' he hollered, banging down the glass. Instantly he probed his chest with his right hand. No bitch

31

tits, thank you very much. Stacking was the key here. He went back to work. There were fifty packages to post before close of play.

Downstairs, Karen folded over the newspaper and tossed it to one side. She was three clues short of completing the cryptic crossword she did a few times a week to prove to herself she hadn't gone completely thick living in this place.

She heard Damon shout and winced. He made her nervous these days. His dubious sideline along with increasingly erratic behaviour had forced her to confront the thing she'd been putting off for too long – sorting out her life. She had a degree in zoology yet had spent nearly ten years doing low-paid jobs that bore no relation to it. Six years ago she had become the carer for her mum, following her dementia diagnosis. Carol begged Karen not to come back but Karen wouldn't hear of it.

'You're the one with the brains, you should be concentrating on your career after all that education,' she advised her more than once. Soon she forgot what Karen had studied. Eventually she couldn't remember who she was.

The old woman, not that old actually, managed almost three years at home before she had to go into care. Karen stayed on, visiting twice a week. Carol died from a stroke six months later and the house had gone to Karen and Damon.

Job options locally were slim unless you fancied being a cleaner or an entertainer in one of the holiday camps. For the past eighteen months she'd been a swimming instructor at the local sports centre. In the summer months she did shifts as a lifeguard. The new season had commenced two weeks ago.

To give Damon some credit he paid the bills, but Karen earned so little there wasn't a great deal of choice. She would much rather they split the place and go their separate ways but that was never going to happen while he had his little gig going. He'd refused her suggestion that he buy her out, at a bargain price too.

The only option left was to disappear. She'd been working on a plan for six months, saving carefully, and it was time to put it into action.

Chapter Four

Who Knows Where the Time Goes

At the far end of the road, triage was in process.

Jack had gone to shower while the others sat downstairs making jokes at his expense. He limped back into the kitchen fifteen minutes later.

'I can't see the damage properly it's on my sole.'

'You ain't got no soul, brotha,' said Matt.

'Sit on a stool and hold your foot up, you big jess,' demanded Ed.

When Jack complied, he examined the bottom of his foot, taking his glasses off and squinting at a small red mark.

'There's no spines sticking out, or teeth marks. It's just a cut.'

He put his thumbs together and squeezed the wound.

Jack yelped. 'What the fuck?!'

'Nope, can't see anything. I reckon you just stood on a small bit of glass. It could do with some antiseptic cream and a kiss. Weever fish, you arse!'

'It felt like a bite, I'm telling you. And I thought I saw something in the water.'

'Probably a condom,' suggested Matt.

Ed went up to his room and came back down with a plaster.

'Best I can do. Had a look in their bathroom cabinets.

Nothing to clean a wound. We could stitch it with needle and thread, there's some in the kitchen drawer.'

'Fuck off, you will.'

'I've got the solution,' Matt dashed upstairs and returned holding a bottle of Scotch.

'I'm not in that much pain,' Jack protested.

'Isle of Jura, single malt. For medicinal purposes only, of course, and consequently perfect for an emergency like this. Give me your foot.'

'No way! It'll burn like acid!'

'Do you want it to get infected? Come on, man up.'

Reluctantly, Jack lifted his foot.

'Lie on your back and lift your foot up so I can pour it accurately. I'm not wasting a drop more than I have to.'

Jack hesitated, then lay down and assumed the position. Ed giggled.

Matt carefully poured amber liquid into the cut.

Jack howled.

Matt and Ed howled.

'Keep your foot up,' shouted Matt, holding it tightly as Jack squirmed.

'Jesus burger-flipping Christ! That stings like a bitch!'

Shaking with laughter, Matt wiped it carefully with a clean tea-towel and applied the plaster. Ed brushed away tears.

'There. All done. Who's a brave soldier, then?' he said, taking a generous swig from the bottle.

A voice came from the hall.

'I can hear screaming, what's up? Are you being tortured by burglars? If so I'm going straight back home.'

Thom was standing in the doorway wrapped tightly in a Belstaff jacket. He held a helmet in one hand and a leather backpack in the other. Like Jack he was in good shape for his years. He was the tallest of them, trim, with silvery hair and a finely clipped goatee. Had Robert Redford's Sundance Kid managed to settle down in Bolivia and lived to be fifty, he might have looked a bit like Thom. A silver fox with a stylist.

'Has he got cramp?'

'He's been speared by a narwhal,' explained Matt. 'Though I've seen him just as distressed when he spilt coffee on his white Fred Perry polo shirt.'

'Actually, he was attacked by a school of piranhas swept into the English Channel by a tsunami,' Ed corrected him.

'I was swimming and I stood on a piece of glass left by some anti-social twat,' spat Jack.

'Serves you right for going in the sea. Treacherous place. Didn't some people die here a year or two ago?

'Yes, shark attack, I recall,' agreed Matt.

'They got stuck in quicksand a long way out when the tide turned,' said Jack, rolling back to his feet and hobbling to a chair.

'The tide was high. But they weren't holding on,' suggested Thom. 'Before I kick off my boots and get back to my roots I need to get some booze in, not enough room in the panniers. Anyone fancy accompanying me?'

'We could do with more coffee,' said Ed. 'There's bound to be a supermarket up the road.'

'I'm not going anywhere,' said Jack grumpily. 'Anyway, someone needs to be here to let in Paul when he eventually materialises.'

'Suit yourself, Captain Miserable,' said Ed, picking up his keys. 'What time is he due?'

'Not sure. Said he was leaving after work. Should take what, a few hours from Hastings on two wheels? If you're shit and old, that is. Anyone else could do it in half that.'

Paul, last to arrive, as usual, was perhaps the least obvious member of the Boys. His rigorously rational disposition – Jack always maintained that he was 'on the spectrum' – sometimes gave the impression he was humourless but he could be deliciously droll. He was frequently the butt of the others' jokes, a role he had filled since school, but he played the part well and, subtly, gave as good as he got. He was gentle, considerate and restrained, a useful check to the others, especially Jack and Matt.

He also had the most long-standing and stable relationship of the Boys in the shape of a twenty-five-year marriage to a Brazilian woman called Francisca who nurtured his spiritual inquisitiveness and generally doted on him. The couple had a grown-up son, Lucas.

'Right, hold the fart,' said Ed sweeping out of the room. 'If you're staying here you might order some fish and chips. Probably wise on a Friday with the barbarian hordes camped at the gates.'

'Ed. Marching on his stomach again,' said Jack.

Thom blew Jack a kiss as they filed out. Jack pulled a sour smile like a child told to be good.

Outside, Ed eased the ice-white Beamer between the Scirocco and Thom's bike and they rolled slowly along the track, gravel crunching and popping beneath the tyres. Another new-build was going up in the middle of the row between two shabbier properties. At the far end, just before the main road, a glowering black pick-up was parked incongruously in the drive of a run-down house.

Turning left, they drove away from the holiday camp, past a row of shops and a grim 1970s pub with torn net curtains hanging in its windows. A piece of cardboard was taped over a hole in one corner. A little further up, they found themselves by a couple of shops and a small local supermarket. Ed pushed on in search of somewhere with more choice than 'Foster's and Lambrusco'.

'Why, why, would you come on holiday here?' asked Thom, having an attack of middle-class vapours.

'Not everyone possesses your impeccable taste and fine breeding, Thom,' replied Matt, whose dad had been a builder, albeit a successful one with a large, detached house.

'True, but you can bag a package holiday to Lanzarote for a couple of hundred quid. A caravan in Camber? I mean, it's a lovely beach but there's not much else round here, is there?' noted Thom. 'Apart from a million other caravans.'

'You are now entering Brexit country,' said Ed in a grave voice as they rolled past a house flying the flag of St George.

'For God's sake don't mention the B word round Paul,' said Matt, alarmed. Paul's Marxist principles were at odds with the EU, which marked him out among the rest of the group. Arguments had raged for years until Will had banned the subject in impolite company.

'Gentlemen,' he had declared holding his hand up during one particularly heated discussion. 'We must respect Paul's opposition to the European experiment and the fact he is a raging Trot. But I do not wish to hear another fucking word about it when we're together. It's a complete waste of good drinking time. When he's not here,' he said pointing at Paul, 'we can have a reasoned discussion and behave like the liberal metropolitan elite that we are. Otherwise Brexit is henceforth banned.'

And so the topic remained off limits.

Matt surveyed the car's pristine interior. It had a new smell about it. The sound-system cranked out the insistent percussive clatter of The National's "Bloodbuzz Ohio".

'How long have you had this toy then?'

'Oh, about six months.'

'You must be doing well.'

'OK,' said Ed, giving a cyclist a wide berth.

'Don't you have anything more upbeat?' asked Matt.

'Some Steps maybe?' snorted Ed. 'You sound like my wife.'

'No, you know, something with a groove.'

'I don't do "groove", I'm not built for "groove".'

'I am. Born to groove.'

'Born to lose.'

Matt began to fiddle with the touchscreen in the console.

Ed slapped his hand. 'In your car you choose the tunes, in mine I choose.'

'I remember that old Golf GTI your dad bought you, Ed,' said Thom, turning the subject back to automobilia. 'Everyone wanted a Golf, then.'

'I loved that car. I was gutted when I wrote it off,' said Ed, shaking his head at the memory.

'Not as much as your mum, it was on her insurance.'

'She went nuts. Handbrake turn that went wrong. But the worst thing was I had to drive a Ford Popular for a year.'

'You had an Escort, didn't you, Matt? With a muffler? The noise. My dad used to complain about the racket it made and it was a complete tip inside.'

'But the sound-system I put in was immense,' smiled Matt. 'You had a lurid yellow Astra GTE, Thom, I recall. Always broke down.'

'I wrote that off, too,' admitted Thom. 'Went into the back of a bloke who pulled up sharply as the lights changed on the North Circular.'

'You were speeding then,' offered Matt.

'Only a bit. Will was in the car with me. He began yelling at me, saying I could have killed him. The guy who was driving the car I hit very nearly did. He was enormous. He was about to do me serious damage when a police car pulled up. I've never been so grateful to see Old Bill.

'The cops made us exchange addresses and because his

car was roadworthy they told him to get going. He went off cursing me. I got done for careless driving, though. Fifty quid fine and a couple of points on my licence. On the plus side I ended up driving my dad's two-litre V6 Sierra, which wasn't too shabby and much more accommodating for the ladies than the Astra.'

'Will's red Mark II Ford Capri with the black vinyl roof was the car we all wanted,' recalled Ed. 'He adored it. All that was missing was the his and hers sunstrip. He behaved like his dog had died when it got stolen. Wouldn't come out for three months because it meant getting in someone else's car.'

'Actually their dog did die around then and I can confirm he was more upset by the loss of the motor,' agreed Thom.

Any prospect of a proper supermarket or off-licence materialising before they reached Rye had disappeared, so Ed turned round, carefully skirting a vast lake of rainwater on one side of the road. They pulled up outside a small supermarket opposite Pontins and made straight for its booze aisle.

'You're all right for Thunderbird here, decent bottle of claret? Forget it,' sniffed Ed picking up a bottle of red as if it were infected.

Thom shuffled down the aisle to the whites. He was examining the label of a bottle of Hungarian Pinot Grigio doubtfully when an old man rounded the corner. He was bent over a stick, his head clamped down almost at right angles so he appeared to be scanning the floor for something. Yellow, paper-thin skin torsioned around his head, revealed vast gums and a few gapped, brown teeth. Thom recoiled momentarily.

Talk about the skull beneath the skin, he thought. What a choice: die young, well, relatively young like Will, or end up like one of those miraculously mummified corpses they find preserved in the tundra. It wasn't the poor old fella's fault age was literally eating him away.

Thom had given age a lot of thought and he had come to a decision that he was not going out like that. The moment he started to lose his mental faculties or the big C came knocking, or any other fatal affliction announced itself, he was on a one-way flight to Zurich. Not that it would be necessary. In a few years they'd be offering assisted dying at the local chemist.

The one thing that might make ageing easier to bear was sharing it with someone else. A slow, gentle, mutual decline. He was unlikely to find his soulmate now, though. And what if he did find her, say at sixty? What a bitter joke. All those lost years. Did Matt feel the same? He made a big show of enjoying his own space but he must still harbour hopes of a meaningful relationship.

Someone was calling his name. Thom put the bottle back on the shelf and hurried to the checkout. Back in a car now stacked with more alcohol and snacks than a supermarket delivery van, he attempted to cheer himself up.

'We should check out a local hostelry. You know, research for later.'

'That's the first sensible thing you've said all day,' agreed Matt.

They located a pub called The Owl just behind a line of dunes bordering the beach. Ed went to the bar to order while Thom sat down in a quiet corner where the sun cut through a window, illuminating the table like a spotlight. Specks of dust jiggled in the air. Matt put his phone and wallet on the table and made for the toilet. He returned just as Ed placed three freshly-pulled pints onto the table. Thom was examining his phone.

'You got a text.'

'Oh yeah? Now what?' said Matt, taking it from him. Its screen was starred in one corner.

'I wouldn't have read it but I noticed it was from Annie

when it flashed up. 'It says "Hope you have a great time, say hi to everyone for me".'

'That was nice of her,' said Matt sipping from his pint, slowly, and reading it.

'Yeah, poor love. How come she texted you?'

'I suppose my name came up first on her phone. Anscombe, alphabetical innit? Anyway, to Annie, and to Will,' said Matt, raising his glass.

'Annie and Will!' chimed Thom and Ed, clinking theirs vigorously and slopping some of Matt's beer onto his hand.

'Did you both spill my pint?' he asked, giving them a comedy psycho stare.

Chapter Five

The Lost Art of Keeping a Secret

Back at the house, boredom was setting in, adding to Jack's gloom. He was wondering if he should have come, given events at home.

He tossed a copy of *Private Eye* to one side, stood and hobbled round the room, casting an eye along the bookshelf, which contained a couple of old Jamie Oliver recipe books, several well-thumbed crime novels and some chick-lit. He was tempted to put them in alphabetical order or dust the shelf. Instead he went round the room turning all the mains plug points to off.

Jack always behaved like this. He was a bundle of nervous energy who found it hard to relax, especially when he had nothing to do. Something was always eating at him. He was fine with the Boys but edgy, often fractious, much of the time. Ed used to say he could pick an argument with himself for pissing on his own shoes in an empty urinal.

He was also a bit of a loner with few real friends outside the Boys. There was another designer, Colin, he had worked with on some dreadful shitshow of a project a decade ago. Its complete and utter awfulness and the client's idiocy had served to bond them. They still spoke regularly, though rarely met. That was pretty much it in terms of solid mates. He had lost a close friend in Will but six was enough for anyone, he reasoned.

A speaker dock stood on the mantlepiece next to a large

plastic seagull and an arrow sign with the words 'The Sea' pointing helpfully towards the beach. He fished out his phone and was about to sync it when he noticed a missed call.

Janice, his wife. Soon to be his ex-wife. She had been giving him constant grief since their split. This weekend provided a welcome opportunity to forget about domestic strife. She was aware of this and appeared to be doing everything in her power to derail his plans, attempting to foist the kids on him because they had an inset day.

Asking him to look after his own children, Simon, thirteen, and Skye, fifteen, was deeply ironic given she had been attempting to stop him from having any contact with them since they parted.

In the end, he'd agreed to stay until lunchtime. They were old enough to be trusted alone for a few hours and their neighbour Mrs Wallace – Jack could never remember her first name – a retired widow, was always around. She liked having the kids now hers had grown up and moved on.

He turned up at their Sydenham semi when he was sure Janice had gone to work and busied himself retrieving his vinyl collection in case she gave it to a charity shop. The kids had kept to their rooms. At midday he went round to Mrs Wallace's to let her know he was leaving. She was her usual cheerful self. Barney, her plump black lab, waddled round in circles wagging his tail. Simon would probably take him for a walk later. He looked like he could do with one. To Brighton and back. Simon was always begging for a dog. He would probably get one now, Jack thought ruefully.

'How are things?' asked Mrs Wallace, looking hopeful.

'Oh, you know...' offered Jack, vaguely.

'I'm so sad you two have fallen out. I hope you'll come round, the pair of you, you're such a lovely couple and they're such nice kids.'

'You never know. We just need a bit of space.'

'Well, have a nice time with your chums, won't you?' she said as Jack retreated out of the door.

He popped back to remind them to behave. Skye rushed over and hugged him, prompting a lump to shoot into Jack's throat. Simon turned away and walked off.

He left the house crestfallen. He'd been overjoyed to see them but their pain and incomprehension was visible. Jack's parents had divorced when he was young, so he understood exactly what they were going through. He was simply perpetuating the cycle.

He synced his phone to the speaker dock. The strains of Radiohead's "Pyramid Song" filled the air, its solemn piano and strings complementing his melancholy mood. He contemplated changing it but slumped on to the couch and stared in silence at the back of the house where shafts of sunlight sliced through the windows scattering geometric shapes on the floor.

Listening to them took Jack back to Glastonbury, 1997. He and Will had worked their way to the front in sticky, pungent mud as the band took to the stage and launched into "Lucky". Will leapt up and down in delight. He made Jack put him on his shoulders for a while before someone shoved him in the back and they tumbled over.

Matt had accompanied them that year but they'd become separated during the Prodigy's set. He failed to return to the tent that night, too. Later it transpired he'd dropped a pill and spent all night tramping the same square of turf inside an all-night rave tent in a distant field and slept it off for much of the following day. They were finally reunited on the Sunday by which time he'd lost his voice and his shoes.

The last time Jack saw Will it was hard to look him in the eye. Sat limply on the couch, he was a shadow of himself.

He'd been such an athlete. Thom was fit, too, but he didn't have Will's build or his hand-eye coordination. He could play any game half decently. And he had become increasingly careful about his health, blitzing up repulsive health drinks composed of green sludge, cutting out red meat and avoiding alcohol midweek. There was a lesson there.

'Wassup?' Jack had said breezily, taking off his jacket and putting it over the back of a chair. The room was uncommonly warm.

'Oh, you know, busy dying,' said Will nonchalantly. A bowl of food lay untouched on the coffee table next to a glass of water.

Jack eyed his sheepskin slippers.

'Comfort footwear?' he asked, ignoring Will's morbid humour.

'I know. Who'd have thought?'

'These things come to us all, in time.'

'I remember those pixie boots you used to have.'

'Nearly got me killed,' nodded Jack. 'That was your fault. Not for the first time, or the last.'

The incident had taken place on a drab Saturday afternoon in early October while they were at uni. Will and Jack had met in a pub for a pint and a ploughman's in town. Later, they wandered round clothes shops and a record store where Jack bought The Smiths' *Meat Is Murder*. He was deep into his Johnny Marr phase at the time, wearing a black polo neck jumper and a long fake pearl necklace over the top. White jeans were tucked into a pair of battered burgundy pixie boots.

Late in the afternoon as they were preparing to leave, they wandered past a pub with a group of Leeds fans standing outside. There were derisory comments and a few wolf whistles. They had reached the corner when Will spun round, yelled, 'Dirty Leeds!' and took off.

Jack gave him a look of horror before a roar went up. The sound of glass breaking shocked him into action. They sprinted down the street pursued by half-a-dozen angry fans. Jack, hampered by the wrong footwear for the occasion, began losing ground. Will sped away. A bus pulled in at a stop and he leapt on its platform. There was a pause then it began to move off. Jack accelerated, the record bag flapping from his wrist was dragging him back. In an instant he flung it away and reached towards Will's extended hand. He snagged the pearl necklace and it broke, spraying beads across the road. For a moment the space between them appeared to be too great but the driver took his foot off the accelerator as a car pulled out ahead and the gap closed. Suddenly Will leant out and yanked him in powerfully. Jack stumbled but somehow ended up in a heap on the back deck. A glass arced towards the bus but landed short, shattering on the tarmac. The irate mob receded into the distance as the bus pulled away, speeding through a set of lights just as they turned amber. They staggered to a seat and sat panting in silence for several minutes.

'You fucking idiot,' gasped Jack eventually. 'You owe me an album. And a new necklace.'

They didn't speak for the rest of the journey home.

That was Will for you, thought Jack. Act first, think later. Life was never dull, though. He was thumbing through his tunes trying to decide on something else to play when the phone rang.

He sighed. Now what?

'Hi.'

'Just checking you got there OK,' came a faint voice. It sounded like it was coming from another continent.

'It's a shocking line. What's up?' said Jack, examining his phone. He had one bar. Quite convenient, actually.

'Nothing. Just, you know... How were your kids?'

'Fine,' Jack didn't want to get into this. 'Did that client brief come back?'

'Yes. I'm just checking through it now.'

'Great, you can bring me up to speed on Monday.'

The voice said something Jack didn't catch.

'What?'

'Where are you again?'

'Camber.'

'With old school mates.'

'That's right.'

More words were lost in the ether.

'What? I'm really having trouble hearing you!'

'Try finding a better signal then,' came the disconnected voice.

Laughter came from the front door. A key shunted into a lock.

'Look, I'll tell you all about it on Monday. I gotta go.'

The voice at the other end mumbled something.

'Same!'

He hung up just as the others tumbled through the door, giggling.

'Who were you shouting at then?' demanded Ed.

'Eh, oh work,' said Jack. 'Couldn't hear properly. Crap signal. We're falling off the bottom of the country here.'

Swiftly he selected The Chemical Brothers' "Battle Scars". The tinny speaker worked hard to fill the space. He turned the volume up to maximum.

'Oooh, it's just like being in Fabric, isn't it?' said Thom.

'When was the last time you were in Fabric, Grandad?' snorted Jack. 'And it's the best they've got.'

'Big fish, little fish, cardboard box,' hummed Matt, miming.

'You lot have been to the pub, haven't you?' said Jack, accusingly.

'Just a sneaky snorkel. And we've come back because we decided to take a spin over to Dungeness. Fancy coming?' said Matt.

'I'm not exactly mobile, am I?'

'Oh come on, it's only a nick, you big jess,' sneered Thom.

Jack contemplated refusing but decided, on balance, he'd rather not be alone for hours. They could hide the keys for Paul and drop him a text.

'Go on then. Shotgun the front seat though, so I can stretch my foot out.'

They all climbed back into the car and rolled back along the track.

'Who left that shitheap there?' asked Ed, skirting a blue Fiesta parked by the house.

'Fuck off posh boy,' said Jack, defensively. 'Not everyone can afford a new car every year. It gets me around. And Jan has got the Hyundai now, obviously.'

'Result,' snorted Ed.

You sneer mate, thought, Jack. Ed couldn't help let you know how well he was doing. Every year there was a new motor and holidays in the Caribbean or South Africa. The most exotic trips Jack's family made were to French campsites. Ed didn't really mean to rub it in, he just had a tin ear.

'Jesus Ed, take it easy,' gasped Jack, tensing up as the car lurched sharply round a corner. 'Are you sure you're OK to drive?'

'I only had one, stop mithering,' Ed replied, gunning the car more rapidly past yards of wire fencing erected around MOD land. Another, smaller, holiday park appeared on the left, sited directly beneath a pylon.

'Oooh let's go there next year!' said Matt. 'What a location. You can keep Amalfi and the Maldives, Camber is now the discerning global traveller's resort of choice.'

'I think it was on the cover of *Condé Nast Traveller* last month,' said Ed. 'Top ten undiscovered destinations.'

'Imagine what its guests are like?' said Thom. 'Paedophiles, ex-UKIP councillors and retired prison wardens.'

'That's one resident, what about the others?' replied Jack.

They crossed a small roundabout, passed rows of anonymous seventies terraces, then turned off into the Dungeness estate whereupon the bland residential geography vanished abruptly.

A vast carpet of grey shingle speckled with clusters of broom, and sea kale stretched towards the horizon. A few old fishing boats lay collapsed on their sides, paint and rust flaking from their hulls. Heavily rusted slabs of iron machinery squatted alongside a handful of dilapidated huts. The door of one swung back and forth gently. A trail of blue and orange fishing net stretched towards the sea, lifting occasionally in the breeze. Wooden boardwalks criss-crossed the shingle.

'Apparently this is the closest thing we get to desert in this country,' offered Ed, as they slowed to a crawl.

'Not counting your hairline,' added Jack.

Halfway down the long, straight road Thom ordered Ed to pull over.

'What's up?' asked Ed. 'Car sick, sonny?'

'Derek Jarman's garden at Prospect House,' said Thom, pointing out one of a handful of architect-designed, tar-coated shiplap dwellings along the road.

'And?' asked Ed.

'He left behind this odd, architectural garden. It's a local landmark, saved for the nation not long back. Worth a stroll around.'

They parked up and wandered around the open garden. Thom noted a nearby house which appeared to be clad completely in rubber.

'It's all very artful in a desolate way but I'm not sure I'd want to live in a giant dildo,' said Jack, capturing a panoramic shot that took in a sweep of the nature reserve with his phone.

'Actually, I can see Thom living inside a giant dildo,' said Matt.

Miniature stone dolmans were piled randomly around the garden while pieces of weathered flotsam were inserted into the shingle among delicate plantings of red valerian and yellow santolina. Rusty springs had been fashioned into garden ornaments and a large rowing boat listed to one side.

'It's very quirky but you could imagine going slowly mad if you lived here for any length of time,' said Ed turning through 180 degrees.

'Imagine what it's like in winter,' agreed Thom.

'Bit bleak?' offered Matt.

'Fucking desperate,' said Ed, flatly.

'Perfect for a misanthrope like Jack,' said Thom. Jack signed back with his middle finger. They made their way slowly back to the car.

'Well I was as impressed with that as I was his movies,' said Ed bluntly, snapping his seat belt in to place.

'*Jubilee* is now accepted as the great punk movie,' declared Matt.

'I recall taping its TV showing for a glimpse of Jordan's breasts. *Caravaggio* was all right; pretty daring in its time for its depiction of homosexuality.'

'It was all a bit much for me, then,' said Jack. 'Not that I had a problem with gay people.'

'Some of your best friends are gay, aren't they?' goaded Matt.

'No, I mean he was trying to rub your face in it and I wasn't ready for that as a teenager.'

'Wasn't allowed that then, rubbing your face in it.'

'No. He was championing something I had no interest in and cared nothing about.'

'He was making a statement about a way of life that was still criminalised. He was putting it on the agenda, asking questions. He was challenging a country still locked in the Dark Ages,' said Matt. 'He's the defining British artist of the eighties. Discuss.'

'If you say so,' said Jack, peering through a window.

They returned to the car and drove further down the road past small gauge rail tracks and a squat white pub until they reached the old lighthouse. Gulls wheeled around a blue sky daubed amateurishly with big wisps of cloud. Ed pulled up as the elegiac strains of Bowie's "Where Are We Now?" commenced.

'We've not amounted to much, have we?' announced Jack, picking up on the mournful mood of the music. 'Look at poor Will. If any of us was going to leave a mark it was him. When he finally looked like he might get one of his scripts off the ground the poor bugger got sick.'

'Ed's doing all right, aren't you Ed?' suggested Matt, generously.

'I am, Matt. My ship's coming in any day now,' said Ed, breezily.

'There it is! Over there,' said Jack causing everyone to look in the direction of his finger. A hulk lay rusting on one side in the shingle.

'He left two lovely kids behind, didn't he?' offered Thom. 'That's the best most people can hope for. Remember what the less famous Will wrote: "Make thee another self, for love of me, that beauty still may live in thine or thee". That's his legacy and it's not a bad one. I don't lie awake wondering if there will be a glowing obituary about me in *The Times* when I join the choir immortal. Most popular cultural achievements will be forgotten. Most films and novels will be long gone unless they are absolute classics. Look at pop music. No one remembers the pop songs of the Edwardian era any more, do they? The youth won't be singing along to "Parklife" in fifty years' time.'

'Maybe not, but people will definitely be singing "Hey Jude" and "The Sound Of Silence",' countered Jack, 'And "Heroes".'

'I blame Bowie for dying,' said Ed. 'It all went to shit after that.'

'Christ, cheer up you lot. If I wanted to be miserable I would have stayed at home drinking on my own. Are we just going to sit here or is there a plan?' asked Matt, tiring of their navel gazing.

'We could climb to the top of the lighthouse? Who fancies that?' suggested Ed, looking up at a liquorice tower across the road.

'Great idea! I'll hop up every step,' said Jack.

'OK, not you, cripple boy. Anyone else?'

'Not me,' said Thom. 'Vertigo.'

'It's not far to go, I've parked right opposite it.'

Thom made a cymbal crash sound effect.

'Come on Ed, it's you and me, the real men here,' said Matt decisively.

Ed swung the door open and pulled the seat forward.

'To the lighthouse!'

Thom and Jack sidled over to a wooden bench as Matt and Ed disappeared through the door to the tower pretending to race each other with sped up walks. A few people sat outside a café across from the miniature train station drinking from steaming cups. A carrier bag wafted into the road then rose up, spasming in invisible eddies.

Jack lit a cigarette after several attempts and took a few

drags in silence, tapping ash onto the grass with a slender finger.

A morbidly obese man in a tracksuit cruised past them on an electric scooter, fat spilled over his hips in large folds beneath a faded black Motörhead T-shirt the size of a tent. Three large dogs on leads trotted ahead, tethered to the handlebars by long leads.

'Look, a mobility sled,' said Jack. 'Mush, mush!'

'Do you think he got fat because he's disabled or he's disabled because he's fat?' mused Thom as the team disappeared down the road.

'Some people like Will are unfortunate enough to become ill, others make themselves sick and they all get treated the same,' replied Jack. 'It's an odd form of free will to be a lazy, inconsiderate slob whose sole contribution to the state seems to be to suck on it like a tick till it drops off.'

'At least you're not judgmental.'

'You and I are paying for him to be like that. I wonder when the last time was that he put in anything. He looked younger than us.'

'He might have had a hard life,' suggested Thom, charitably. He stood up, stretched his back and began to walk towards the beach.

'Where are you off to?' asked Jack.

'Thought I'd take a look at those shacks over there. Coming?'

Jack sat there for a moment as he wandered off, then stepped on his cigarette and limped after him with a sigh. They crunched over shingle then on to boards leading to a small cluster of whitewashed wooden shacks with a small, weather-beaten caravan parked to one side. The word 'Gallery' was painted on a piece of plywood nailed to a stake by a picket fence. They stuck their heads inside, unsure. Framed paintings lined the walls. One side held several beach scenes while abstracts lined the other. They wandered inside for a closer look, their steps sounding uncommonly loud on the wood floor.

Thom peered close-in at one, a panoramic landscape in which the power station glowed radioactively against a dark night sky. In another, a rusty boat listed to one side surrounded by heavy smears of grey streaked in chalky white. The same orange glow hung in the sky above the horizon line.

'These aren't bad, actually,' observed Thom.

'Can I interest you in one?' the voice came before its owner appeared in the doorway, a small man with a white beard and blue-framed glasses.

'Mmm, not sure,' said Thom, put on the spot. 'How much are they?'

'Which one,' said the gallery owner, seemingly determined to make him squirm.

'Umm, the power station.'

'That's sold, that's what the red dot means in the corner.'

'Oh, shame. Are they yours?'

'Not that one, mine are the abstracts. Those are my partner's.'

'You live and work here?' asked Jack.

'Yes. Have for twenty years now.'

'What's it like?'

'Like nowhere else. It has an otherworldly quality to it that's quite inspirational.'

'It's very isolated.'

'Like being on the edge of the world,' agreed the gallery owner. 'Oddly peaceful.'

'What about the power station, isn't it unnerving being that close to all that radioactivity? Aren't you worried about a leak or something?'

'I've not grown any extra toes yet. If something happened I wouldn't be any safer in Dover or Hastings. I'd be a lot less happy, though.'

'S'pose not, well thanks,' said Jack, retreating to the door.

'Bye then,' added Thom, following.

The gallery owner followed them out, then branched right into the other hut.

Thom and Jack made their way back along the boardwalk. A huge gull blocked their path.

'Jesus H, it's an albino pterodactyl! Is he sure about the radioactivity around here?' gasped Jack.

The gull eyed them arrogantly for a moment then took off, only to land on the roof of the gallery where it proceeded to relieve itself proudly.

'Oh, look, he's doing a little painting of his own. "Dungeness Dump, mixed guano and gouache",' said Jack.

They made their way back to the bench and sat down. Thom eyed the lighthouse. There was no sign of any activity at the top. Jack glanced at his phone.

'How are things with you and Jan?' asked Thom suddenly. He'd been waiting for an opportunity when they were alone.

Jack pulled a face.

'That bad.'

'Yup. She's still barely communicating. Tried to ruin my weekend by dumping the kids on me. First time she's let me near them in months. Looks like I'm going to have to find a lawyer to sort out some proper access.'

'No chance she'll forgive and forget?'

'No. It's broke.'

'That's a shame.'

'It's my fault. Actually, it isn't. Not all of it.'

'Want to share?'

'Not really. Not yet. I'm officially the guilty party but it's not that straightforward. Yet I'm the one who stands to lose the house and the kids. I worry she'll turn them against me. Simon doesn't seem to like me anymore.'

'I know how you feel, believe me. You need to keep the father-son-daughter stuff up. I don't have that option.'

'If she'll let me.'

'She will. She'll have to. At least she's not kidnapped them and taken them to the other side of the world,' he said bitterly.

Thom's predilection for the opposite sex was well documented but it had caught up with him four years ago when his American wife, Amy, had decided enough was enough. She had left him and returned to her St Louis home, taking Connor, their then nine-year-old son, with them. Thom had understood her reaction but her decision to move back was devastating. He saw the boy once or twice a year now, prompting him to entertain the idea of moving to the States. Would he get a Green Card? Perhaps he could be an escort for women looking for dapper older men. Englishmen. There was probably a market.

* * *

Breathing hard, Ed and Matt climbed the last few steps of the spiral staircase that coiled around the inner wall of the old lighthouse. They emerged from a small door onto a narrow balcony rail running around the storm-paned lantern room. Ed was gasping for air like a chub tossed onto a riverbank. Matt was in even worse shape. The climb was the most exercise he'd done in months. Sweat ran down his face, his legs were jelly.

He smelt fresh air and reached for the rail to steady himself, glancing over involuntarily. The vertical drop suddenly leered into view. He recoiled instantly, feeling horribly exposed. His stomach also decided it had had more than enough and in one violent reflex expelled the contents of their liquid lunch, sending a jet of vomit arcing over the edge. He staggered back from the rail and through the door, brushing past Ed who was still fighting for breath and thus unable to express his derision.

'I'm going back,' gasped Matt abruptly. He began to descend, pressing his body tight to the wall. Ed, rattled by Matt's sudden turn, sat down on the top step to compose himself. Leaning forward he glanced over the stair rail. Its helical spiral was like staring down the barrel of a large cannon. He imagined falling from the top, splattering like a watermelon on the stone floor. Time to go. Gripping the handrail tightly he began to descend slowly.

A little way down, Matt had sat down but was still descending, step by step, sliding on his backside, breathing carefully through pursed lips to centre himself. Ed reached quietly for his phone. A third of the way down, a family crossed on the way up, chattering loudly. Matt pretended to look at his phone as they passed. The father buttonholed Ed as they crossed.

'Did you pour something over the edge?'

'Sorry?' replied Ed, confused.

'We were heading through the entrance when all this liquid hit on the ground, splashed the back of my trousers.

'Why would I pour anything over the edge?' asked Ed. 'Are you sure it wasn't a seagull? They're bloody enormous round here.'

The man turned away with a snort of disgust.

Ed began to trot down. He overtook Matt halfway, wordlessly. By the time he reached the bottom he was breathing hard again. Matt, who had managed to stand upright two-thirds of the way down, was slowly completing his descent, muttering quietly to himself. Recovering quickly, Ed began to snigger at his halting progress.

'Come on you sorry, geriatric fucker.'

Matt ignored him, heading swiftly out of the door.

'Fuck that was horrible!' he sucked in deep draughts of fresh air.

'What came over you? You were Chris Bonington at the bottom, a kitten stuck in a tree at the top. I thought I was going to have to call for a rescue party.'

'Fuck off. I didn't see you stopping for a selfie,' said Matt spitting on the ground.

'I was too busy laughing.'

'Wheezing like an asthmatic on a nebuliser, you mean. Right, not a word about this, OK?' he wiped his hand across his mouth.

'Understood,' nodded Ed.

They walked back to the car where Jack and Thom were waiting.

'You took your time,' said Thom. 'Didn't even see you waving at us from the top.'

'Matt got the fear and lost his dinner,' grinned Ed.

'You grass!' Matt shot back accusingly.

'What, after all that, you had a senior moment?' smiled Thom, raising an amused eyebrow.

'High anxiety!' sang Jack.

'Projectile vomited from the top then slid down the steps on his backside like a Jack Russell wiping its arse. Seven-year-olds skipping past him,' grinned Ed. 'Look!'

He produced a video of Matt shuffling down the steps on the seat of his pants.

'More intimations of mortality,' laughed Jack uproariously. 'Put it on YouTube quick.'

'Don't you dare! You complete bastard Simmons. I don't

know what came over me,' said Matt, still in shock. 'I suddenly felt dizzy and nauseous. I had an ear infection a couple of weeks ago. It must have been that along with a pint on an empty stomach.'

'Ear infection!' boomed Ed. 'Balls infection more like.'

'What a bunch of Prufrocks,' said Thom, shaking his head, '"Time to turn back and descend the stair, With a bald spot in the middle of my hair."'

'If you say so,' shrugged Ed.

Laughing helplessly they climbed into the car and swept back to Camber accompanied by the strains of Pulp's "Help The Aged".

Chapter Six

Shut Up and Drive

Damon trotted down the stairs, dragging two plastic mail sacks in his wake. It had taken a couple of hours but the deliveries were now packaged up. The Roid Room was locked down, ready for another batch next week when the powder finally arrived, and the menagerie had been fed and watered. Everything was in its place.

The army had instilled a sense of order he hadn't possessed as a child. And order and cleanliness was important to home chemistry. Contamination could destroy his rep overnight and reps were hard-won in this game. Someone was always ready to move in, there was always a new wonderbatch. Herbs, spices, inflated claims of rapid muscle mass gain. It wasn't miracle grow. Not far off, mind.

He stopped at the downstairs bathroom to examine his face in the mirror. An angry zit stared back at him just above his top lip. He leaned in to the mirror, placed both thumbnails either side and brought pressure to bear on the festering mass. It ruptured, sending a satisfying jet of yellow pus onto the mirror. He snapped a piece of toilet paper off the roll, dabbed it, threw it down the toilet and wandered into the kitchen.

Karen was waiting patiently by a kettle as it came slowly to the boil. She was tall with long bleach-blonde hair that curled and split at the ends from the chlorine in the water at the baths. Her job helped her maintain the sort of figure women in their early thirties were struggling to hold on to. Not having children had its physical benefits even if the ticking of her body clock was growing ever louder in her head.

It had been her intention to move out and find a better job ever since the death of her mother but Karen was currently drifting, becalmed. She'd always imagined herself working in a marine profession but it just hadn't worked out. A long-term relationship kept life in check, then it collapsed. Dennis was eight years her senior, clever and well-travelled. Karen found older men more attractive for some reason. She has given it some thought and wondered if it was down to losing her dad so young but it seemed like cod psychology. She wasn't looking for a father figure.

Dennis had done his wandering. He wanted to settle down and start a family but Karen wasn't ready. She was determined to have a career, although she lacked the confidence to make it happen. Lack of self-esteem ate away at her.

Their father, Iain, had died while she and Damon were still in their teens. He was an Australian from Mooloolaba on the Sunshine Coast who had backpacked to the UK in his early twenties and never returned. He met Carol at Glastonbury Festival in the late eighties; a hippy with pink hair and a muddy vintage lace dress. They had neighbouring tents in what turned into a giant bog of animal slurry following heavy rain. He used to joke that they were in the shit from the moment they fell in love.

Iain had been killed instantly when the crane he was operating collapsed on the construction site of a city skyscraper. He had waved them cheerfully goodbye one morning and never come home. He was a happy grafter who had escaped a repressive family life back home and followed his dreams of a second life but his luck ran out.

Carol had bought the house with the compensation money but had never recovered from the loss of her husband who had rescued her from a drab, suburban life. Karen was fourteen at the time. She had made a good pretence of keeping it together but Damon, just over a year older, had struggled without a father to keep him in line. Always hyper, he became disruptive at school. A minor incident with a teacher during his GCSEs escalated and Damon had hurled a chair. He was excluded and didn't bother sitting the remaining exams. They were arts anyway and Damon didn't do arts, or languages. He was, however, good at maths and science, largely through the support of a teacher, Mr Archer, who did his best to direct Damon's interest and give him some responsibility. He was made lab monitor, which gave him the opportunity to mess around with chemicals and nick strips of magnesium foil, which he'd ignite on the beach at night watching them burn neon white, lighting up the darkness with furious energy before they swiftly turned to powder on the pebbles. The residue reminded him of his dad's ashes when he had once peeked inside the urn hidden in Carol's bedroom.

It was Karen who held the academic qualifications, but it was Damon who supported them. And he felt that gave him a say over everything his sister did. She was aware he was involved in something unusual before she moved back home. It soon become apparent it was less than legal, too. The first time she brought it up, it was made abundantly clear she was not to pry.

She had no intention of ever going in his office or whatever it was, anyway. The spider appalled her. She'd had a phobia of them ever since she woke one morning to find a huge, dead wolf spider curled up in her bedclothes like a rusty broach. Had it crawled over her? She ran out of the room screaming and her dad had rushed in.

'It's dead, Kaz!' he yelled after her. 'Can't harm yer! You should see the ones in Oz!'

Karen had no desire to hear of monstrous horse spiders but she loved listening to his stories about Australia, the animals in the rainforest and the billions of fish swimming in the Great Barrier Reef. He was going to take them there when he had enough money saved. That was the plan.

His stories inspired her love of the ocean. Not the grey mass across the road but the fabulous electric blue waters above the reef. Before emigrating he had worked briefly as a diver in marine construction.

'You should see it down there Kaz, so many fish, rainbow colours everywhere you look,' he said. 'It positively glows beneath the waves, I'm telling you.'

Iain taught her to swim, something she took to readily, and promised he'd pay for a diving course as soon as she was old enough, but he had died too soon. So she saved the money herself. Passing her PADI a few years ago was a bittersweet moment, but it opened up a whole new world of possibilities.

Damon had no interest in the sea but he was interested in manufacturing potions, and bugs. The day after Karen had found the spider Damon found its body on the grass in the garden where Iain had tossed it. He produced it with glee. She ran off down the street and hid at a friend's. His dad made him throw it on the fire.

It was the beginning of Damon's fascination with arachnids. Now he had an exotic housed in a tank upstairs. He had taken the monster out once and began to pet it carefully and she nearly fainted. That night she had a nightmare about it stalking her, had to get up, put the light on and check the bedclothes, just as she had when she was a child.

'Do you want a cup?' she said, chewing on a Marmited slice of toast, smacking glossy scarlet lips as he entered the kitchen.

'Go on, then,' said Damon, toeing the sacks to one side. She dropped a tea-bag in a stained blue mug and poured water over it while Damon fiddled with his mobile.

'Awww, have a look at this,' he said, holding out the phone.

'What?'

She took it. A short video clip played in which a man rescued an injured baby deer in danger of being eaten by wolves, nursed it back to health and returned it to its mother in the forest.

'Lovely, but it probably got eaten, anyway,' she said, handing it back.

'Don't say that,' frowned Damon. 'The guy did a lovely thing.'

'The wolves will probably starve now,' she countered.

'You're a heartless cow, aren't you?'

'It's nature, isn't it Damo? Survival of the fittest and all that. That bloke disrupted the food chain.'

'No danger of you doing that. You live on toast. What are you up to tonight?'

Keeping tabs on her again.

'Pub maybe, might see Ayesha later.'

'Right, I better get going,' said Damon, satisfied. He downed the rest of his tea in one long gulp and banged the empty cup down on the counter-top. He threw the sacks out of the front door and held it open.

'Be careful you don't hit any baby deer,' she called.

'Fuck off. Come on Drog, let's go, mate!'

The dog lifted its head from the rug at the sound of its name. It trotted quickly out to the car. Damon opened the passenger door, it hopped in and sat on a tartan blanket folded on the seat while Damon put the sacks in the back. Then he jumped in, gunned the engine and reversed swiftly out, just as a white BMW sailed past.

'Whoa, where did that cunt come from?' he muttered, flicking the Merc onto the sideroad and pulling sharply away with a rip of gravel.

The Beamer went off in the opposite direction while he turned left towards his first stop, a post office up in Rye. He liked to spread the parcels around a couple of branches and stick others in post boxes en route, rather than send it all through the same office. He had a franking machine in the Roid Room so, ordinarily, he would just drop them off but it had run out of money, necessitating some be paid for. He preferred not to be seen dispatching packages but he had no choice today.

Fortunately it was quiet in Rye. He used a self-service machine for half-a-dozen packets and moved on. On the way out he paused to shove several more packets into a nearby mailbox before heading back towards Camber. Holding the wheel with one hand, he thumbed on the radio, absent-mindedly massaging his left breast through his T-shirt with the other. Sun flickered through trees, strobing him with light. He reached for a pair of sunglasses and slipped them on. As the car rounded a corner a black object appeared in the distance. It was a cyclist, clad head-to-toe in black Lycra. Bent over the handlebars, he was mashing hard on the pedals but making little progress. Two overstuffed panniers protruded either side of his rear wheel.

Lost in thought, Paul was almost oblivious to the effort he was putting in. He had been looking forward to the Boys' Weekend for weeks but it was going to be overshadowed by Will. No change there. He might have departed but he still managed to command centre stage. He always was that bit louder, that bit more alpha. He dominated things without even realising he was doing it sometimes, yet he was generous to a fault.

When Paul came back from travelling, Will let him have the spare room in his flat, rent-free, for months until he found work. Without an audience he was a different beast, quieter, more considerate. The more people you added to the mix, the louder and more competitive he became.

He was like a brother to Matt, an only child, but Paul, the youngest of four from a large, non-Orthodox Jewish family, had his siblings to look out for him. At the same time his bond with the Boys was unbreakable. They'd grown up together, now they were growing old together. That was how it should be. Will just had to be different.

If Paul was closer to any of them, it was Ed, whose clownish humour was gentler, more inclusive. Ed also shared some of his geekier passions – astronomy – if not his more strident political convictions and distaste for material objects. Ed could not help himself with his ostentatious spending. He had to have the latest gadget and remind you where he had just flown in from.

Matt was a natural show-off, he always made you laugh but he had an excessive streak that disturbed Paul. He never knew when to quit and behaved like he was still in his twenties when he had a drink inside him. It had started to look self-destructive to Paul. Like the nasty cut he had sustained to his head before Christmas. 'Pissed again!' he'd laughed. The burst blood vessels around his nose were starting to give him away.

Thom was witty and cultured but rather self-obsessed, a bit too impressed by himself sometimes. He was also permanently on heat, like a stag in season. You could be talking to him and he'd be eyeing up something half his age behind you.

Jack was more introspective, tense and he could be brutally sarcastic, often for the sport of it. He and Will frequently traded barbed insults that made outsiders believe they were about to come to blows.

The last time Paul saw Will was late November. Will wanted out of his 'cell', so once Annie had swaddled him in jumpers and a thick scarf, they climbed into Paul's much derided Toyota Prius – actually his wife's – and set off. They drove in silence with just the radio for a while. A talk show debated the week's politics. Will turned it off without asking permission. He opened the glovebox, found some boiled sweets and popped one in his mouth. Rows of empty football pitches swept past. A few kids played in an empty goalmouth with no nets. Will let out a sigh as he watched them.

'Do you think there's a God, Paul?' he asked suddenly. 'Yahweh, Jehovah, whatever.'

'I very much doubt it, I'm afraid,' said Paul, glancing at him. Paul had lapsed out his faith a long time ago.

'Shame. I'd like to punch the cunt in the face,' said Will.

They both laughed out loud. The memory popped into his head as he churned the pedals in slow motion. On Monday he had gone to see the vice chancellor at the university to be informed politely that his course would not be part of its syllabus for the next academic year. It was a blow but not an unexpected one. The university had been winding down its operations in Hastings and focusing on more vocational courses. Everyone had to be engineered into job readiness these days, he lamented. Academic achievement as an end in itself was so twentieth century.

But there was another agenda, which was all to do with his role as a union rep in an ongoing dispute about pension cuts. In some respects he was OK with it, he'd get a decent redundancy package and it solved the reservations he increasingly had with what he was teaching, but it irked him that he was being singled out for his activism. He was torn between escalating the issue or letting it go.

Looking ahead he spotted a vast puddle where the road

curved. Given it was too dangerous to negotiate on the dry half of the road he opted to pedal slowly through it.

'Fuck me, a gimp. Look at that clown, Drogba!' said Damon, spotting a cyclist in the distance. He had complete contempt for anyone on two wheels.

Pumping the accelerator he caught up rapidly and entered the lake of rainwater just inside its lip, engineering a sheet of water that arced over the unsuspecting cyclist. For a moment he looked like a surfer negotiating the barrel of a wave, then the spray hit him.

'Wipeout!' yelled Damon. The dog began to bark in excitement.

Surprised, Paul jammed on the brakes mid-crossing. His back wheel fishtailed uneasily and he nearly came off. With a frantic jerk he attempted to unclip his right foot, failed, and toppled into the water.

Howling with laughter, Damon slowed to enjoy the scene in his rearview mirror, before pumping the accelerator once more. The Merc shot off at warp speed.

'Oh, that was fucking priceless. I wish I'd recorded it.'

The dog turned to look at him, appearing to grin. Its huge pink tongue flapped to one side of its mouth.

Damon stabbed a button on the dash and the radio sparked into life. A local station was playing The Feeling's "Love It When You Call". He began to sing along. 'I found a switch, you turn it on, I hit the ditch, you carried on!'

In Camber he turned off the main road and parked across from the post office on double yellows. He hauled a supermarket carrier bag of unfranked envelopes from the boot and headed for the door. He was about to leave the dog but thought better of it. There was a good chance he'd chew on the leather seats if left alone too long.

'Come on.'

Drogba hopped out and trotted obediently after him. As they crossed the road a filthy Peugeot 406 with a torn spoiler appeared at a side road. Sitting behind the wheel was a man with a tattoo growing like ivy around his neck. Scrawled in the dirt on the driver's door was the legend, 'Cunthead'. He must have known the word was there but had made no attempt to erase it, as if he were proud of the sobriquet.

For a moment the two locked eyes. Damon recognised Geddy. Total roidhead. Barred from his local gym, Repz, which took some doing. Damon gave him a cursory nod of recognition before the car sped off, its muffler roaring petulantly.

Still humming The Feeling song, Damon strolled casually into the post office, a dingy, rundown shop, manned by a middle-aged Sri Lankan couple awaiting its imminent closure. He flipped the sunglasses on top of his head.

There was one other customer at the counter, a man with a ponytail dangling from behind a leather cowboy hat with a brightly-coloured fishing lure in its band. He held two envelopes.

'I want to post this first-class but I want the envelope inside stamped for return with enough money for the object to be placed inside, which is a mobile phone.'

'You can't send phone through post,' said a woman in an orange patterned sari sitting inside a glass booth with a shake of the head.

'Why?'

'Battery may catch fire.'

'Everyone has a phone, I don't see people being hosed down in the street with fire extinguishers. Phones don't catch fire.'

'OK but I have to put sticker on saying "Danger".'

'Don't you have one that says, "Mobile phone inside, please help yourself"?'

Damon shifted from foot to foot. He could feel the sands of his patience, a very short timer, already running down to their final grains.

Standing behind the other counter, wearing a blue anorak, the husband counted newspapers, and tied them into a bundle. The post office doubled as a corner shop but aside from rows of snacks and confectionary, its stock was poor. A few bottles of milk sat inside a dirty cabinet with several tins of fizzy drink. A single aisle contained a pick and mix of washing powders, a row of soup cans, some pots of instant noodles, a few loaves of sliced bread and, inexplicably, a lone pack of dried porcini mushrooms.

The woman sighed. 'What is weight of phone?'

'I don't know, if I had my phone I wouldn't be here would I?'

'I put enough for one kilo.'

'A kilo? It's not 1986. Can you get a move on? Fucking thick Paki.'

Her husband stopped what he was doing. The woman looked like she might cry.

'Oi!' said Damon, tapping him heavily on the shoulder. 'Mind your mouth!'

The man span round. He blinked. His mouth twitched.

'Apologise to the lady,' said Damon, nodding towards her. 'Go on!'

'Sorry about that, I got Tourette's,' he stammered.

The woman clucked her tongue, ran off a stamp. The man pasted it on the envelope, placed it quickly inside the other one, sealed it, paid and left without another word.

'Some people got no manners. I served with a coupla Asian lads, they never let me down,' explained Damon, stepping forward and emptying the bag on the counter.

'I want these all to go second-class UK. They're all the

same weight so do one and just print off twelve labels,' he said, putting the first packet on the scale.

'No, I must have postcode for each one.'

'Really? Surely it doesn't matter where they're going,' he replied defensively.

'It's the way machine works,' said the husband, chipping in.

'Fair enough,' he said with a forced smile.

Finally, with the batch stamped and stowed in a mail sack ready for collection he made to leave. Something caught his eye. Under the glass shelf, where the husband bundled up returned newspapers, was a six pack of large fireworks emblazoned with the title, Sky Dragon. Damon had a childlike fondness for pyrotechnics and they both sounded and looked impressive.

'I'll have those.'

The man, counting, ignored him.

'I. Want. To. Buy. Them. Fireworks,' said Damon reciting each word as if the man could not hear him.

Muttering numbers the man finally wrote a number on a piece of paper and looked up at Damon.

'Fifteen pounds. My friend.'

'Fifteen? You're 'avin a laugh! They're six months old.'

'Firework not loaf of bread, not go off.'

'If it not go off then it no good,' countered Damon.

'No, they are fine, just no sell-by date.'

'Go on then,' he tossed two ten pound notes on the newspaper bundle. The man handed him the change and the pack. Damon spun around and held the door for the dog who wandered out. An old lady appeared in the doorway, he stepped back and waved her in theatrically before stepping out in the sunlight and sliding the sunglasses back onto his nose.

'Daylight robbery,' he muttered, examining the pack of rockets. Long sticks poked from blue plastic cases with conical red tips. He felt a tingle of anticipation.

'Maybe we'll let some off later, eh, mate?'

He opened the boot, placed the fireworks inside, let the dog back in and threw the door shut. He was about to climb in himself when he remembered something.

'Stay. I'll be back,' he told the dog and jogged across the road to the supermarket where he made for the vegetable aisle, selected two bags of spinach and made for the till. Ahead of him, in a short queue, stood a cyclist in cleats. Water dripped onto the tiles. Damon bit his lip with amusement.

'Has it started raining?' he asked aloud.

The cyclist turned round to examine him. There was no flicker of recognition.

'No, some cock in a truck went through a big puddle at ninety miles per hour and drenched me.'

'Some people don't like cyclists.'

The words were delivered with no discernible trace of sympathy.

'You're right. Drivers in this country are utterly negative towards anyone on two wheels. Do you cycle?'

'What, me?' said Damon, offended. 'No, fuck that, too dangerous. And you look like a bit of a nonce in the gear. No offence.'

The cyclist turned his back. He reached the front of the queue, paid for some tissues and stalked out of the supermarket's sliding doors.

On returning to the motor he was relieved to find Drogba sitting patiently. The dog had resisted the urge to chew up the interior. Damon jumped in and revved the engine. Along the street Paul attempted to recompose himself. He looked up at the aggressive noise just in time to see a black truck disappear off into the distance.

He watched it recede rapidly and took a few deep breaths. He adjusted his helmet, climbed on the bike and sat gingerly on the saddle, feeling the damp penetrate into every nook and cranny. Finally he set off, pedalling slowly in the same direction.

Chapter Seven

All My Friends

Back at the holiday rental, the Boys were milling around the kitchen.

'Time we got on it,' announced Matt.

'I thought you were feeling queasy?' asked Ed, surprised.

'It's passed now,' said Matt, extracting a bottle of lager from the fridge.

'Hold that beer then and try one of these.'

Ed held aloft a bottle of orange liquid.

'Tizer?'

'Aperol.' He grabbed five tumblers and filled them with the orange aperitif, rummaged through the freezer for ice and then popped the cork from a bottle of prosecco.

'Wow, these couldn't be any more gay unless they came with an umbrella and a disco soundtrack,' said Jack, examining his.

'Wait till you try it.'

'Oooh,' smiled Matt. 'That's nice. I could be sitting in a piazza in Cortona.'

'Or eating pizza in the back of a Cortina,' suggested Ed.

The spritzers went to work and soon they were laughing and talking nonsense loudly.

A doorbell chimed over the din. It rang several more times before Matt went to answer.

Paul stood waiting impatiently, bike in hand.

'What happened to you?' his grin slid off at the sight of Paul's expression. He was shivering, despite the sun.

'Some bonehead in a redneck truck thought it might be fun to soak me,' scowled Paul.

'You look like he hosed you down.' Matt stood back as Paul wheeled the bike in, propped it against the banisters, hauled off his cleats and tossed them into a corner. He began to strip off soaking clothes leaving damp sock prints on the floor.

'Paul's arrived. He's bit wet,' announced Matt, returning to the kitchen.

'We know that,' said Jack.

'Did you take a wrong turn through a car wash?' asked Ed, pushing his glasses up his nose.

'Some nutter in a truck deliberately doused me. I fell over and nearly drowned in an inch of water. I could hear this big dog barking inside as it swept past.'

'Why, what was his problem?' asked Jack, setting down his drink.

'People don't need an excuse to pick on cyclists. It's open season.'

'No need to shower at least,' suggested Jack, breezily.

'Have a drink Paul,' said Matt, proffering a bottle.

'I'd rather have a cup of tea, actually. In fact I'll have a hot shower first. Got a bit of a chill.' He stood up, unhooked two panniers from the bike on his way through the hallway and disappeared up the stairs still wearing his helmet.

The others went back to baiting each other.

Fifteen minutes later Paul came down wearing a T-shirt and baggy shorts. A cup of lukewarm tea waited on the island. He took a sip of the brew and sat quietly on a stool.

The others were busy ribbing each other and competing

for laughs as usual. Paul wasn't in the mood but he felt better just for being there, all the same.

Bowls of snacks lay around. He helped himself to some crisps.

'Don't suppose anyone brought any cake, did they?' he asked, hopefully.

'As it happens...' said Jack. He reached into a box and raised a tin aloft.

'Raspberry sponge, home baked.'

'I don't care what anyone says about you, Jack,' Paul's face lit up at the prospect of sugar.

'I always said you were a bit of a fruitcake, Jack,' said Matt.

Jack cut him a generous slice, placed it onto a plate and handed it over. Paul took a large bite and felt his mood lift instantly.

'Mmmm,' he smacked his lips and washed it down with a swig of tea. 'Very, umm, moist.'

'Better? Is it releasing the endorphins?' asked Jack, cutting himself a slice and sweeping crumbs off the counter-top.

'No endorphins round here,' said Thom. 'Just sharks.'

'Jack got stung by a box jellyfish, earlier,' announced Ed.

'Really?' asked Paul, raising an eyebrow.

'No. He stood on some glass, poncing about in the sea.'

'Serves you right,' said Paul. 'Swimming in these waters is madness.'

'No cake for you now,' admonished Jack, pretending to confiscate the plate.

The banter ratcheted up a notch. Paul finally accepted a drink, Thom and Matt became involved in an intense discussion about classic British motorbikes, Ed went off for a 'shit, shower and shave' threatening to use Matt's en suite to execute the first stage of his plan.

'Don't you dare!' shouted Matt after him.

Late afternoon wound into early evening and the bottles began to pile up. As the conversation grew louder, Matt gravitated to his usual role of DJ.

The minimalist Reich piano loop of LCD Soundsystem's "All My Friends" began its insistent build. He moved to the centre of the room, suddenly his dancefloor. Ed nudged Paul and they watched in amusement as he began to pull jerky shapes to its rhythm. He threw his arms out making patterns with his hands as the pulsing beat and nagging guitar began to propel the tune. He became increasingly more animated, even moonwalking poorly at one point. Then he began to mime the song's lyrics. At "one of the ways we show our age" he pretended to walk shakily with a stick. He shielded his eyes for "if the sun comes up" and lurched around at "I still don't want to stagger home". Everyone was now watching the floorshow. Matt looked them all in the eye and beckoned enticingly with a forefinger.

Jack was first to accept the challenge. The pair faced each other and began to cycle through vintage dance routines like The Swim and The Mashed Potato, re-enacting *Pulp Fiction*. Matt then signalled furiously at Thom, Paul and Ed. Thom gave in and joined them, bumping bottoms with Jack. Matt then grasped Ed by the hand and pulled him onto the floor. Ed gave him a pleading look but quickly began to side together enthusiastically. Matt was yelling the words passionately now, 'And where are your friends tonight?' he sang, extending his arms beckoningly. Then he gathered each of them in and they all linked arms, singing. Paul finally joined the circle and they hollered the climax in unison at the tops of their voices, 'If I could see all my friends tonight, if I could see all my friends tooooooooniiiiight'.

As the tune faded out, they laughed and high-fived.

Matt slumped to the floor and lay there, arms and legs starred.

'One dance and I'm knackered. How did we manage to club all night?' gasped Ed, slumping into an armchair.

'We danced. You dozed, remember?' said Matt, supine.

'There were no guitars, Baggy arrived just in time to save music. Right, who's ready for fish and chips? I'll go if someone comes with me,' offered Jack.

'Trust you to be the first to think of food,' tutted Thom.

'I ordered while you were out, like you suggested,' said Jack.

'Veggie pie for me, I hope,' demanded Paul.

'No I asked for dolphin and chips fried in whale dripping, Ghandi.'

'Sustainably caught dolphin, I hope,' said Paul, looking over his reading glasses.

Ed and Thom cruised cautiously to the chippy.

Its windows were completely steamed up despite the door being jammed open by a queue of customers that snaked outside. Behind the counter it was a hive of activity as an entire family in white coats fried and wrapped furiously. Angry sizzling filled the air and the aroma of boiling oil hung heavy.

Wearing a grey hoodie, Damon stood near the front of the queue, holding Drogba by a chain lead in one hand and perusing his phone with the other. The queue at the post office had been bad, this was worse. He looked up as the two entered the shop. Obviously London types. Actually they looked familiar, he realised. Those blokes staying in the flash palace down the street.

Damon looked back at the mobile in his hand. Its screen displayed an image of Karen holding up her dive training certificate on her club's website news page. He was aware she had been studying for a test of some kind. It was something to get her out of the house she had said when he asked, but there was more to it than that. She was up to something. He knew it. Was she going to do a runner?

Then it would be just him. Everyone he'd ever been close to had left him in the end: Dad, Mum, Mr Donovan his science teacher, Andrezj. All gone for one reason or another. 'We're all on our own in the end,' his mum had mused aloud once. He knew what she meant now.

He didn't have any real mates locally – he didn't count the other gym rats. There was Treggers but he could barely look him in the eye. He had an exit plan. Another couple of years would suffice then he'd quit Camber and head for Spain. Karen could come with him.

'What can I get you Mr Damo, usual?' asked Angelo, the proprietor, snapping him out of his brooding. Deep bags below Angelo's eyes made him look doleful, as if life behind a deep fat fryer was not what he had envisaged for himself.

'The usual, Angelo mate,' replied Damon with a sigh. Angelo went to work rapidly, scooping chips onto crisp white paper. Dark oil stains leached into it.

'Pickled egg for you, Mr Damo?'

'Yes please Mr Angelo.'

'Nice and shiny like your head, eh?' grinned Angelo.

'That's right mate,' said Damon slapping his bald pate vigorously. It was an in-joke between the pair to which Damon had given his consent.

'Best give one to my friend here, too. He slapped Ed lightly on the head. Ed, lost in his phone, reared back in surprise.

'Ha, ha, no offence mate, good for the follicles,' Damon winked.

'Caused by too much testosterone,' smiled Ed, polishing his head in an attempt to defuse the moment. The shop was quiet. Everyone was watching.

'Maybe I can pay for your supper since you were kind enough to return my wallet earlier,' asked Ed.

'Not necessary mate, got my own business. Doing nicely thanks.'

'Your own business? Good stuff,' nodded Ed, approvingly. 'We entrepreneurs need to stick together. What do you do?'

'Oh, buy and sell, you know.'

'Good for you,' Ed nodded approvingly.

'Absolutely. Anyway, nice to meet you. Enjoy your supper, gentlemen,' said Damon breezily as he exited the chippy with the dog in tow.

Ed, Thom and the entire line of customers watched the pair climb into the Mercedes truck parked on double yellows. It did a swift U-turn and sped off.

Their order arrived and was swiftly stuffed into bags. Ed paid and they made their way back to the car.

'That was a bit odd, wasn't it?' said Thom, delving between papers and fishing out a couple of chips.

'A bit, maybe it was his way of being personable,' said Ed, cracking a window to avoid the smell penetrating the upholstery.

'Funny way of going about it, oh, look there's his motor!' Thom pointed at the pick-up as they reached the end of their road.

'Must be, how many black X-Class Mercs do you think there are round here?' agreed Ed.

'About one,' said Thom, throwing another chip in his mouth. The tart vinegar made him pull a face.

Inside, Jack and Paul were sitting around the dining table engaged in an improbable discussion about the perfect cheesecake. They stood up and began to open the paper bags and divide the food onto plates.

'Where's Anscombe?' asked Ed, pinching a chip from a plate.

'Upstairs. Oi Matt! Yer fish supper's on t'table!' hollered Jack.

Matt was sitting on the toilet casually thumbing through his phone. He glanced at Annie's text again. He wondered how she had remembered the date of Boys' Weekend. Had he mentioned it? Maybe it was written on a calendar somewhere. He began to type a reply but got stuck halfway through and erased it.

The last time he had seen her was a month after the funeral. They'd met for a coffee in a busy café on the Thames by Wandsworth Park. It was a bitter day and Baltic air raced upriver. Fragile flakes of snow fluttered from a pallid sky. She was wrapped up in a heavy woollen jacket, black jeggings and leather boots. Long dark chestnut hair tumbled out from a wool baker boy hat that was a little too young for her but she carried it off. They made small talk for a while then went for a walk in the park. Matt apologised for cutting out so soon at the wake. She understood, she said, in fact she'd barely noticed she was so busy.

'The whole day had an unreal quality about it, I was on autopilot.'

Matt inquired gently what she'd done with Will's ashes.

'We threw him off a bridge,' she said matter-of-factly.

'Nice touch. Any particular one?'

'Putney. We held a ceremony early one Sunday morning as the tide was going out. Steven held up his phone and played "Atlantic City". On family holidays Will would always put it on in the car when it was time to go home. Even the kids would sit and listen in silence.'

'It's the bit about dying and coming back, isn't it?' nodded Matt. He began to sing the chorus. Annie joined him and they sang together softly. He was reminded just how good her voice was. She had fronted a soul covers band for a few years, which was how they had initially met.

They walked on in silence for a few minutes. The grass and the surrounding brick houses appeared tonally flat as if the weather was draining colour from the air.

'So what are your plans?' asked Matt eventually. An empty pleasure boat rolled and pitched downriver.

'Oh, there's plenty to do, a lot of loose ends. Like what to do with his agency.'

'And what are you going to do?' asked Matt, kicking a conker. It bowled pleasingly along the tarmac. Mentally he celebrated a goal at the Clock End.

'Still haven't made up my mind. Shelley and his team sent me an email about buying it out a couple of weeks after the funeral.'

'They didn't waste much time.'

'No, but I suppose life has to go on and they have their jobs to think about. It's only a small set up so it's not worth a great deal without Will but I could do with the money really. He put everything into it. We cancelled our life insurance a few years back to free up some cash.'

'Oh.'

'Yes, I know. I'm not sure how long we can afford the mortgage. Illness is an expensive business.' Her heel caught on a rough patch of the path and she stopped to examine it for a moment.

'What does that mean?' asked Matt frowning.

'Downsizing I suppose.'

'That's a shame. Would you stay round here?'

'Maybe. Steven's still at school so I hope we can survive a couple more years where we are and bite the bullet when they're both at college or whatever.'

'And how are they coping?' he ventured as they fell back into step.

'Charlotte's carried on as if nothing's happened. She's putting on a brave face for me but I think she's OK. I'm more worried about Steven. He's become very withdrawn. Doesn't want to go out and keeps complaining of mysterious aches and pains.'

'Sounds like he's suffering,' nodded Matt. 'It's understandable, losing his dad like that. I could have a word with him, maybe use Will's season ticket and go to a game. It might help get him out of his shell.'

'That's a good idea. If you wouldn't mind,' she glanced at him.

'No, it's not a problem. Actually watching West Ham is a problem but I'm prepared to make sacrifices for my godson.'

'It's a big ask, I know,' she laughed. 'I could never understand why Will cared when they gave him so much grief. He'd be in such a bad mood when they lost.'

'Christ, he must have been foul most weekends, then,' said Matt.

They stepped aside as a cyclist wrapped up like an arctic scuba diver whirled past. He put his hand on her arm.

'What about you? Have you got anyone to, you know, talk to?' he asked looking her in the eye.

'Not really,' she shrugged, glancing at him then away quickly. 'My folks are both gone, I've taken the kids to see their grandmother a couple of times. We've never really seen eye-to-eye.'

'What about the others?'

'The Boys? No!' she snorted, derisively. 'I was Will's wife. No Will, no reason to stay in touch, is there?'

'I'm here. I'm around.'

She stopped and put her hand on his arm.

'I know you are.'

They had reached the exit to the park. Her house was a ten-minute walk away. Matt was overrunning on a meter.

'I'd better go. I'll be in touch with Steven. Ask him to take me to a game, make it difficult to get out of,' said Matt breezily.

'Good idea.'

'And I'll see you soon, right?'

'Definitely.'

They hugged, Annie pecked him on the cheek and Matt trotted off without looking back.

He'd tried a couple of times but failed to persuade Steven to accompany him. Now there was only one home match left in the season. He resolved to try again on Monday or buy tickets for an England game.

* * *

Jack's shout drifted up the stairs. He sighed, put his phone on the sink, pulled his trousers up and flushed.

Downstairs the conversation had tailed off as chips were fed into mouths. Jack raised his eyes when Matt trotted down and promptly emptied half a bottle of ketchup onto his plate.

'Where's my battered sausage?'

'At the home for battered sausages?' suggested Jack.

'Like battered sea sausage dog home?' enquired Thom.

'I suppose they forgot it,' said Ed, sprinkling more salt on his chips.

'You should have checked, you completely useless, mildly overweight twat,' said Matt prodding his fish with suspicion.

'Stop complaining,' scolded Paul. 'And enjoy your unsustainable marine catch.'

Conversation lulled as they worked their way through the greasy piles on their plates then, as they sat back licking fingers and lips, Ed decided it was time to draw attention to the elephant in the room.

'So are we going ahead with this grotesque idea of watching Will play question master?' he asked, filching a piece of batter from Thom's plate. In the background a playlist rotated through old funk and soul numbers.

'Of course we are,' said Matt, drumming his fingers on the table in time. 'He didn't make it so we could bin it and go down the boozer.'

'It's what he wanted,' agreed Jack.

'What he wanted was to live,' pointed out Ed.

'I'm not particularly comfortable with it,' said Paul. 'It's going to feel very weird, him sitting there, casually playing Paxman, setting us pop poseurs when we all know he knew his time was up. The vibe is all wrong.'

'Let's pass – Will did!' urged Jack sarcastically.

'Absolutely not,' said Matt. 'He obviously considered that but he still went through with it. He can't be here but he's here in spirit, that's the point. The least we can do is... play along.'

'If he's here in spirit, we should get out the Ouija board and ask him,' said Thom abruptly. He flipped over a tumbler and began sliding it around the dining table jerkily. 'Hang on, I'm getting a message... D... A, no, E,' the tumbler zigzagged frantically. 'M... O...' The glass jerked around wildly under his hand, '... N!'

He then scooped some mushy peas from a small Styrofoam cup into his mouth and made a pantomime retching noise before opening it to reveal the contents.

'Good lad, eat your greens and you'll grow up to be an evil presence,' said Paul.

'Enough devilment,' said Ed standing up with his plate. 'Are we going to stay here and hold an exorcism or are we going down the pub for some holy water?'

'Be ready in twenty minutes?' suggested Jack.

They wandered off to their rooms to change.

***

Ed sat heavily on the edge of his bed and sighed. He felt a little bloated. Picking at Thom's batter had been a mistake.

He kicked off his chinos, pulled on a pair of jeans and a jumper, rubbing his gut tenderly in the process. Then he flopped back on the bed to gather himself for a moment. He was going to have to go through with the quiz. Hopefully it would be a painless bit of fun but you could never be sure with Will. He could be a contrary bugger, they'd all witnessed it often enough.

Perhaps it helped take his mind off things but the thought of them all sitting around drinking and laughing without him can't have been helpful.

His mind wandered back to their youth. There was a camping trip they'd all taken to Devon during a classic English summer thirty years ago. Walking one afternoon they'd found a swing hanging over the River Dart. Spontaneously they'd stripped off and spent an hour hurling themselves into the water, whooping and laughing. Life hadn't served up many more idyllic moments than that since, nor was it likely to. The afternoon was rounded off by Will mooning an unsuspecting family who had the misfortune to appear on the opposite bank, much to their amusement. The father had been deeply unimpressed, uttering threats, which made it even funnier. Pure Will.

There was another holiday when Ed saw another side of Will when he accompanied Ed's family to the south of France.

It was a difficult time for Will. He had lost his dad, Don, five months previously. Ed's parents offered to take him along because the families were close.

Will had taken a week off school in the immediate aftermath, then returned behaving as if nothing had happened. None of the others made any attempt to raise it. It wasn't the sort of thing you did then, and Will certainly didn't bring the subject up. He was ploughing on. Being Will. Even more so, winding up teachers, provoking other kids. He was given extra licence and he used it.

The pair spent a happy week in Fréjus cadging cigarettes from girls dispensing them in trays along the beach, eating frites dripping in wine vinegar, dancing in the site's disco and trying to get off with girls. Naturally it was Will who scored, disappearing off with a tall German girl for long walks making Ed jealous. Thankfully, Eva Braun went home after a few days and they were back doing bro things again.

One evening they were lounging outside the caravan surrounded by empty bottles of French lager. Don came up in the conversation, somehow. Ed probed gently and Will suddenly began to open up.

'He was fifty-two years old. Fit. You realise life hangs by a thread. I get palpitations sometimes now, feel a bit faint. I don't think I'll ever be old either,' Will admitted.

Ed attempted to mollify him, told him he was talking rubbish but Will was having none of it. He was a total mess and he'd been putting up a front ever since.

'I don't want kids,' he announced. 'I couldn't bear to leave them like that. Dad would be devastated if he knew he'd left us. Life's shit.'

'He wouldn't have wanted to miss out on you or your sister, I know that, Will, whatever was going to happen. He was happy, he didn't know anything was wrong with him. It was just one of those things.'

'But what about me, though?' Will asked. 'What about me?'

He was crying like a baby. Ed put an arm round him and pulled him close. Will put his head on Ed's shoulder and sobbed for a while. Then he wiped away the tears and disappeared 'to clear his head'. An hour or so later, when he hadn't returned, Ed went to search for him, feeling concerned. He strolled up to the bar and there was Will deep in conversation with a pretty blonde. He gave him a wave and a smile. Neither ever mentioned the incident and Ed never saw Will show that side of himself again, not even when he was gravely ill.

Dead at fifty-two, just like his dad. At least he had time to say goodbye, Ed thought.

Enough. He sat up, pulled on his shoes and walked slowly downstairs where the others were already pulling on coats. They then stood around waiting for Thom to appear.

'There's always one,' sighed Jack.

'Come on! It'll be last orders by the time we get there,' shouted Matt. The clock ticked on a few minutes before Thom appeared at the top of the stairs. He was wearing black trousers, cherry red brogues and a burgundy jumper under a grey tweed jacket.

'Come on, for heaven's sake it's not a fashion shoot,' said Paul.

'Just because you look like a tramp doesn't mean we all have to,' said Thom dismissively, pulling on a checked cap. 'And will you all please hurry up, you're keeping me waiting.'

He barged past and stepped outside into fresh night air.

Chapter Eight

I Need Some Fine Wine and You,
You Need to be Nicer

Matt reached into his top pocket, produced a spliff and lit it.

'That absolutely stinks, Matt,' said Paul, stepping away from him suddenly, repulsed. He had never considered drugs anything less than idiocy.

'Calm down, calm down. It's just a harmless bit of weed.'

'No such thing as harmless when something's illegal. It's probably trafficked by gangs using immigrant slave labour.'

'Actually it's home produce. Lovingly tended by the Jolly Green Giant, a local horticultural acquaintance who grows it in his greenhouse between the tomato plants,' said Matt. 'You'd be surprised how much of that goes on. Pop down your local aquarium supplier. Those hoodie blokes in the queue buying hydroponic equipment? They no keep exotic fish.'

'Not even roach?' asked Jack.

'Well just stay out of my way if you must do it,' snorted Paul, striding ahead.

'Lighten up, Jeez,' muttered Matt. Jack reached across, plucked the joint from his lips, took a long drag and coughed.

'Sweet Mary Jane,' smiled Matt.

They had reached the end of the gravel road behind the

dunes where a rough footpath cut diagonally across a patch of wasteland with a tiny basketball court in one corner. The wind had dropped and with the tide on its way out, the sea was inaudible. They found themselves back in residential side streets outside a pub called the Dunes Bar. Together they entered, stepping over astroturfed decking through a door and into a large busy bar. To one side, tables were full of diners consuming plates of fish and chips. The rest of the pub was packed with a mix of weekenders and locals.

'Empty table,' said Jack, indicating a spot near the door about to be vacated by a group. 'Wife beater,' he added, making a beeline for the space before it was snapped up.

Paul joined him while the other three went to the bar. They returned bearing pint glasses and packets of crisps.

'Your fizzy piss,' said Thom, handing Jack his lager.

He lifted his glass.

'Will!'

They all clinked glasses.

Jack, Ed and Thom promptly produced their phones.

'Oi! No phones,' said Paul. 'You're worse than a bunch of teenagers.'

'I was just checking for messages,' protested Jack.

'Me too,' agreed Thom.

'I can't believe anything that important might have broken in the past ten minutes.'

'And I was checking work emails,' pointed out Ed.

'My point entirely. You're chained to the thing.'

'Oh, I hear the sound of a horse being saddled up,' sighed Matt, feeling nicely woozy.

'That so-called tool of liberation has you enslaved,' said Paul pointing a finger accusingly at the iPhone in Ed's hand. Ed reared back slightly in mock surprise.

'You can't step away from your job, your apps are tracking

your every move and every search you make leaves a crumb trail of data for corporations to build a detailed profile of your life.'

'Alternatively it's a remarkably sophisticated device, one about a million times more powerful than the computers that guided the first moon landing and all in the palm of your hand. It's a portable entertainment centre, a bottomless source of knowledge and a very useful distraction when pub bores start banging on,' countered Ed.

'I'm with Paul,' declared Jack. 'He's right. There's this app in China that pretends to log your creditworthiness. It began innocently enough but it's ended up rating people how good they are as citizens, i.e., how much they tow the party line. Dissidents, troublemakers get a bad ranking and then find they can't access any care services.'

'That's where Orwell got it wrong,' said Paul. 'He thought there would be cameras everywhere to monitor people, he didn't think we'd be stupid enough to monitor ourselves.'

'The difference being, we don't live in a one party police state,' said Ed, using a beer mat to scrape ale onto the carpet.

'Have you read the papers recently?' returned Paul.

Thom stood up and excused himself.

No one paid much attention to him as a debate over surveillance ensued. Ed and Jack went to work, gleefully winding Paul up.

Matt zoned out as the argument went to and fro and let his eyes wander round the room. 'Hey, have you seen Thom?' he asked eventually.

'He went off to the loo,' said Jack, looking up.

'No, he's over there chatting to that tall woman at the bar,' he said, nodding towards the far corner where Thom was deep in conversation with a handsome woman wearing jeans tucked into leather boots.

'Wow, he's unbelievable,' said Jack. 'How old do you reckon she is?'

'Can't help himself,' agreed Ed, attempting not to sound jealous.

Abruptly the woman downed her glass, pulled on a coat and made for the door. Thom sauntered back to the table.

'Who was that?' asked Paul.

'Just a friend,' said Thom, making no move to sit down.

'A friend? You don't know anyone round here.'

'I do now.'

'You're kidding,' said Jack, suddenly appalled. 'You haven't pulled on a Boys' Weekend?'

'I'll see you back at the house,' said Thom, blowing them a kiss and making for the door.

'Thom!' Paul called after him, but Thom failed to turn round. 'I don't fucking believe it.'

'That's pretty poor, I have to say,' snorted Jack.

'Agreed,' said Ed. 'She was, what, thirty?'

'It's his life, who are we to judge?' said Matt, rising to his feet. He still felt stoned.

'If we wanted to have women here we'd invite the WAGs to come with us, well those who wanted to come with us. It's not called a Boys' Weekend for nothing, is it?' said Jack, scowling.

'Forget it. I'll get another round in,' said Matt, leaving them muttering into their beer like blazered gentlemen who have just been informed there's a woman in the club.

He headed for the toilets first where he relieved himself in a cubicle. He glanced at the ceiling, checking for cameras, then reached into his jacket, produced a small baggie and a tiny silver spoon from inside his jacket, dipped it in and took a small bump up his left nostril. With a loud sniff he thrust everything back into his pocket, flushed, snapped the latch and exited, stopping briefly at the mirror above the sink to check his top lip before leaving the bathroom.

Thirsty drinkers crammed round the bar. He had to push past groups and squeeze between two stools to reach the counter. Five long minutes later he turned round with a tray full of pints only to find himself hemmed in by a bulky figure with his back to him. The man was holding court to an older couple who seemed to be hanging on to his every word.

''Scuse,' said Matt.

The figure carried on, his head bobbing slightly as he held forth.

'Excuse me!'

The man showed no sign of moving. The older woman had spied Matt but made no attempt to interrupt.

'Can you move? Please!' shouted Matt, prodding the man lightly in the back with the tray, then stepping back.

Damon spun round, lips pursed tightly. Matt realised his mistake instantly.

'Did you want something?'

'Sorry, I was just trying to get past.'

'You don't raise your... voice... to... ME!' Damon spat out the last word. Faces turned in their direction.

'I didn't think you could hear over all the noise.'

'There's nothing wrong with my hearing. You didn't say, please.'

'I did say please, I can assure you.'

'There you go again, suggesting I have a hearing problem,' said Damon, irked.

'No I didn't. I mean it's very noisy in here so maybe my words got lost,' said Matt. A pleading tone had entered his voice.

Damon leant across Matt and set a pint of lime and soda on the bar. Matt stood holding the tray, boxed in. Damon leaned in.

'I know what I heard and you better not be here when I leave,' he hissed into his ear.

Matt stared back at him, trying not to show he was intimidated, although he most certainly was. Damon stepped to one side. Matt slid swiftly past him and headed quickly back to the table.

'Er, boys, I think I've just accidentally upset someone.'

'What do you mean?' asked Paul, draining his glass and setting it down.

'The big geezer at the bar. I tried to go past him but he wouldn't move. I raised my voice and he got all upset.'

Ed glanced at the bar. Damon's gorgon gaze was locked onto their table like he was trying to pull it in with a tractor beam.

'Isn't that our mate? Now ex-mate. Nice one, Matt!'

'I think we should drink up swiftly and head back pronto. He muttered something about me not being here when he left,' said Matt anxiously.

'Exit pursued by stare,' nodded Paul.

'Exit means exit,' said Ed flatly.

'Jesus, this is like having Terry Dolan waiting for me at lunch break,' said Matt, recalling an encounter with a school bully, still firmly imprinted in the memory like a thirty-five-year-old boot mark. His pint remained untouched.

'This may be worse than a quick pasting behind the bike sheds,' noted Jack.

'I gave a good account of myself that day, actually,' replied Matt.

'I saw it. A black eye and a fat lip was a let off when you consider how bad it might have been,' nodded Ed. 'It was over in seconds.'

'This isn't school, though, is it? It's pathetic,' said Paul. 'I'm not going to be intimidated by some thug.'

'Easy for you to say, you're not the one he wants to batter,' said Matt sullenly.

Damon moved over to engage another group close to the door, cutting them off.

'Matt's right, we should probably drink up and go,' announced Jack, taking a large swig of his pint and burping loudly.

They went to work on their drinks, except Matt whose thirst had suddenly diminished. A few minutes later Damon placed his glass on the bar and headed towards the toilets.

'He's gone for a piss, let's go,' said Jack, grabbing his jacket and heading straight for the door. The others followed suit with comic haste. Outside, as they pulled on their coats, Matt peered through the front window. There was no sign of Damon.

'Come on,' he said, spinning on his heel and heading for the patch of wasteland. He burped loudly. Someone echoed him. They sounded like a group of frogs staking out their territory.

'Whose idea was Camber, anyway? Thanks Will,' muttered Jack.

'Don't think we can blame Will for the local wildlife, can we?' said Paul.

'Oh, shit! He's just run out of the pub and he's got an axe!' said Ed, urgently.

Matt's head span round.

'Only joking.'

'You bastard, Ed,' said Matt. His heart had momentarily skipped a beat.

'Come on Matt, you can take him, let's go back. The harder they come and all that,' grinned Ed.

At the far end of the path they all turned round to look back but no hellhound stalked their trail. Matt took one last look around to check for pursuit before he slid the key in the front door and let everyone in. Then he bolted the door.

'Phew! I need a drink after that,' he gasped, his appetite for alcohol rapidly returning.

'Wait a minute, what's that?' asked Jack frowning.

They stood still for a moment. Cries could be heard coming from upstairs, a woman in the throes of ecstasy. The backbeat of mattress springs kept time with her moans.

'He's only brought her back here!' gasped Paul.

'Wow, and I bet he's not using his own bed either because he had a single,' noted Ed with some concern.

'It's like a porno version of the Three Bears, "Who's been shagging in myyyy bed!"' giggled Jack. '*Hot Grizzlies.*'

Matt unbolted the front door, opened it again, then slammed it loudly. The coital soundtrack ended abruptly. Shaking heads and tutting, they filed into the living room, poured drinks and slumped into comfy chairs. Matt put his phone in the dock.

The strains of Prince's "Sexy MF" sprang into life. Everyone laughed.

'Perhaps it should be Fleetwood Mac's "Sugar Daddy"?' Paul offered.

'Seriously, I've never known anyone put it about so much. He behaves like a randy teenager,' sighed Paul.

'He thinks Screw Fix Direct is a dating agency,' shot Jack.

'Randy!' snorted Ed. 'There's a word you don't hear any more. Like "shag". Does anyone "shag" anymore?'

'Is that an admission about your sex life or an etymological question?' asked Paul.

'Slip her one, do the dirty deed, bonk…' threw in Jack.

'Tup… Shakespeare,' offered Matt.

'Educational, too. The conversation really has gone to

another level, I must say, that's why I come away on these weekends,' observed Paul.

'You don't think she's staying, do you?' asked Jack, suddenly worried.

'Nah, he wouldn't do that, would he?' said Ed, sounding unsure.

'Do what?'

Thom was standing in the doorway, barefoot in a pair of tracksuit bottoms and a T-shirt. He strolled in, extracted a clean tumbler from a cupboard and poured himself a glass of water and downed it. He had the air of a man who should be wearing a smoking jacket.

'She's not staying, is she?' demanded Jack.

Thom sat in the last spare armchair and took a long swig from his glass. 'Oh, I shouldn't think so, she's a local lass. Passing ships and all that.'

'Was it really necessary to get off with a bird on a Boy's Weekend, Thom? Couldn't you keep it in your pants for a couple of days?'

Thom shrugged.

'It wasn't like that…' his voice trailed off. 'You lot are back early?' he said, attempting to change the subject.

'There was a bit of an incident in the pub,' said Ed. 'Matt managed to upset that bloke we met, the big guy who returned my wallet when we were on the beach, the one in the chippy.'

'He's a bit odd and very big,' said Thom. 'I wouldn't want to get on the wrong side of him. What did you do Matt?'

'Nothing! It was a misunderstanding, he got the wrong end of the stick.'

'We made a swift exit,' said Jack, flicking a bit of paper at Matt. 'Caught you with your pants down.'

Heels clattered on the hallway's wooden floor, then

Karen appeared in the doorway, hair brushed and make-up reapplied. A tiny smudge of ruby lipstick was visible in the corner of her mouth.

'Aren't you going to offer a girl a drink, Thom?' she said, hoisting her handbag onto the kitchen table. 'Don't worry, I'll help myself.'

Jack shot Thom an angry look, Thom pretended not to notice and sat down.

Karen rummaged through cupboards. Unable to find a clean glass she picked up a dirty one, rinsed it under the tap, emptied a bottle of red into it and piled a handful of peanuts into her mouth. Pearly teeth flashed briefly.

They sat watching her silently like a group of monks in a monastery confronted by a supermodel at vespers.

'Aren't you going to introduce me, Thom?' she said finally.

Thom stood up with a cough. Karen slid straight into his seat and crossed her legs very deliberately. Ed, sitting to her left on a couch, found himself inadvertently reminded of Sharon Stone in *Basic Instinct*.

'Erm, Karen this is Ed, Jack, Paul and Matt,' he said, pointing each of them out.

'Nice to meet you. Thom's told me all about you. Fancy being friends for so long,' said Karen, toying with her glass. 'I don't have any friends left from school.'

'You seem to make them easily enough,' said Jack, a touch sarcastically.

'Jack, wasn't it? Don't you like girls, Jack?' Karen asked, tipping her head to one side.

'I get on fine with them, thanks, but I don't know you and this is supposed to be just about us, a bunch of lads getting away for a few days. It's not a Club 18–30 holiday.'

'I don't think you qualify any longer, if you don't mind me saying,' she smiled.

Thom cleared his throat. 'Err, look, how about I walk you home?'

'One of you died, didn't he?' said Karen cutting him off. 'Is this a kind of a wake? Are you going to scatter his ashes in the sea or something, like that film?'

'That's not what I said,' said Thom, looking at the others, embarrassed.

'But someone died, didn't they?'

'It's not really any of your business,' snapped Jack, seemingly determined to make the atmosphere as chilly as possible.

'Will, wasn't it?' Karen turned to Thom.

Paul stood up without a word and left the room.

'Gosh you boys really don't like girls, do you?'

'Umm, Karen...' Thom began.

'I'm just teasing you all... come on. I'll be on my way in a minute, be gentlemen and indulge me. I'm curious because you're a funny bunch if you don't mind me saying and this is an interesting story,' she said, draining her glass and handing it to Thom. 'A quick refill wouldn't go amiss.'

Thom hesitated for a moment then walked over to the kitchen. All the bottles on the counter were empty but he found a fresh one in a box, cracked the cap, poured her another glass and one of his own.

'Lovely place,' said Karen, looking around the room. 'They built it last year. I had a peek through the windows when it was finished. I'd love a kitchen-diner like this.'

'Anyone else?' Thom called breezily.

'So this friend who died... Will. You're here to remember him?'

'Not really,' said Thom, perching on the arm of her chair. 'He booked it. We've been doing these little weekends for a few years and he always organised them. But he couldn't make it this time because he passed away a few months back.'

'That's sad.'

'Yes it is,' said Ed.

'What did he die of?'

'Why are you so interested in us?' asked Matt, feeling more than a little drunk again.

'You're interesting. So what happens to the women; the wives, girlfriends.'

'We explained, it's an annual mates get together. Just us. We went to school together, our women didn't. There's nothing wrong with them but there's a different dynamic when we go out with them together,' said Ed, patiently.

'They don't all get along in other words.'

'That's not what I said.'

'You're a bit cliquey then. Wrapped up in yourselves. Impressed by each other's wit and repartee.'

'Is this twenty questions? If it is, you're running out rapidly,' sneered Jack.

'I've got a few left, come on. What did he die of? Will.'

'Leukaemia slash rotten luck,' said Thom quietly.

'Nasty. Was he very unhealthy or something?'

'Superfit, never smoked in his life. You're out of questions by the way,' said Jack.

'Do you all have a role?' Karen asked, pointing at them in turn. 'Sneezy, Sleepy, Stoney Not Bashful, definitely. And you must be Grumpy.'

Thom and Ed grinned. Jack smiled, despite himself.

'You're not exactly Snow White, honey,' he said in a Sam Spade voice. 'And there's only five of us.'

'What was he like, this Will guy? You act like he was a legend.'

'What was Will like?' asked Thom, considering the

101

question. 'Funny, generous, intelligent, charismatic in a way that made people overlook his flaws. A genius to us, anyway.'

'And what were his flaws?' asked Karen.

'He could be rude to the point of obnoxious, loud, overbearing, arrogant...'

'And that was on a good day,' added Ed.

'He sounds adorable,' smiled Karen.

Chapter Nine

The Stars Are Indifferent to Astronomy

Drogba bolted madly up and down the moonlit beach. He'd been left at home while Damon went to the Dunes and, having relieved himself, was now burning off pent-up energy.

The dog was no longer allowed to accompany his master to the pub because he was barred. In his defence the woman had stood on his tail but it was an ugly scene and she had been lucky to avoid more than a sharp nip. Tom, the landlord, quietly but firmly suggested it would be best if he didn't accompany his owner in future, though the reverse might have been an equally acceptable arrangement.

Damon stalked along behind the hound as it pirouetted in the sand, barking at him. Wrapped up in a heavy khaki jacket with a fur collar, he held the pack of fireworks in one hand and jammed the other inside a pocket. Watching Karen go off with Thom had soured his mood. His mate with the tray of drinks had only compounded his irritation.

He had an idea she was up to something when she slid off round the other side of the bar and stood on her own, ignoring him. Damon had watched her out of the corner of one eye as he buttonholed Squits about weight loads. Squits, real name Colin, had earned his nickname following an unfortunate incident at the gym when he had followed through while squatting a couple of hundred pounds. He'd attempted to explain to the rapidly emptying room that his loss of bowel control was down to the fact he was suffering from 'the squits' after eating a dodgy sausage roll.

Damon was rambling on about progressive loading when he caught sight of Karen wandering over to an older guy at the bar. He had said something in her ear and she'd laughed. Then she said something into his ear and he'd laughed. He'd bought her a drink and they'd begun to talk. Barely fifteen minutes later they had left. Just like that. She had studiously avoided any eye contact with him on the way out. Shocking behaviour, especially with a bloke who was obviously much older, but then Karen had always had a weird thing for older men.

She was a good looking woman, he reasoned. She could have a decent, regular bloke, easy. She'd had one eighteen months back. He was older, too, mind. They been going out for a while then one morning she had returned home sporting a black eye after an argument, so Damon felt honour-bound to chastise him.

It was a shame. Dennis was all right for a Palace fan, but he'd crossed the line. Damon went round to his place, knocked politely on the door and kicked it hard the moment the latch turned. The door swatted Dennis several feet down the hallway. Damon stormed in and kicked the stunned figure still in his dressing gown in the balls before he could get back to his feet. Then, as he retched onto his hall carpet, Damon had delivered a stiff lecture before leaving just as abruptly.

Unsurprisingly, Dennis hadn't shown his face around since. Karen had cried for a few days afterwards but it had ended. Quite rightly, too.

Up ahead, Drogba paused to relieve himself on a fence near the Boys' holiday let. Damon let his mood fester. The idea of an older man lying on top of her turned his stomach.

'Dirty old bastard!' he muttered aloud.

It was almost two years since Damon's last relationship. Tanya had packed her bags after a row, never to return. She had tired of finding herself some way down the pecking order from football and bodybuilding. She told him he was married to the gym, and there was some truth in that. In fact Damon had reached the conclusion he derived more satisfaction from pumping iron than he did from having sex with her. When she texted him to say they should call it day, it came as no great surprise. People always let you down in the end.

He strolled towards the back of the Boys' house and examined it for signs of activity. Several figures were clearly visible at the back, Karen was one of them. The muscle in his jaw flexed in irritation. He turned on his heel and marched in the direction of the sea until he was standing in damp sand.

'Target identified, bearing zero-six-five. Six rounds.'

He took the rockets from their plastic wallet and laid them carefully on top of the sleeve, ensuring their touchpapers remained dry. He selected one, blew it then inserted it loosely into the sand. He called Drogba over and ordered the dog to sit behind him. He stood back up, held a damp finger in the breeze briefly then crouched over the firework and realigned it. Satisfied, he reached into a pocket, fished out a lighter and thumbed the flint. A flame appeared then disappeared. He clicked it again, this time shielding it from the breeze with his other hand. The touchpaper glowed a soft orange colour and began to fizz. Damon felt a little thrill of anticipation and took a step back.

He began to count aloud, 'Five, four, three...'

That instant the rocket shot out of the sand with a loud whoosh. Damon inhaled sharply as it disappeared upwards, fishtailing with a loud hiss. It detonated loudly overhead, illuminating the night sky in pleasing cauliflowers of green and red sparks. He turned round to check on the dog, but Drogba, sitting patiently, had not so much as flinched.

'Lovely. Now, lower elevation,' he muttered.

He knelt down and selected another projectile from the pack, slid it into the sand but pushed it gently forward so it was leaning at a steep angle. He stepped back and eyed it up, like a golfer lining up a putt. Then he lit its touchpaper and stood back expectantly.

'Fire in the hole!' he barked.

The firework hissed, a thin wisp of smoke curled up its shaft before it shot out of the sand and streaked towards the back of the holiday rental, clipping the roof and deflecting with a shower of green and red sparks and a loud bang.

'Oooh, close! Noisy. Almost as loud as an eight-one-millimetre.'

He knelt down swiftly again, selected all four remaining rockets and planted them in a line in the sand. He snapped the lighter and lit each touchpaper, swiftly moving from left to right, then stood back feeling a childlike buzz of expectation rise as the fuses smouldered.

'Incoming!' he bellowed.

The four rockets launched in rapid sequence. The first two cleared the roof, igniting above the main road, the second clipped it and ricocheted over, the third hit one of the top windows. The double glazed glass held but sparks showered down onto the patio.

'Yes!' Damon began to perform a jig of delight in the sand. Drogba stood up and began to bark and run around him in circles. Damon stopped abruptly to look at him, howled like a wolf and recommenced his war-dance.

* * *

Karen was still toying with male egos when the second rocket clipped the roof of the house. A faint whistle was followed by a thud upstairs. Ed frowned, Thom cocked an ear, Jack started. At the far end of the couch Matt had fallen into a stupor.

Paul came running downstairs wearing a faded T-shirt from a sponsored run and a pair of shorts.

'Did anyone hear that? I was reading in bed.'

'Sounded like fireworks going off,' said Jack, standing up.

At that moment a sequence of detonations went off. Something collided with the upstairs rear window, sparks showered into the back garden.

'What the hell's going on?' Ed leapt up and ran to the back window and peered out.

Part of a rocket burned on the patio, yellow flames licking from its shell. Burning embers flickered in the breeze.

'I think we're under attack.'

Jack and Thom joined him at the window.

'There, someone's over there.'

'Where?' said Jack, cupping hands round the windowpane and looking into the distance.

'Towards the shore. Dancing round a dog,' said Thom.

'Let me have a look!' Karen stood up and squeezed between them.

'It's Damon. He bought some fireworks this afternoon. Thinks he's still in the army, firing rockets everywhere.'

'Who's Damon?' asked Thom, looking confused.

'My brother. We live at the end of the road.'

'That bloke is your brother? The guy with the dog?' asked Thom incredulously.

'Afraid so,' nodded Karen. 'Do you know him?'

'You might say we've met,' said Ed.

'You didn't tell me that you had a possessive brother,' said Thom, visibly worried.

'Why would I?' asked Karen. 'It's not the sort of thing you boast about. You've met him?' she raised an eyebrow quizzically.

'He returned my wallet earlier but Matt somehow managed to upset him in the pub,' explained Ed.

'He's very polite, but he takes offence easily,' explained Karen, biting her lip tensely.

'And now I've had carnal relations with his sister,' groaned Thom.

'His bark is worse than his bite,' said Karen, trying to mollify them.

'Are we talking about him or the dog?' asked Jack.

'I hate dogs,' said Matt, now awake and peering over their shoulders into the distance.

Karen drained her glass. 'I'd better be going.'

She retrieved her handbag and left without another word. The door slammed behind her. There was a moment's silence. Matt ran after her and bolted it.

'Nice one Thom,' said Jack accusingly.

'What did I do?' asked Thom, extending his hands innocently.

'Err, shagged the local psycho's sister?'

'How was I to know?'

'Why was it necessary to have a sexual encounter on a Boys' Weekend in the first place?'

'Because.'

'Because what?'

'Because I felt like it. I don't have to explain myself to you, right?'

'Now the *son et lumière* is over, I'm going back to bed,' said Paul. He padded out of the room and mounted the stairs.

'All right, calm down everyone, it's not worth getting worked up over,' said Ed, acting as peacemaker. 'Whose bed did you use by the way, Thom?'

'Err, it might have been yours,' said Thom, guiltily.

'Oh, for fuck's sake. You total bastard. Nothing changes!'

'It's OK, I put a towel down and cleaned up, you wouldn't know, I promise.'

'Oh, thanks for that,' said Ed stomping into the kitchen and pouring a glass of water, which he drained immediately. In their teens, he'd held a party at his parents' house. Thom had shut himself in Ed's bedroom with a girl and left a damp stain in his bed. Ed had had to wash the sheets the next morning, prompting questions from his mother. *If only*, Ed had thought.

'Let's have a nightcap. We can clear up the mess outside in the morning, eh?' Matt held up the bottle of Scotch. 'Who'll join me?'

'Go on then,' said Thom. Matt scoured the kitchen and rinsed off some tumblers. He then poured a couple of fingers in each. The four of them sat round the dining table.

'This is nice, very mellow,' nodded Ed.

'Mellow is good after this evening,' agreed Jack.

'Sorry everyone,' said Thom apologetically.

They sat back savouring the Scotch quietly. Jack stood up and began to tidy away, stacking newspapers, putting empty crisp packets in the bin and filling the dishwasher.

'So Karen was pure chance, Thom? You just turned your famous magnetic charm on her,' said Ed.

'Spur of the moment, honest, carpe diem and all that. The signals were unmistakable and I just switched on to auto. I shouldn't have done it I know but these options don't present themselves every day. I usually rely on Tinder.'

'You use Tinder?' asked Ed, unable to contain his curiosity.

'Occasionally,' admitted Thom, swilling the amber liquid in his glass.

'At his age,' called Jack, in the voice of a scandalised spinster.

'So the options do present themselves fairly often. How often?' carried on Ed.

'Don't know. Maybe twenty, twenty-five.'

'That many? And are they worth it?'

'Some are, some aren't. It's a lottery.'

'Lucky dip,' chipped in Matt.

'Are they all half your age?' inquired Jack. 'And I trust you took precautions young man, you don't want a paternity suit or a dose.'

'Of course. I used a wotsit,' said Thom exasperatedly.

'A wotsit? What, like this?' said Jack, holding up a corn snack from a bowl. 'How? Did you shove it down the eye?'

'A condom, you twat.'

'I quite like the idea of a cheese snack as a prophylactic,' observed Ed. 'Did she nibble said cheesy knob? Were other snacks employed? Maybe a Hula Hoop as a cock ring?'

'It's a bit of Twiglet, if I recall,' said Jack, raising an eyebrow.

'He definitely has a small bag of nuts,' added Matt.

They sniggered like children for a while. There was a brief lull while each mulled over potential new lines of engagement. Jack was first in.

'But there must be a danger of STDs with these encounters... Shit Tinder Dates.'

'Yes, there's been a few.'

'Go on,' urged Ed, refilling his glass.

Thom hesitated, then continued leaning forward as if letting them in on a secret.

'There was one really quite attractive woman in her forties, an events manager. We went to her place, had a glass or two of wine. She seemed perfectly normal until we got down to it. She was clearly not getting much out of the encounter. I asked what the problem was, whether there was something that got her off and she straight out asked me to urinate on her.'

They all exploded with laughter.

'Oh my. Did you oblige?' asked Ed, appalled.

'No I did not! I don't mind servicing people's kinks within reason. I said I'd been before I came out. Then I got dressed and baled.'

'You pissed off rather than piss on her,' noted Ed.

'Surely she should have mentioned her scatological proclivities on her profile?' mused Jack.

'Fifty Shades of Yellow,' said Ed. 'Any other standout moments?'

'There was another. We met in a café. I spot her in the red beret she said she'd be wearing but when she stands up she's clearly about six months pregnant. I mean, heavvvvyyyy with child.'

'You're sure she wasn't just a porker?' asked Ed.

'No, she was expecting.'

'And you were unsuspecting,' added Jack. 'Or was it yours from a previous encounter?'

'Ha. Turns out the boyfriend had done a runner. She was lonely and very messed up. I stayed for a couple of coffees, bought her some chocolate cake and then wished her luck in her search.'

'That's quite sad.'

'Yeah, it was.'

Matt poured himself another couple of fingers and set the bottle in the middle of the table. Jack wiped down the island, eyed it for smears, then threw the cloth in the sink.

'Right, I'm off to bed. Night.'

'I'll be up in a minute darling,' said Thom.

'You've had quite enough for one evening,' said Jack, starting the dishwasher. Water began sloshing around.

Jack climbed the stairs carefully. He felt drunk. He opened the door to the room he was sharing with Thom. He peeled off his clothes, used the bathroom, then slid under the sheets and glanced at his phone. The screen bathed his face in light. Nothing to report. He put the phone into its charger cable and lay back. Ten minutes later Thom came through the door. He kicked off his shoes, stripped to his underwear and climbed into bed with a sigh.

'Can I have a bedtime story?' asked Jack.

'Goldilocks and the Three Bears? Red Riding Hood?'

'The Three Little Pigs might be more appropriate.'

'Hmmm, this house is built on sand but at least its walls aren't straw.'

'The big bad wolf, the big bad wolf...' chimed Jack.

'Yeah, or its owner to be more precise. Maybe we're making too much of it, though. He's just a bit of an angry twat. I doubt he's actually dangerous.'

'I don't particularly want to find out,' said Jack. 'I'd rather not see hide nor hair of him again.'

'Not a hair of his chinny chin chin,' agreed Thom, plugging his phone into a charger and turning off his light.

They lay silently in the dark for a while. A toilet flushed in the bathroom down the hall.

'Are you asleep?'

'Good grief, Jack. Not yet. Why?'

'The Tinder thing. Do you get a buzz out of it?'

There was a long silence.

'After Amy moved back to the States with Connor I was at a bit of a loss. I had no desire for a proper relationship but I still liked being with women and, yes, I still enjoy having sex with them. Tinder is very handy for that. Is it satisfying? Not always but it serves a purpose. And maybe I will meet someone eventually. It is a dating app after all.'

'Are they always younger?'

'Usually but it's not like I pretend to be younger than I

am. Some women go for older guys. It's not a crime. And no, I have no interest in teenagers or even women in their twenties. What would you talk about?'

'You talk to them? Well done. What about Karen? Will you see her again or did that scratch an itch?'

'Well things ended rather abruptly but I doubt it. Although she was intriguing. There's more to her than meets the eye and she's quite easy on it, too. But there's obviously stuff going on, too.'

'You gave her your number, didn't you?'

'I might have done but I won't go there again. Boys' Weekend, after all.'

'Jesus Thom, you're driven by your libido like no one else I've ever met. Anyway lights out, eh? Night Jim Bob.'

'Night Mary Ellen.'

Jack turned on his side. Soon he was breathing rhythmically. Then he began to snore gently.

Thom lay still, waiting for sleep to arrive. The drink should have been enough but he was buzzing. Karen had been unexpectedly, if all too briefly, brilliant. He also felt faintly embarrassed. It was a bit out of order, a whim addressing his needs and no one else's. Was Karen unacceptably young? Was he a predator? Absolutely not, he decided, frowning in the dark. She could have changed her mind at any point and he'd have done the decent thing. Everyone wanted to rush into judgement these days. They were consenting adults, everyone else could piss off.

He closed his eyes in the hope that sleep would ensue but the mattress was uncomfortable. His eyes sprang open, involuntarily. His thoughts drifted to Will, the quiz, and back round to Will.

The last time he saw him was just before Christmas. Festive light shows flickered on and off outside homes in the streets surrounding their house. There were a few decorations up at Will's, a token attempt to fall into step with the season of goodwill but the mood inside was understandably downbeat. He had a brief conversation with Will's son in the kitchen. Annie made a couple of cups of tea, took him to the study then disappeared, leaving them to it. Will looked pale and paper thin.

'How you doing?'

'Never felt better.'

They sat in silence for a while. Will tapped away casually on a laptop keyboard. Thom found himself at a loss for words.

'How's work?' asked Will eventually, attempting to reboot the conversation.

'Good actually, I've been working on a communal housing project on a piece of brown belt in North London and doing some drawings to turn a vintage ice cream parlour into a house while retaining its original, err, flavour.'

'Ice cream is one of the few things I still have an appetite for,' said Will. 'Proper Italian sorbet. Do you remember the ice cream we had that day in Santa Fe after we'd been walking for hours in the blazing heat? Chocolate and sea salt. Amazing.'

'Yes, it was absolutely fantastic. A little Mexican-style café, I recall.'

'I found these,' Will climbed stiffly to his feet, shuffled to a filing cabinet in his slippers and pulled out a paper wallet full of photos from a trip they'd taken to the States when they were in their early twenties. Fresh out of college and not especially eager to start full-time jobs, they'd saved up enough money for a two-month tour that took them from east to west coast.

Thom took the wallet from him and began to sift through the photos. It was almost tragic how young they looked. Tall, handsome, ready for everything the world had to offer. Will already had a great physique, Thom, with his blonde, shaggy hair, was merely cute by comparison.

'Oh. Shit. Look at us,' he gasped.

'I know.'

'I still think about that trip. I wish I could do it again.'

'Not as much as I do.'

'And, oh my God, it's the surfer chicks, Candy and Silvia. I haven't seen these pictures since you had them developed. What a blast,' laughed Thom, shaking his head at a picture of two girls they had met in San Diego.

Candy and Silvia were a pair of regulation California girls, tanned, slender, slightly older and infinitely more worldly-wise than the two boys they met in a bar. But the English accents weaved their magic. They were staying in a campervan near the beach and invited them to crash. Just like that. Thom and Will were astonished at their luck.

'Whenever I feel down I always take myself back there,' said Will. 'So I've spent quite a while there, recently. It was like the idyllic bit in a seventies movie. You know, before the hero is shipped off to Vietnam and put through hell.'

'Yes, they were that trip's most memorable moment and for the right reason, unlike the dog incident.'

'Fuck, yes. That was the other side of America. The crazies. You had lots of really helpful, kind people who couldn't do enough for you and the occasional random headcase. Mind you it's probably worse now.'

The pair had been hitching near Lookout Mountain Park, west of Denver, Colorado. Their previous lift had dropped them near the suburbs so they'd bought some food at a store and wandered slowly towards the highway. Two hours later they were still there. Hills rose up steeply either side of the road. Morning rolled into afternoon, then, in the distance, a dog was trotting towards them along the empty highway. It kept coming, straight down the middle of the road. Further back a truck appeared, travelling quickly in the same direction. The dog, now identifiable as a Labrador, continued its progress but shifted across to the safety of the other side of the road. It was barely fifty metres away from Thom and Will when the truck caught up with it, swerved suddenly and ran straight over it, smearing the unsuspecting animal into the warm tarmac. Blood squirted out from under the tyres. Thom and Will yelled in horror as the truck driver roared past them laughing and banging his fist on the steering wheel.

Will lost it and chased after the truck in fury, screaming abuse and waving his arms. Thom caught him up and joined in. Suddenly the trucker stamped on the brake bringing the truck screeching to a halt in the road. Will immediately dived for cover but Thom stood his ground. The truck reversed backwards at speed and stopped abruptly a few feet away from him. Will, hiding in the undergrowth shouted at Thom to run, sensing he was in big trouble. Thom, now petrified, remained motionless. The driver, a man not much older than them with a moustache and a trucker's cap jumped out. He had a pistol in his hand. He raised the gun and pointed it at Thom.

'Did you say something to me, boy?'

Thom stood, petrified.

'That your dog?'

'No,' stammered Thom. The crotch of his shorts stained dark. Will shut his eyes and held his breath. He wondered whether to stay put or run if the guy opened fire.

'Hey, you're pissing yourself, you little motherfucker. I guess you're sorry now!'

'Yes,' said Thom quietly.

'I didn't hear you,' he cocked the hammer.

'I'm sorry,' shouted Thom desperately.

'Damn right you are,' said the redneck. Laughing hysterically, he climbed back into the truck and drove off with a screech, leaving a bloody tyre print in his wake.

Thom staggered to the edge of the road and collapsed in a heap. Will ran over to console his friend who was sobbing with fright. Thom rolled over on his side and vomited. They sat there in silence for a while, recovering, then rose, walked back into town and took a bus instead.

Thom sifted through more photos. There were shots of them at US tourist landmarks like the Empire State Building, the Statue Of Liberty and the Golden Gate Bridge. He stopped at a picture of Will's aunt who owned a ranch near Sacramento where they'd stayed for a week, The scene had resembled a UK remake of *City Slickers* with the pair floundering around attempting to deal with life on a big farm. It was shockingly hard work.

'She was a lovely lady your aunt. Even if she was a bit of a slave driver.'

'She's still going strong, too,' replied Will.

Thom ignored the implication and carried on leafing through the pictures. There was a well-composed Edward Hopperesque image of an old gas station with vintage pumps and a few shots of clouds of Monarch butterflies fluttering in the air in San Diego's Wilderness Garden Preserve. One photo was simply of a huge plate of sticky ribs taken in a barbecue shack.

Another photo had captured them outside CBGB on Bleeker Street. They'd gone in for a drink and returned that night for a Tom Tom Club gig. All that was missing was an impromptu set from Springsteen at The Stone Pony. They did venture out to Asbury Park and found the bar only to discover it was almost empty apart from a DJ playing R&B covers.

'Happy days. I wanted to stay longer,' said Thom wistfully. 'In fact I'd go back tomorrow if I could.'

'Do it, Thom.'

'If only it was that easy.'

'It is, you know, don't wait till it's too late.'

Thom slipped the photographs back in the wallet and pushed them over to Will.

'You may as well keep them,' said Will, pushing them back.

Thom gave him a baleful look but accepted them without argument.

'I'd better be off,' he said, picking up the wallet and putting it in his coat.

'Take care Thom,' said Will. Thom smiled. He was tempted to shake hands or hug him. Instead he simply gave him a little salute. Why on earth hadn't he hugged him?

He tried to visit again a few weeks later but Will refused.

Finally sleep began to creep over him, an incoming tide washing away thought and memory, submerging him in its warm depths. He genuinely believed he was going to die on that stretch of highway. Instead here he was and Will was dust.

* * *

Ed staggered past the twin room and stood swaying in the doorway of his room feeling completely pissed. He kicked off his clothes, plunged the room into darkness and felt his way to the bed. The room started revolving. He opened his eyes and attempted to centre himself to make the sensation go away. What an odd day. Not as relaxing as hoped, in truth.

The weekend was a much-needed break from domestic dramas that had assailed him in the past few months. His son had started hanging out with a bunch of local lads in the evening. There was drinking, probably dope. At the same time his daughter had suffered a meltdown after an ex-boyfriend had posted an intimate image on social media. Her friends had been supportive but she had quit her internship at an agency, convinced everyone would judge her. Ed had taken an injunction out ensuring the images were taken down, and the man was being prosecuted, but the damage inflicted on her was unquantifiable. She was back at home, slowly attempting to rebuild her confidence.

To cap it all there was Will's death, a truly horrible event and an unpleasant reminder of the precariousness of life. He had vowed to lose weight, eat better, cut back the drink and do more exercise but it was proving impossibly hard. Chaos circled round him like midges.

He pushed everything to the back of his mind and focused on something comforting: sex. An image of Thom fucking Karen slid straight into his head. His hand slid into his boxers.

Matt was also now flopped drunkenly onto his bed. The laptop lay where he had left it. He was tempted to boot it up again, then he remembered the battery. Once the booze had started flowing he'd forgotten to ask Paul if he'd brought a cable. That was his first priority tomorrow. Will could wait for his moment. His final scene, badly edited by fate but now carefully restored. The Quiz: The Great Director's Cut.

He put the laptop on the floor, kicked off his shoes and fell asleep on top of the duvet, fully clothed with the lights blazing.

Chapter Ten

Softer Than Shadow and Quicker Than Flies

The whiteknee tarantula lifted a leg as if to scratch itself then continued its slow passage across the wooden kitchen table. Damon dropped a dried cricket in its path. The tarantula paused as if to consider where, or why, such a delicious and unexpected gift had appeared from nowhere, then it advanced rapidly towards the bug, its legs fluttering like fingers over piano keys and enveloped it in its jaws. A soft crunching could be heard as it munched on the treat.

'Attaboy, ain't you clever?' said Damon, softly peering closely at the spider.

At that moment Karen half stumbled through the door. He stood up as she entered the room and she yelped in shock.

'Jesus fucking Christ, Damon, put it away!' she backed out and slammed the door. The spider froze, as if aware it was the source of the consternation.

'Don't you worry about her JT,' cooed Damon. Gently he corralled the arachnid towards a small plastic tray covered in straw. 'Come on fella before angry lady gets her panties in an even bigger twist.'

He picked up the tray carefully and walked into the front room where Karen sat wide-eyed.

'Get rid of it now. Lock it up!' she snapped, shrinking back in the chair and pulling her knees to her chest.

'Maybe I should drop it in your hair,' said Damon, taking a sudden step towards her. The spider lifted a leg to steady itself.

Karen squealed and grabbed Ossie from the arm of the chair. The cat struggled in her lap. 'If you bring that one step nearer I'll throw the cat at it.'

'He might very well end up with his paws in the air then,' replied Damon softly. 'Acanthoscurria geniculata is not to be trifled with. Hair trigger temper, one inch fangs with enough venom to kill him. We wouldn't want that, would we Ossie?'

Karen held the cat tight in her lap. It eyed the beast cradled in Damon's hands.

'Shame you don't devour your partner after mating like some of the females.'

Karen kept her eyes locked on the tank. Damon stared hard at her.

He gave a loud sniff and headed for the stairs. Doors banged briefly before he trotted back down again minus the insect.

'There. All tucked up... in your bed.'

'Piss off Damon, you're not funny,' she let the cat go and it stalked off, disgusted to have been used as a shield.

'What's the difference between JT and that dirty old bastard? They're both predators.'

'He is not a predator. I met him of my own free will and he's a perfectly nice, polite guy.'

'He might have been a serial killer for all you knew.'

'Don't be ridiculous. I don't see the worst in everyone, like you. They're old friends on a weekend break. One of them died not long ago, that's it. This is my life Damon, just because I live here doesn't mean I have to get clearance from you.'

Damon pulled a face.

'Enjoy the lightshow?'

'No I didn't, it was embarrassing and foolish. I worry about you.'

'Hope I didn't interrupt anything.'

'No you didn't. It was pathetic behaviour. Thank God they couldn't see it was you, though I think they had suspicions,' hissed Karen.

'They want to stay out of my way!' snapped Damon standing over her. 'And you'd better stay away from that old fart.'

'I don't know what's got into you, Damon, but if you think I'm going to let you dictate what I do with my life you're bonkers,' she said, eyeing him furiously.

'What did you tell him about me?' demanded Damon.

'Nothing, we had better things to do than discuss your sad little world!'

Damon lunged forward without warning and seized her by the throat, pinning her in the chair. He tightened his grip for a moment and they locked eyes. Satisfied he saw fear, he loosened his grip, turned around and stalked off upstairs. Karen gasped for air and felt her neck tenderly. Tears began to roll down her cheeks. She put her head in her hands.

Upstairs Damon clicked open the browser of his computer and opened Karen's bookmarked emails. She had changed her password a few months ago but it was easy enough to crack with a bit of off-the-peg software. He was going to have to move the Roid Room. It had never been his intention to run the business from home. It was a basic error, compounded by complacency. An old static caravan on a downmarket site on the way to Dungeness would serve from next month now he had restored it and added some home comforts. A floorboard protested as she padded quietly past his room before a door clicked quietly down the hall.

He sighed heavily and put his head in his hands. He shouldn't have done that. Grabbing her was out of order. He had lost it, not for the first time recently. Roids did that to you if you weren't careful. He should probably look at the stacking, address doses. But she needed to understand he had her best interests at heart. She just didn't seem to get that. She would though. She had to.

***

Down the road Matt jerked feverishly in his sleep. A small moan pierced his lips. A large figure was stalking towards him, a lurching human with a dog's head, like something on an Egyptian tomb. He wriggled on top of the bed sheets as it came closer. The dog man had him cornered, then it reached for its head and peeled off a mask. Will stood there staring at him. Matt moaned. His feet pedalled on the duvet. Will leaned in, much closer and opened up a mouth full of razor sharp teeth.

He snapped awake, sweating, blinking uncomfortably under the overhead light. His stomach churned, his bowels quaked. He staggered for the toilet unsure which issue to address. Then his stomach reached the line first and he vomited. Swiftly he reversed position, just before his bowels exploded. He sat there for a while until it was safe to rise and proceeded to clean up. He tottered uncertainly to the sink where he rinsed his mouth out and spat several times, avoiding his reflection in the mirror. He felt like death. Why not? It would be closure if his heart just stopped. They warned him at the hospital that there was damage. The coke had left its mark.

He staggered his way back to bed, glancing at the bedside clock: 4.18. He found the lights, slid under the duvet and fell asleep immediately.

Down the hall, Jack listened to the orchestra of evisceration. It didn't take much to wake him these days. He hadn't slept

123

properly since the kids were born. Now they weren't there, he slept even worse. Thom lay comatose. As silence descended back on the house he closed his eyes and recommenced the wait for temporary oblivion. How did Will feel when he shut them at night towards the end? Hope I die before I wake?

Chapter Eleven

Everybody Knows This Is Nowhere

Ed wandered bleary-eyed downstairs to find Paul reading a newspaper and eating an apple. An empty cereal bowl was balanced on one arm of his chair.

'You're up bright and early.'

'I went for a run and bought a newspaper,' replied Paul, pulling off his glasses, breathing on the lenses and cleaning them vigorously with his T-shirt.

'Very healthy,' observed Ed, pulling a face as if the idea appalled him, which it most certainly did.

He strolled to the window to gaze at the beach where the Channel glittered beneath an almost cloudless sky. Despite his aversion to exercise he was almost tempted to run outside and dive in the water, it looked so tropical. Of course it was absolutely perishing. Air blew in gently through slightly parted doors. A few grey embers stirred on the paving slabs.

Further down the beach, huge kites zigzagged above a group of surfers. He watched intently as the figures performed tricks, swooping rapidly across the surf. They looked graceful and dynamic. Ed wished he could do something like that. He needed a hobby aside from computer gaming. Kitesurfing might be too big an ask now, though. Maybe an e-bike, he thought. Just let the motor kick in on nasty hills.

He wandered back to the kitchen and made a cup of tea,

helped himself to the discarded sports section of Paul's paper and sat down.

'Why isn't the plural of moose, meese?' asked Paul, looking up.

Ed stared at him blankly. The question hung, stupefied, in the air for a moment before Paul went back to his paper. He functioned like a bad algorithm sometimes, thought Ed.

Five minutes later a pained voice came from the hall.

'Fuck!'

'Jack has now entered the conference,' intoned Ed.

'Stubbed my fucking toe coming down the stairs,' Jack complained, pulling a pained face.

'You're a disaster, you are. You need one of those big alarm units round your neck in case you have a proper fall and can't get up,' said Ed.

'I have no problem getting it up,' Jack's voice came from the kitchen.

He poured a bowl of cereal and sat spooning it automatically into his mouth at the dining table as he thumbed through his phone.

'Who threw up last night?' he asked without looking up.

'Not guilty,' said Paul.

'I've got a bit of a woolly head but that's it,' said Ed casting the paper to one side. It lay front page up, leading with a story devoted to the day's Chelsea v Manchester City match.

'Must have been Matt then,' said Jack, eyeing the Scotch bottle that stood nearly empty in front of him. 'Good job he's in a bedroom on his own. The isolation tank.'

'Drunk tank,' corrected Paul.

Jack stood up and turned on the speaker. Vintage ska clanked into life. Mouth still full of cereal he began to search through the cupboards.

'God, you're hyperactive, Jack,' sighed Paul. 'You should

try Ritalin for breakfast instead of cereal.'

'Look, board-games,' Jack said, pulling out several boxes. 'Why don't we play one? Monopoly? No, Ed the voracious capitalist baron would win easily. Cluedo? Colonel Thom in the bedroom with the rope? Not again! Oooh, Risk! Do you remember the epic encounters we used to have round Will and Matt's flat? The Great Risk Wars. They went on so long we had to use rocks to represent our armies because they grew so large.

'I am not playing Risk,' said Paul flatly. 'I know what happens. You all gang up on me like you used to and I'm first out.'

'Oh, come on Paul, that's all in the past.'

'Absolutely,' said Ed, pounding a fist into his hand.

Jack stood up and emptied the box on the table, unfolding the board and stacking the cards. He was wearing a faded Doves T-shirt. A coffee stain was visible on the left breast.

'Who's in?'

'Me,' said Ed sitting down eagerly.

'No fucking way. Definitely not,' said Paul.

'Come on Paul, don't be soft. We need three at least.'

Paul sighed, and took a seat at the table.

Cards were dealt and everyone placed their pieces then Jack took the first roll and threw a six. 'Attack Kamchatka.'

'I fucking knew it, you massive twat!' cried Paul, offended.

'It's strategic, nothing personal,' said Jack, holding his hands up innocently.

Paul eyed him fiercely.

Ed rolled and took his turn.

'Attack Kamchatka.'

'Oh, you complete and utter bellend!' shouted Paul, throwing his hands up in the air.

'Calm down, Paul, you're the only serious option I have,' said Ed.

Paul squealed like a small hedgehog surrounded by hungry foxes.

At that moment the mastiff charged through the open rear doors of the holiday home. It was as if a sudden ball of energy or a canine twister had just risen from the ground as the dog ran back and forth barking and snarling at the three of them.

Paul yelped in surprise and stood on the table, Ed leapt behind his chair and Jack jumped on the island.

Moments later Damon stood framed in the doorway with a self-satisfied smile of one who could bring a halt to the chaos or redouble it.

'Down, down! Bad dog! Heel!'

Drogba immediately ceased barking and strolled to his master's side.

'Sorry! he just ran off, he gets overexcited sometimes, smells things,' he explained, innocently. 'You aren't cooking sausages, are you?

None of the Boys spoke.

He strolled around the room taking it in once more, nodding occasionally. He peered at the artwork and pulled a face.

'These sort of gaffs are going up all over the place round here now. No one lives in them. No one real. They're holiday homes for the likes of you. A grand a weekend. I see them sitting out there on the patio, sneering, not deigning to mix with the scum on the beach.'

Paul stepped down from his perch.

'Excuse me, but this is a private residence. Would you mind taking your dog and leaving?'

'The cycling gimp, isn't it?' Damon took two quick strides and put his face within an inch of Paul's. Paul took a step back and toppled into a chair.

'Since I'm here, I could do with a cup of tea.' Damon span

ninety degrees and walked to the kitchen where he flicked the switch on the kettle. Jack slid off the island but kept it between them. Damon found a clean mug, blew in it and threw a teabag in. He began to whistle tunelessly as it boiled, not looking at anyone. An uneasy silence reigned. Ed flicked his eyes at Paul who remained expressionless. Damon poured hot water over the teabag, added three sugars and milk.

'I should apologise for that little display last night,' he said, blowing the liquid. 'It was just a bit of fun. No hard feelings.'

'I think you should go,' said Ed. 'Or I'll call the police.'

He brandished his mobile.

'My dog just ran off, he found his way in here and I came to fetch him,' shrugged Damon. He took a swig from the mug. 'You could be more neighbourly. I mean I might have lost him. He's my best mate.'

Drogba wagged his tail on cue.

'Whatcha playing? Oooh, Risk! I used to play that with my old man. Someone's getting a bit of a beating by the looks of it.'

He sat down and examined the board.

'Who's Kamchatka?'

'Me,' replied Paul.

'They're picking on you, aren't they?' he eyed Ed and Jack with suspicion.

'It's just a bit of fun,' said Paul. 'I'm a bit crap at it, too.'

'No one likes a bully,' declared Damon without irony. 'You just need a bit of military strategy. Fortunately I've combat experience, so I am well placed to assist. I think we can rescue the situation with a bit of courage and a pair of reinforced steel balls.'

He picked up the die and slammed them down on the board keeping his hand on the top.

'Oooh sixes! Attack Alaska. Come on, who's Alaska then?' he gave Jack and Ed an inquiring look.

'Look we've got to go out now, it's time we packed up,' said Jack, waving his arms.

'Sure, in a minute, but first we got to finish what you started,' said Damon. 'Are you the generalissimo in charge of Alaska?'

'Yes but...'

'Well sit the fuck down and take your turn, I've attacked!'

Jack looked at Paul and Ed. He shuffled back to the table cautiously and sat down. Clearly the only answer was to humour Damon and hope he would withdraw peacefully at the end of the encounter. Jack had considered quietly extracting a knife from the chopping block but thought, wisely, it would only make matters worse.

Ed joined them at the table in a show of support. Jack picked up the defence die and threw low numbers. Troops were routed. Damon rattled his die in a gnarled fist once more and slammed them down.

'Sixes! Attack Alaska!'

'Umm, can I see the dice please?' asked Jack, tentatively.

'Are you suggesting I'm cheating?' asked Damon, fixing him with a frown.

'No, no, of course not, but...'

'Right, so attack Alaska.'

Jack sighed and threw weakly again.

'There!' grinned Damon. 'Fortune favours the brave.'

He massed his troops into Alaska flicking Jack's vanquished pieces aside with contempt.

'That's how it works in the real world. Superior firepower and the will to employ it ruthlessly. I know this because I was in Iraq doing your dirty work, you see?'

'I'm not following you,' said Ed.

'I was in the army. Iraq. I fought. People died. My best mate lost his legs.'

'Sorry to hear it,' said Paul warily. 'But I didn't want the war.'

'I expect you were one of them lot protesting. Try protesting against a towel-head in a suicide vest, see what happens. We didn't have a choice, we just went. We always do. Then people like you snipe away.'

'I don't blame you, it's the politicians,' said Paul, sympathetically. 'They lied about it.'

'What's new?' said Damon with a derisive snort.

'We lost a mate not long ago,' offered Jack, in an attempt to strike up some empathy.

'Shit happens,' said Damon. 'Kaz told me you lost a comrade. I know what that's like. You lot are tight, I like that, respect it. When the enemy approaches you stand arm-in-arm. Hello, looks like someone's been having a crafty spliff. Very daring,' he extracted a half-smoked roll-up from the ashtray and sniffed it. 'Skunk. Nasty shit.'

He had the moral high ground now.

'Class B drug this. Criminal behaviour. Could be a matter for the feds.'

'Not sure that's necessary, is it?' said Ed, somewhat alarmed.

'Nah, probably not,' said Damon, dropping the butt. He stood up abruptly. 'Where are the others? You know, Jimmy Saville and Gobshite?'

'They went out,' said Jack. 'To the shops... in Rye.'

'Did they? Very nice,' said Damon, not looking entirely convinced. 'Well I must be going, the gym calls.'

With that he headed out the back door, with the dog at his heels. Rapidly the energy levels in the room dropped back to normal. The three of them watched him exit with relief. An ugly scene appeared to have been averted.

'Jesus paddleboarding Christ,' said Jack. 'That was tense. I thought we were toast.'

'Thank God he didn't go upstairs,' agreed Ed.

'God, yes, it would have kicked off big time then,' said Paul. He stepped out of the back doors into the garden where debris still lay from the previous night's rocket attack.

'There's a black mark on the ground,' he called, rubbing it with his hand. He wiped it on his pants. 'Good job the windows are thick.'

Ed joined him and together they cleared up, tossing the pieces in a small bin in the corner.

'We should get going soon if we're going to make lunch,' said Paul, looking at his watch.

'Yeah, I'll get the others up,' said Ed.

Paul tossed a handful of gravel at the top floor window.

'Get up Anscombe, you lazy bastard!' he called.

Ed made his way upstairs. Thom was already on his way down.

'Has he gone?'

'You heard him?' asked Ed.

'Too right, I hid under your bed.'

'Very wise. I'm not sure what would have happened if he'd seen you.'

'He'd have been struck by how dashing I am,' said Thom jogging past him. He had the spring in his step of a man who had narrowly avoided a pasting.

Ed knocked on Matt's bedroom door. Silence greeted him. He rapped louder. Still nothing. He knocked again and opened the door a crack.

'Matt? Matt are you going to get up? We're leaving soon.'

He knocked again and entered the room unsurely. Matt lay still in the bed with his back to him. Suddenly, concerned, Ed moved forward and gave him a shake.

'Huuuhhh!?' Matt sat up suddenly.

'Sorry, I was trying to get you up. It was like waking the dead.'

'Well I'm awake now, aren't I?' Matt grumbled. His hair stood on end as if he'd been tasered in his sleep.

'We're. Leaving. Soon,' said Ed, attempting to let each word permeate.

'Leaving where? What do you mean? Did I miss the 'melter? What happened? Who won?'

Ed gave him a funny look, unsure as to whether he was messing about.

'No, you fucking stoner. We're going to walk to Rye for lunch, remember? You missed the nutter, fortunately. He dropped in for some sugar.'

'What the fuck are you on about?'

'Best you never know.'

'Whatever,' Matt scrubbed at his pubic hair. 'Give me ten minutes to freshen up.'

Ed pulled a face, left him and returned to the kitchen. Upstairs a power shower kickstarted into life.

'He was still asleep.'

'What a feckless but very fortunate pair of bastards they both are,' declared Paul, locking the back door firmly.

Chapter Twelve

Dark Side of the Gym

Bracing himself, Damon let out a loud hiss and heaved the loaded barbell above his chest. His pursed lips made a good impression of Dizzy Gillespie. With a loud grunt he began to pump the weights slowly.

'Fuck you,' he hissed.

A single bead of sweat popped from just above his brow.

'No, fuck you!'

More beads emerged.

'And you, and you, and you!'

Like a powerlifting penitent he reeled off ten fuck yous and hefted the weight back on the stand, which rocked in protest.

'Cheers, Cry Baby. Want me to spot you?'

Cry Baby eyed the load, unsure.

'Go on then,' he said, saving face. They switched positions on the bench. Damon lifted the weight off the rack and popped it into Cry Baby's open hands. Bracing himself, he received the barbell and managed four quivering reps, sobbing loudly between each lift as he always did. His face bloomed a bright shade of red like a cartoon temperature gauge.

'So how was sex with that Down's Syndrome bird last night?' asked Damon casually.

Cry Baby froze with the weight fully extended above his

head. He attempted to focus. A twitch of mirth flickered on one side of his mouth. Then a snort of laughter and a jet of snot shot from his nostrils. The weight began to sink steadily until it was touching his Adam's Apple. His left foot flailed about in a wild polka, an odd gurgling noise churned from his throat.

Damon sighed, lifted the weight from him and dropped it on the rig.

'Bit too much for you, I'd say. Maybe use smaller plates next time?'

Cry Baby sat up and had a coughing fit. He looked around for his drink bottle only to see Damon walking off with it. He placed it on a machine several feet away.

Here at Repz, Rye's least exclusive gym, Damon was master of all he surveyed. He bossed the place, dispensing advice whether it was wanted or not. He even dictated what music was playing over the sound-system. Strutting around the mirrored room in red vest and baggy shorts he was in his element, last night's eruption soothed by a wave of endorphins.

Damon walked away and advanced towards the Smith machine. A younger man heading in the same direction stopped and waved an arm deferentially.

'No, you carry on mate,' said Damon. 'I don't do squats, they stunt you.'

The youth hesitated for a moment as he attempted to digest this nugget of bro-science then stood under the weight regardless.

Damon eyed him for a moment. He'd never seen the kid in the gym before. Obviously a newbie. Damon reached for the weights rack beside it and pulled out a twenty kilo handbell and sidled over to the mirror. He paused for a moment to admire himself, turning an arm side on. Unlike most of the amateurs in the room, his body remained almost completely unadorned with tatts. No Celtic symbols, Sanskrit verse, Chinese philosophy nor runic hieroglyphs gilded his pink-porcelain skin. In common with many in the bodybuilding community Damon shunned tattoos for the way they ruined definition. Ink obscured veins and sinews. The exception was a small blue lion rampant, regardant, on his left buttock, an area that rules dictated had to be covered in competition, though not at home where Damon frequently strolled around naked, much to Karen's consternation.

His mate Blue Tony had a huge crest on his back complete with gilt edging. It looked good on the beach but Tony was about sixteen stone and most of it was flab. Jumbo, a squaddie in his regiment had had a pair of elephants ears tattooed either side of his penis. He called it 'the trunk of junk'.

He lifted an ice-white trainer, placed it on the bench and began to pump his arm very deliberately.

'Who's a pretty boy... who's a pretty boy,' he muttered, staring intensely at his reflection.

He switched hands and repeated the exercise before wiping the bar clean with a rag cloth that hung from the waistband of his shorts and sauntering over to the youth who was now seated at a machine doing overhead raises.

'Son, that pump feel you get in your arms, it's the same as when you get a hard-on. It's blood rushing in, and it's fucking AWESOME!'

The kid regarded him with wide-eyed surprise. Cry Baby giggled and sucked on his bottle.

Ten minutes later the young man approached Damon as he stood pretending not to admire his reflection.

'Err, what kind of supplements do you take?'

'You ever hear of HFW?' asked Damon jutting his head towards him as if about to share a secret.

'No, can you buy it online?'

'Hard. Fucking. Work. You should try it,' he said, raising an eyebrow.

'Seriously mate, you don't use… err, steroids, do you?' the youth spoke quietly, glancing round the room.

'Do I look like a user to you? Eh? You think this is down to roids?' Damon hoisted up his vest to show off a tubular six pack.

'No, but…'

'What do you want to take steroids for, son? You want to look hunky for the chicks, is that it? Or are you queer?'

'Yes, I mean no. Yes, I want to look good for girls. They all want a bloke that's buff these days.'

'Do you know what the darknet is? Clue, it's not a search engine for blacks,' smiled Damon, amused at his own wit. 'Have a look for some stuff called Ironman. Top brand. And do a bit of reading up or you'll end up with a pair of titties like a twelve-year-old bird breaking out.'

The kid nodded and went back to his routine. Damon sat down at the fly machine and hissed his way through a set of reps, then he headed for the changing room where he showered.

While he was towelling off the youth entered, stripped, and stepped into the shower. Damon dressed, then sat on the bench thumbing idly through his phone with his bag between his legs. The youth re-emerged and began to towel off. Damon watched him. Aware of his presence, the young man turned his back.

'You need to work on your glutes mate,' announced Damon. 'And your right deltoid is bigger than your left.'

'Er, right, thanks,' said the youth, hauling up his boxers hastily.

Damon picked up his kitbag and left the gym, heading towards The Pipemakers for the lunchtime game.

Chapter Thirteen

The Joke's on Us

Finally, after much faffing about, everyone was ready to leave.

Paul, dressed in a checked shirt, long black cargo shorts and a pair of walking boots, was already waiting outside when the others emerged. He had a backpack on one shoulder, and was perusing an Ordnance Survey map. A walking pole dangled from one wrist as he held his arm up to examine his watch.

'Christ Paul, we're going for a stroll not a Himalayan expedition,' snorted Jack.

'Fail to prepare, prepare to fail,' declared Paul, who had the air of a Victorian missionary dealing with uneducated natives about him. 'We need to get going.'

'Route maps? Why not just download an app?' asked Ed.

Paul gave him a disgusted look.

'Dib dib, then,' said Matt, whose preparation had gone as far as procuring a straw pork pie hat.

They turned off the gravel path onto the beach and began walking west. The tide was on its way out, streams of seawater flowed in rivulets in the dark sand. Three women on horseback rode slowly past. One wore a day-glo gilet with the word 'Polite' on the back. Colourful umbrellas, striped windbreaks and mini tents were already scattered up and down the beach. Groups of children ran around kicking up sand and shouting in excitement. Two families had set up an encampment of tents and windbreaks. The parents were sitting in fold-up chairs, chugging cans of lager while their kids dug holes.

The intrepid five arrived at a café where a small queue gathered around a window. A woman turned away from the kiosk holding a cardboard box filled with ice creams and steaming cups of tea. Matt promptly sat down at a wooden table.

'What are you doing? We've only just got going,' asked Paul in exasperation.

'Got sand in my shoe,' he said, pulling off a suede Adidas Gazelle and emptying it.

'That's because we're walking along a beach, Matt.'

'Yeah, well it's a pain,' said Matt.

'You should have worn sandals,' said Ed, waggling a Birkenstock.

'And look like an old paedo? No thanks,' sneered Matt, shaking a trainer out.

'Hey, Jack, what does Ed use for grooming?'

Jack looked at Matt for the answer.

'Facebook!'

Paul walked off towards the car park as Matt flapped sand from his socks and stuffed them in his pockets. They stood absently chatting before he reappeared a few minutes later.

'Where have you been?' asked Ed.

'For a leak.'

'But we only just got going. As you recently reminded us,' said Matt.

'The coffee went right through me. We all bow to the demands of the prostate in the end.'

'Christ you're fifty-two, not seventy,' said Matt, appalled.

'Benign prostatic hyperplasia can affect anyone over forty,' explained Paul patiently.

'Another of life's ways of taking the piss,' explained Thom.

'Shall we get going?' inquired Paul impatiently, striding off like a scoutmaster.

They recommenced their journey. Ed jogged ahead, reached for his phone, dropped it, blew on it and took a group photo as they walked towards him.

Ahead, two small boys played with a yellow frisbee. As the five approached, the disc flew over the nearest boy's head and landed at Matt's feet. He picked it up and sent it back with a deft snap of the wrist towards the smaller of the two. However, the child was caught out by the speed of the throw. He reached out a hand to catch it too late. The frisbee collided with his forehead and he collapsed with a cry.

'Oh shit! Sorry!' Matt raced towards the stricken boy.

'Jesus Matt, it's always you!' sighed Ed, rushing over, too.

They all gathered round the sobbing boy. An elder, blonde-haired boy stood watching, apparently dumbstruck.

'What's his name?' called Matt, looking around anxiously for an irate parent. None appeared.

'William,' replied the boy. 'He's nine,' he added helpfully.

'Hey Will, can I call you Will? I'm really, really sorry, are you hurt?'

The boy rubbed his head and wiped away tears but remained mute otherwise. A red mark was visible just below the hairline but, thankfully, there was no blood.

'I had a mate called Will,' said Matt, thinking of something to say.

'Where is he?' sniffed the boy.

'He couldn't be with us.'

'Is he dead?' asked the child abruptly.

'Err, yes,' replied Matt, taken aback.

'My dad's dead,' announced the boy, climbing to his feet.

'I'm sure he'd be proud of you, Will,' said Matt. 'Hey, can we stay and play for a minute? I promise not to throw it as hard next time.'

'Is this a good idea?' asked Ed, also looking around for an irate adult. 'I don't want to be mistaken for a bunch of paedos.'

'You shouldn't have worn those sandals then,' said Jack.

'Come on!' urged Matt, 'Everyone has to catch the frisbee in turn before we move on, including these chaps,' he pointed at the boys. 'And Paul, so we might be here till sundown.'

'We don't have time for this,' said Paul, keen to avoid sport.

Ignoring him they spread into a circle and began tossing the frisbee around. The smallest boy proved a little tentative following Matt's attempted beheading but his confidence soon returned. Paul, being hopelessly uncoordinated, proved the weak link as he always had been in these challenges. Finally, they managed an almost complete round with one last throw in the chain remaining. Ed launched the disc but threw too hard. It sailed tantalisingly over Paul's head.

'Catch it, you spazz!' screamed Jack.

Galvanised, Paul span round and chased after it. The frisbee began to glide sideways back to earth in slow motion. Paul dashed towards it gamely. He misread its flight initially, then corrected, put in a spurt, stumbled and launched himself full length as he fell, somehow clutching hold of the disc before it hit the ground.

'Yes!' they all yelled, breaking into applause.

'Howzat?' cried Paul climbing to his feet and holding the frisbee aloft in triumph.

They said their goodbyes and continued walking along the beach. Soon, they reached the mouth of a river. A muddy channel flowed swiftly through damp brown sand into the sea. Behind them the white sails of a cluster of wind turbines rotated slowly.

'What's this then?

'The Rother,' said Paul.

'Bother the Rother, we can't get across,' said Jack.

'Oh, well, taxis it is,' said Matt with unvarnished delight. All the running around had made him feel queasy again.

'No, we just walk along the river bank,' said Paul. 'Rye's upriver.'

'Right,' said Matt, crestfallen.

'The far side is Winchelsea, it's a nature reserve. Further along the shore you might be able to see the Mary Stanford Lifeboat House. The lifeboat launched from there in the 1920s to rescue a ship caught in a storm but capsized, drowning all the crew. It's a memorial now.'

'That's cheered me up no end,' said Ed. 'Any more local history to brighten the day?'

'The sea looks as benign as Paul's prostate today, but I guess it isn't, is it?' said Matt regarding the agitated waters at the mouth of the estuary uneasily.

'Looks can be deceptive,' agreed Paul. 'The new lifeboat station is up the estuary, we pass it.'

He tutted, bent down to pick up a discarded day-glo water bottle half buried in sand and put it in his backpack.

The group turned north and began to walk upriver. Just behind the dunes was a well-manicured green with a flag fluttering from its hole.

'Is there any stretch of countryside in Britain that doesn't have a fucking golf course?' asked Jack.

'I doubt it. Scafell Pike possibly?' suggested Paul. 'I think Trump built a course on Helvellyn.'

'A good walk wasted,' observed Matt. 'Not unlike this one.'

The path continued to take them upriver. On the far bank, saltmarsh and saline lagoons containing an archipelago of micro islands stretched towards Winchelsea. Seabirds wheeled above a horizon collapsed beneath an azure sky. A solitary red-roofed hut contributed an arthouse look to the composition of the surrounding landscape.

Paul and Thom had fallen into step as Paul explained about the rare birdlife that populated the nature reserve. Thom listened politely, wondering if he could find a reason to drop back. Paul bent down mid-stride to pick up a crisp packet lying in his path.

Jack caught up, then thought better of it, dropping back alongside Ed and Matt.

'They're talking about plovers,' said Jack, sniggering.

'Well Thom's had a few, hasn't he?' replied Ed.

'He loves birds,' agreed Matt.

'But tits are his favourite,' added Jack.

They dissolved into gales of laughter at the childishness of the exchange.

A small harbour came into view. A handful of small boats were moored up to a rickety jetty. Just inland a group of children in wetsuits were learning how to windsurf on a lake. Sails floated in the water and heads could just be seen clinging to boards.

'Is that a pub over there?' inquired Matt.

'Looks like it,' said Paul, examining the map.

'Bother the Rother, again. How deep is it at this point?'

They walked through the car park and rejoined the path which zigzagged around a tributary and skirted a field populated by sheep with turquoise paint marks daubed on their flanks. A few gathered around an old bath used as a water trough.

'Look, if we steal that bath, put wheels on it and push it

down a hill we can become a real life tribute act to *Last of the Summer Wine*,' suggested Jack.

'It's a reality TV series in waiting,' agreed Ed, beginning to whistle the theme.

Matt joined Paul and Thom, providing Thom with some relief from ornithology.

'How're the kids?' Jack asked Ed.

'Making my life hard,' sighed Ed. 'Luke's mocks were a disaster. I can see him not getting the grades. He just can't be bothered and it doesn't matter what I say. He'd rather spend his time gaming. We just end up rowing. Fathers and sons, you know?'

'What about Jade?' asked Jack.

'Yeah, she's making progress, it was a horrible experience for her. Hopefully she'll emerge from it stronger, though. Yours?'

'Yeah, you know, coping,' said Jack with a shrug.

'It was all pretty abrupt, wasn't it?'

'Yeah, it was,' agreed Jack quietly.

Ed waited for him to elaborate, but he didn't. That was the thing with Jack. He bottled everything up. You ended up doing a lot of giving but he rarely shared. Sometimes he wondered how well he knew him.

The path turned at an outlet cut into the bank, and skirted behind some marshes. Paul shook his head at the junk that had washed up among the reeds: a plastic jerry can, a mildewed caravan door and a plastic car bumper. Across the other side of the estuary lay an industrial plant. Paul eyed it suspiciously, as if it might spew toxic waste into the water at any moment.

They passed a house close to a golf tee and eventually came to a halt where the path ended at a small brick hut. It emerged onto a road that forded the river via a small iron bridge. Paul stopped again, this time to pick up a carrier bag that blew around his feet. He eyed it with disgust and added it to the collection of waste in his back pack.

They crossed in the direction of town, strolling past sports fields and a skate park where a few youths in baggy T-shirts could be seen see-sawing back and forth on boards.

They took a road towards the town centre, passing a couple of pubs, forcing Paul to bar the doors to Matt and point him firmly onwards. At an ancient castle gate tower he gave everyone a short history lecture about the Cinque Ports, Rye's early mediaeval French occupation and subsequent sacking.

'Bloody French. No wonder they voted for Brexit round here,' observed Ed.

'What did Will say? Remind me about the B word, Ed,' admonished Jack.

'Yet they still managed to leave their mark despite everything,' said Thom, pointing out a bistro.

They continued through narrow streets. Jack ducked into a shop and emerged with a bottle of water. He took a sip. Matt held out his hand and Jack passed it over.

'Cheers,' he said handing the empty bottle back with a belch.

'Paul, Paul, I found another empty bottle, can I put it in your backpack?' asked Jack in a child's voice. He unzipped his bag and stuffed it in with the rest of the rubbish.

A little further on they came across a large pub with the name The Pipemakers Arms in Gothic script.

'Right, it's lunchtime and I've worked up a proper thirst now,' said Matt, crossing the road. He put his hand on the door-handle and turned to look at the others.

'Not that one! Hold on a little longer, you alky, the pub I've booked is just up there,' called Paul, signing a road to the left. Matt sighed and followed behind, grumbling.

A few minutes later they were sat at a reserved table in a white walled pub called The Ship. It was doing a busy trade and it took a few minutes for the waitress to arrive with menus.

'Bring us your finest wines!' shouted Matt.

'Shut up Matt,' said Jack, smiling at the waitress who pulled a fake smile in return, sensing she might be in for a difficult afternoon. 'Excuse my friend. He's not had a drink since he poured vodka on his morning cornflakes, would you mind please bringing him the wino list?'

Drinks were ordered and the first of a succession of bottles began its journey to the table ensuring everyone was soon feeling 're-vine-drated', as Matt put it. A cute gamine placed a couple of baskets of bread on the table. Thom flashed her a big smile. She smiled back. He winked.

'That's a yellow, Thom,' said Jack, wagging an imaginary card. 'She's young enough to be your daughter.'

'Or mine,' added Ed, affronted.

'I was just being friendly,' protested Thom, outraged.

They returned to perusing the menu.

'What happened to Will's ashes in the end,' asked Paul suddenly.

'Woah, straight outta leftfield. Again,' gasped Jack.

'No, no, I saw a starter with the goat's cheese in ashes and my mind did a lateral jump.'

'Spastic fucking lurch more like.'

'Jack, you can't use that sort of language in a public place. It's not acceptable any more,' scolded Paul.

Jack put his tongue into his bottom lip. Paul shook his head and attempted not to smile.

'They were thrown off a bridge,' announced Matt.

'What do you mean, "thrown off a bridge"?' asked Thom, looking up from his menu.

'Annie and the kids scattered him off Putney bridge one Sunday morning as the tide was going out.'

'That's nice,' observed Paul approvingly.

'How do you know?' asked Jack.

'Because I asked her and she told me,' said Matt, returning his gaze.

'Family thing,' nodded Jack.

'What would you like done with your ashes then Paul?' asked Ed.

'Hmmm, I've thought about this.'

'Of course you have,' interjected Jack.

'I want to become a tree. You can have your ashes placed into a bio-urn with a seed planted on top so it draws the nutrients from you as it grows.'

'You sap,' sneered Jack.

'You'd almost certainly turn into a plum,' agreed Matt.

'What about you Ed?' asked Paul, refusing to lower himself.

'You can have your ashes launched into space now, so your remains get to orbit the earth in perpetuity,' said Ed, seizing the last piece of bread and gnawing on it.

'Going round and round interminably. Bit like one of your arguments?' suggested Jack.

'And you, Thom,' asked Paul, moving round the table.

'I read somewhere you could have them turned into a diamond.'

'You are a diamond geezer, after all,' interjected Ed speaking mockney.

'He's just being precious,' added Paul.

'You might turn up on *Antiques Roadshow* in fifty years,' observed Jack, now on a roll. 'Pale, overweight, goth girl with a blue streak in dyed black hair stands there with her massive cleavage heaving at the camera and pants, "My great uncle had his ashes turned into a diamond and they were then set in a ring, what do you think it's worth now?" Expert fixes a lens thing to his eye and examines it for a moment, "Well it's deeply flawed, I'm afraid, half-cut, not so much twenty carat value-wise, more a bag of carrots".'

Thom doffed an imaginary cap. The waitress returned for the food order.

'What about you Matt?' asked Ed when she had gone.

'He'd like them distilled so we could all drink a toast to him,' said Jack.

Paul pulled a face.

'Not a bad idea actually but no, there's a company that turns your ashes into a vinyl record. Life beyond the groove, that sort of thing. That would be pretty cool.'

'You're already like listening to a broken record,' said Ed.

'Do you get to choose the tune?' asked Paul, suddenly interested. 'Say, The Vinyl Countdown?'

'As if I'd do pomp rock. What about, "I Want You Back"? Actually, it might just be a clip of you talking. Copyright issues and all that.'

'Wow, fancy having to revisit your stoned ramblings,' said Jack.

'No one likes you Jack,' said Matt flatly. 'Pray tell us, what would you have done with your ashes?'

'I like that movie *Captain Fantastic*, where the mum asks for hers to be flushed down the toilet,' Jack said flatly.

Paul nodded enthusiastically as if this was a revelation.

'Can we shit on you first?' asked Matt.

'It wouldn't be the first time. Anyway, I'm going to outlive the fucking lot of you.'

A family in the corner turned to look over at their table. Jack waved at them.

'Pardon my French!'

Paul shifted uncomfortably in his seat.

'Well now we've all settled our affairs, just in case... To absent friend,' suggested Ed, lifting his glass. They all clinked.

The starters arrived and they tucked in hungrily, occasionally switching to taste each other's dishes.

'I should have had yours,' said Thom, savouring a piece of squid tempura from Ed's plate. 'I always suffer menu remorse when the food arrives. What's yours, Matt?' he asked, leaning over to examine what was on his plate.

'Oysters, smoked and deep fried with oyster sauce.'

'No oyster foam? And what about some oyster tartare?' asked Paul. 'That dish seems a bit short on oyster options.'

'Keep your distance, I'm allergic to oysters. Just a whiff could kill me,' said Ed, pulling his plate further away. 'Last time I had them I thought I was going to die. I threw up for twelve hours and passed out on a toilet floor.

'That happened to Matt, didn't it, Matt? Had a bad pint. Twelve of them,' announced Jack.

'Sounds like listeria,' said Matt.

'It wasn't hysteria. I swear it almost killed me. I daren't have one again,' said Ed.

'Has anyone else had a near death experience?' said Paul, putting his knife and fork down and wiping his mouth. No one had shown any interest in trying the goat's cheese rolled in ashes.

'You. Every time you tell a joke,' suggested Jack.

'I overtook an old bid on a narrow country road four or five years back,' began Thom.

'Did you signal her to stop, get in and shag her?' asked Matt.

Thom ignored him. 'There was a little hill and I couldn't quite see over it but I assumed I'd have plenty of time, so I pulled out and went for it. Just as I did a car going like stink appeared coming the other way. It wouldn't have been a problem but the old bid sees me and instead of slowing she puts her foot down. Did I mention she's driving a pokey little Renault Megane hatchback? It still shouldn't have been a problem but somehow I miss a gear and suddenly it's squeaky. The driver coming the other way hasn't slowed down at all so I slam the throttle wide open because it's too late to drift back in. I made it with inches to spare. I can still see the face of the guy coming the other way. He clearly hadn't seen me. My nerves still jangle thinking about it now. I had to stop down the road and dismount because I was shaking so much. The old bid just zoomed past without so much as a second glance.'

'You remain the prime candidate for an early death. Will would be gutted he beat you to it,' said Jack, working his finger round his empty plate.

'It's more likely to be you, Jack,' said Thom.

'What makes you say that?'

'Because you can't keep your big fucking mouth shut,' said Thom, brandishing a steak knife at his throat. The family behind suddenly became very tense.

Jack pulled an expression of fake terror. 'Please don't shank me blud!'

'You also had that incident with the redneck on your American road-trip,' said Ed.

'Yes, that was pretty unpleasant. I actually pissed myself I was so scared.'

'That happened to Matt, too,' nodded Jack. 'In fact it happens regularly.'

'Thom's right about your mouth,' said Matt, fixing him.

Jack's mouth hung open in mock surprise.

'I had that crash about ten years ago, you might remember,' said Ed. 'That was pretty close. Car blew a tyre as it overtook me, bounced off the central reservation and took me out. I was ferried to hospital with the driver of the other car. I could hear them trying to revive him in the next cubicle when we arrived. Then it all went very quiet. They came in a few minutes later and had a look at me. All I needed was a few stitches in my head and a neck brace for a bit of whiplash. They were wheeling the other bloke away with a sheet over him as I left.'

'That's pretty heavy,' said Matt getting to his feet.

'Worse still, my Beamer was a write off.'

'No! I hope you sued his family for the damage and distress he caused,' said Paul straight-faced.

'People are so selfish,' agreed Matt. He squeezed out and made his way to the toilets where he relieved himself, then took a small bump with a loud sniff. He flushed and stepped out of the cubicle to find Jack washing his hands.

'Got a cold, Matt?'

'Err, no, probably dusty in here, or a change of temperature. Doesn't take much to set me off.'

They walked back to the table together.

'Have we missed any more near death incidents?' asked Jack.

'I nearly got murdered,' offered Paul casually.

'I'm not surprised,' said Jack. 'Go on.'

'It happened while I was travelling in South America after uni. When I was staying in Rio I met this girl in a bar one weekend. We left and walked around for a while, then found ourselves at the end of a jetty. We started getting very friendly on a bench, she was in my lap and we were going to do it right there. Then out the corner of my eye I see these two guys walking towards us. We freeze but they keep coming till they're just a few feet away. She climbs off me and they start talking. My Portuguese is good enough by then to work out that they're going to rob us, cut my throat and rape her. One says she's a whore going with tourists.

'They pull out knives so we back off to the end of the jetty. I glance round and I can't see a thing but we're toast if we stay there so I grab her and launch us both off. We hit the water, not rocks thankfully. I can't see a thing but we both surface and I grab her, swim underneath and we hold onto the posts. They're staring over the side shouting obscenities, saying they're going to wait till we get out or drown. We begin to work our way back towards land but they're following us. One begins to use his lighter to set bits of rubbish alight and throw them down on to us. She gets a piece on her and panics and they start laughing. Just as it's beginning to look hopeless a group turn onto the jetty. We hear their footsteps and start shouting up at them. They come towards our voices and the hoods decide to retreat. We climb up a ladder on the side of the jetty and appear out of nowhere and explain to the people what had happened. They walked us back to town and we had a drink with them. At the end of the evening I kissed the girl once. We took separate cabs home and I never saw her again.'

'Good Lord, Paul, why haven't you ever told us that?' said Ed, astonished.

'It was never relevant,' said Paul simply.

'It's like having a dinner date with Mr Spock,' sighed Jack.

The main courses arrived, along with more wine.

The conversation slowed while they ate.

'What's that again, Paul?' asked Ed, eyeing Paul's bowl suspiciously.

'Tofu ramen. Have some, it's not bad,' said Paul pushing it towards him.

'I'd rather eat my own liver,' said Ed, pulling a face.

'Try Matt's,' suggested Jack. 'It's been pickled.'

Matt promptly put his knife and fork down and stood

up abruptly. The family behind froze. Then he sat down and continued eating.

Empty plates were pushed to one side. Puddings were ordered. And more wine. The pub, which had been doing a brisk trade when they arrived, had begun to empty out as the afternoon stretched on. The nearby family had decided against dessert, paid up and left swiftly.

'So what's the plan?' asked Jack.

'Stroll round town for a while, then go back, maybe chill on the beach with a few sundowners?' suggested Matt.

'Sounds good,' nodded Jack.

'And do The Brainmelter, yes?' asked Jack, picking his teeth with his right pinkie nail.

'Yes,' said Matt flatly.

'Or we could avoid the whole morbid charade and play games,' said Paul.

'It would feel like a bit of a betrayal if we didn't, given the effort he went to,' said Thom.

'Shit, that reminds me,' said Matt, alarmed. 'Did you bring a Macbook charger with you, Paul?'

'No, why? Should I have?'

'I forgot mine and I'm not sure it's got enough juice. Didn't you all see my text?'

'I generally ignore your texts,' said Jack.

'Me too,' said Paul. 'Rambling and incoherent usually.'

'Thanks for that. I can't be sure my old MacBook battery will last.'

'We're going to have to hope for the best,' said Jack.

'I'll get this,' said Ed producing his wallet and tossing a credit card on the table.

'No you don't,' said Jack. 'We're not your fucking clients. We split it as usual, we don't need any liquidity from the Bank of Ed, thanks.'

'You can never have too much liquidity,' said Matt. 'Put it on my tab. I'll catch you in an hour, I feel a pressing need for fresh air.'

He picked up his jacket and rolled out of the pub in an alcoholic haze. He stood for a moment blinking in the sunlight, lowered his sunglasses and began to walk, unsure as to where he was going. Maybe he could find a charger somewhere. He could not let Will down.

Chapter Fourteen

I Against I

As he was leaving The Pipemakers, Damon's phone began to ring. He stopped in his tracks and fished the mobile from the back pocket of his jeans. It wasn't a number he recognised and he hesitated. Something told him to answer. It was Treggers' mum, Eileen. She explained haltingly that he was in hospital.

She had come home from the shops to find him unconscious in his room. There were a couple of empty packets of his pain medication by his bed and an empty half-bottle of Scotch. They'd pumped his stomach and were running checks to see if there was any lasting damage to his organs. Damon swallowed hard, told her how sorry he was and to let him know as soon as she had any more news. He stood there for a long time, shaking his head, muttering.

Matt spotted him the instant he materialised from the pub doorway and froze in his tracks. No question who it was. Damon had his back to him as his phone began to ring.

Matt's brain computed options with all the speed of a lagging Wi-Fi connection. He couldn't take the chance of walking past and being recognised or running off, which might attract his attention. But he couldn't stand there much longer either, because sooner or later, Damon would look round. He was barely fifteen feet away. Matt considered ducking into the car park but he could see the X-Class parked in a bay, dominating the space like a bull in a field of cows. Instead, he did a slow volte-face and walked softly but swiftly in the opposite direction not daring to look back, in the hope that he looked like just another hipster in a hat wandering around Rye. He took a left at the first side road, sped up and attempted to lose himself in the back streets.

* * *

Damon pulled himself together and turned towards the car park. In the distance he saw a man in a paisley short-sleeved shirt and a straw pork pie hat make a sharp left turn. He looked vaguely familiar.

He pocketed the phone and stood for a moment wondering whether to go home. Instead, he turned and headed towards the quayside. There was no pressing need to head back yet, he couldn't do any work because he didn't have the chemicals, though a check for a package en route would be necessary. Treggers would be OK, surely? He'd go down next week when he was out of the hosi and have a word. He should offer more support to the guy, maybe bring him over for a weekend break? He resolved to make it a plan.

Putting the issue to the back of his mind he strolled up the hill to The Antique Barn, a large wharf-side junk shop. Many of the buildings in the old part of town had been converted into stores selling designer homeware. Not the Barn, which was huge, dusty and filled with bric-a-brac. Its owner, Billy the Yid, piled it high but occasionally he got his hands on a real gem. Billy was Rye born and bred and did not have a single drop of Jewish blood in him. He was a Spurs fan who had picked up his nickname because he was fond of saying his allegiance made him one of 'The Chosen People'.

Stepping through the large wooden doors of the musty

space, Damon sidestepped tourists and climbed a set of timbered stairs hung with cheap prints. On the top floor more rows of junk were spread out on tables and shelves: lamps, pots, glassware, comics, Bakelite phones, toys and ornaments.

People milled around squeezing past one another, idly examining objects and putting them back. A large sign carried the slogan, 'Smile, you're on CCTV'. Something hanging from the ceiling caught his eye, a .22 air rifle with a telescopic sight. He reached up and unhooked it. Billy looked up from his newspaper and nodded, by way of consent. Damon broke open the gun, squinted down the barrel and sniffed it. Then he levelled it and looked down the telescopic sight.

* * *

Having settled a hefty bill at The Ship, the others had departed, splitting into pairs. Ed and Paul went in search of ice cream, Jack and Thom wandered towards the antiques shops, eventually discovering a large two-storey Aladdin's cave in an old fishery. It was the kind of place that held the promise of something valuable but never delivered.

They filed up and down its rows. Thom weighed up a chrome cocktail shaker and pretended to spray it at Jack. Jack examined the bottom of a piece of Poole pottery and nearly dropped it. Thom picked up an old Super 8 camera and pretended to film Jack who played up for the camera, seizing an old bayonet and brandishing it aggressively. A female tourist in a yellow anorak backed away, alarmed.

The pair made for the stairs giggling. A middle-aged woman seated behind a counter full of grubby jewellery watched them disapprovingly. Long brown roots showed beneath her bleached hair. The second floor was crammed with more ephemera. Thom stopped at a cabinet full of toys, beckoned Jack over and picked up a scale model of a motorbike.

'Triumph Bonneville T120, 1967. Classic.'

'Lovely,' said Jack, unimpressed.

'Think I might buy it.'

'Go on then,' said Jack, who had seen enough. His hands felt grubby from handling filthy toot.

They turned towards the counter at the back of the room and froze in their tracks as Damon squinted down the telescopic rifle sight at them from barely fifteen feet away.

Unable to see much beyond a dark blur through a scope, which was much too powerful for the small space, Damon spun back round to the counter.

Thom quietly put the bike down and they retreated gingerly to the stairs without exchanging a word.

'Got any slugs for this?' asked Damon. Billy pulled a face. He had a skin tag just under his right eye.

'Nah,' replied Billy. 'Best go online. Or maybe try the angling shop.'

'What's that?' asked Damon, his eyes alighting on a pistol grip poking out of a leather holster on a shelf. Billy's eyes glanced around the room. The only other customers appeared to have left.

'Antique Very pistol, Webley & Scott. Not sure if it works. Old military type sold it to me yesterday,' he reached behind him and handed the weathered holster over to Damon, who extracted the wooden handled brass pistol, breached it, sniffed it loudly and weighed it in his hand.

'Got any flares with it?' asked Damon, pointing it at the floor and squeezing the trigger.

'Four. Again I can't confirm their state except to say they haven't been fired and they look unmarked.'

'How much?'

'I don't know Damon, you probably need a firearm certificate. I'm going to have to check first.'

'Hundred quid.'

'Ahhhh, really... better err on the safe side, you know.'

'All right you bandit, one fifty. Cash.'

Billy sighed. 'Go on then, but I'll log the sale and the fact I informed you that it requires a firearm certificate.'

'Whatever. Forget the air rifle, I don't have enough cash on me for that as well.'

Damon reached in his pocket, peeled off a roll and dropped the notes onto a glass counter held together by Sellotape in one corner. Billy examined them suspiciously one by one.

'Oi! They're good,' frowned Damon.

'So was one I was given the other day, 'cept it was still wet when I touched it,' sneered Billy. He slid the weapon into a battered canvas bag and handed it over.

'Do be careful with it, won't you? It's not a toy. Could do a lot of damage.'

'Of course,' said Damon, cocking his head. 'Do I look like a nutter to you?'

* * *

Jack and Thom had swiftly lost themselves in the back streets. Thom pulled his phone from his jacket.

'Matt, where are you? That nutter's in town. We've just seen him in a shop. He had a gun.'

'I've already seen him,' Matt's voice betrayed concern. 'What do you mean "he had a gun"?'

'He was looking at an air rifle in a junk shop. It's a miracle he didn't see us.'

'I stood right behind him,' said Matt breathlessly. 'He walked out of that pub I tried to go in on the way here. He would have seen me if his phone hadn't rung. I did an about turn and disappeared before he saw me.'

In the course of losing himself in the back streets Matt had stumbled upon the local vinyl emporium. Thom located the street on his phone and they went to join him. Minutes later the pair stepped inside a room full of second-hand records located in the former classroom of an austere-looking early twentieth-century school on a side street.

'This is a find,' said Thom to Matt. 'We can do a spot of crate digging and hope that the Neanderthal goes back to his cave or gets arrested for scaring tourists.'

They began to work along the racks from A to Z, occasionally skipping entire sections. The shop owner, a man with long grey hair and blue-rimmed spectacles, pretended to ignore them although he was secretly excited. The only people who had been into the shop all day were a gang of teenagers who found the place hysterical.

Matt worked swiftly through crates with an expert touch. He extracted Brian Eno and David Byrne's *My Life in the Bush of Ghosts* and Tom Waits' *Bone Machine* and set them to one side.

'Oooh,' Jack held up a copy of The White Stripes' *Elephant*. 'That's pretty rare... and so's the price,' he noticed, putting it straight back.

Thom made for the funk and soul section and soon had Funkadelic's *Maggot Brain* and the soundtrack to Shaft stacked on the rows of records next to him.

Matt had moved on to a section of electronica. He pulled out an Ólafur Arnalds album and frowned at the cover. He was in the mood to take pot luck, so added it to his pile.

'What's this like?' Jack held up Talk Talk's *Spirit of Eden*.

'Interesting,' said Matt. 'Freeform, moody ambient-rock, critically slagged in its day, now regarded as a bit of a classic.'

Jack pulled the vinyl from the sleeve and ran a critical eye over it. There were a few scratches but nothing needle-threatening. He laid it on top of the rack and continued his quest into the reggae section. He flipped, stopped and examined an old Island compilation before rejecting it when he saw the sleeve had a name scribbled on the back in biro. Why did people do that?

Matt's phone rang. It was Ed saying he and Paul were at the train station. They took their haul to the desk and settled with the grateful shop owner who gave each of them his card to remind them he was online. Jack edged out of the door, looked right and left and signalled the all-clear to the others.

They found Ed and Paul slumped on a bench outside the station. Ed looked tired. Paul looked bored.

'Don't tell me you found a record shop,' said Ed, eyeing their bags with irritation. 'Why didn't you tell us?'

'Didn't want you wasting your billions on jazz, dude,' replied Jack.

'There was a jazz section?'

'Yeah, full of old Blue Note. Rare as hen's teeth some of it, and cheap as chips. Don't think the owner had a clue about beat-bop,' said Jack.

'Be-bop.'

'You selfish gits, you could have told me. Can we go back?'

'Nah, he was shutting up when we left. I think we made his day,' said Thom.

'Never mind your vinyl collection, what about the laptop cable?' asked Paul.

'No joy, I'm afraid, we'll have to hope he doesn't bang on too much, as unlikely as that sounds,' said Matt with resignation. 'I'm out of ideas.'

They hailed a large SUV from the taxi rank and headed back to the house. As the cab sailed out of Rye, Thom and

Jack told Ed and Paul about the incident in the junk shop. Matt then recounted his near miss with Damon.

'It's like being stuck in Dante's Seventh Circle of Hell with that loon,' sighed Paul, slumping into his seat.

'Anyone want to know the football scores or shall we wait till *Match of the Day*?' asked Ed, peering at his phone. Paul groaned.

'We are not watching *Match of the*-Fucking-*Day*.'

'You sound like my wife,' said Ed. 'But at least there's a good reason not to watch *Match of the*-Fucking-*Day* when she objects to it.'

Chapter Fifteen

You Can't Stop What's Coming

The holiday rental smelt of stale booze and fish and chips. Ed headed straight up the stairs to his room and collapsed onto the bed. Paul made a cup of tea and joined Jack and Thom in the garden soaking up the late afternoon sun. Matt came out with a bag and packet of tobacco, sat down and began to roll a joint. Paul shifted in his seat, flapped his newspaper uncomfortably but said nothing as the pungent aroma of skunk filled the air.

Thom suddenly announced he was going for a stroll. He pulled the garden gate shut behind him, lowered his sunglasses and scanned the beach carefully before setting off.

It had emptied out considerably but a few floral parasols and striped windbreaks that were still scattered here and there. Sandcastles lay testament to the day's industry and a sizeable hole had been excavated halfway between the houses and the sea. Above, a child's kite danced in a sky now filled in with fat tufts of cloud. A few brave souls were still messing around in the water on lilos and bodyboards. One family was still gathered laughing and splashing around a large plastic crocodile. A little way further on, a father was packing down a windsurfer with the help of a little girl. *People don't realise how lucky they are sometimes*, thought Thom. He would have loved to spend a day on the beach with his lad. He ordered a cup of tea at the café and sat at an empty table as far away from the kiosk as possible.

Karen joined him a few minutes later. She was wearing a yellow hoodie, bearing an RNLI logo and red shorts. Sand clung to her long legs.

'Wow, it's just like *Baywatch*,' smiled Thom.

'*Baywatch* but with dogshit and empty cans of Tennents,' agreed Karen, sitting down.

'You've not deserted your post have you?' asked Thom. 'Wouldn't want anything to happen out there.'

'No, I'm off duty now,' she said, flicking sand from her hair.

'So what's up? Thought we were a one-night stand and a bad reality show?'

A trace of a smile flickered on her face then a tear rolled down her cheek.

'Woah, what's up?' he got up and moved to her side of the bench. She buried her face in his shoulder and sobbed for a full minute. Thom sat there dumbfounded. A woman holding an ice cream gave him a filthy look. He felt a mixture of confusion and embarrassment. He couldn't even pull off a one-night stand properly these days.

She pulled her head away and apologised, wiping a tear away with the back of her hand.

'I don't know why I texted you, well I do, actually, I'm grasping at straws.'

'What do you mean?'

'I have to get out of that house and I need a room for a few nights. Just a few then I'm gone.'

Oh. Shit, thought Thom.

Karen looked him in the eyes.

'I know this is a huge imposition but I've got to get out of there before something happens to me. I think he might do something.'

'We're talking about your brother obviously.'

She nodded.

Thom wondered why these things happened to him. Normal people had perfectly ordinary sexual encounters. Wham bam, thank you, ma'am. Sometimes they were good, sometimes they were bad, but that was it. No dramas. No postscript. Not him. He got pregnant women, sexual deviants and battered wives. Or sisters.

Karen proceeded to tell him all about Damon. How he had gone from career soldier to unstable steroid dealer in the space of five years.

'He was genuinely OK to be around, a little wild, but joining up sorted him out. He was a model soldier to begin with, but he was different when he came back from Iraq. He saw some bad things there, although he's never told me what happened. I know one of his mates got badly wounded, that's about it. He failed a drugs test a few months after coming back to the UK and they discharged him. Just like that. Thanks for risking your life, off you go.

'After he got kicked out he lost his mojo. Then he discovered bodybuilding, found a new discipline. He also got into martial arts. Did all his belts, became a sensei and started teaching. He moved back down here and started his own carpet-laying business. He had a girlfriend, too, but she left him when he started to go off the rails. He suddenly piled on the muscle. The carpet-laying stopped but he was still making lots of money.'

Thom listened quietly, wishing fervently he had ignored her text.

'I thought he was selling drugs or something, turns out he was, but not street stuff – steroids. He makes them upstairs in the spare room. He keeps bugs in there, too.'

'What, listening devices?'

'No, a giant spider and some hamsters. He prefers animals to people, I think. The room's kept locked but I've seen the pills he makes. He tried to get me involved but I didn't want anything to do with it. I should have left after Mum died but I had nowhere to live so I turned a blind eye.

'Recently, he's started to get more unstable, losing his rag over nothing, trashing things. He beat up my ex. We'd had a huge argument and I ended up with a black eye but it was actually my fault. I went for him and he tried to fend me off. As soon as Damon saw it he stormed round and beat him up, even though I explained it was a genuine accident. Now he's started threatening me. Last night he grabbed me by the throat really hard. I thought he was going to strangle me.'

She pulled the hoodie down at the neck to show him a vivid red mark either side of her throat. Purple bruising was beginning to flower.

'Shit, that's nasty!' said Thom, peering at it closely. 'Fancy doing that to your sister.'

'Totally. I've had enough. I'm leaving. Not just here but this country. I've got a friend in Brisbane who can get me a job working on the Barrier Reef. I completed my diving certificate last week, I'm qualified to teach now, so I'm off. I bought a one-way air ticket this morning. I've got some savings and somewhere to live for a while but the flight doesn't leave till next Friday and I don't want to spend another day in that house, I just don't feel safe with him any longer. You said you lived alone, so could I just kip on your couch till then? He'll never know where I am. I don't plan on telling him I'm going. I'd stay in a hotel but I can't afford to do that for a whole week.'

'I don't know Karen, I mean…' Thom sighed.

She gave him a desperate look.

'I know it's a big favour.'

'Look, give me a while to think about it, will you? It's a

bit of a surprise. I feel like I'm getting involved in something that's nothing to do with me.'

'Sure, I understand completely. I wouldn't ask if I wasn't desperate.'

'Of course you wouldn't,' Thom stood up. 'I'll let you know shortly, OK?'

She nodded. 'I should have gone straight home last night. Sorry. I was a bit pissed and I have to say you lot are quite interesting. You're lucky to be so close.'

'We're just a bunch of old farts. No one else is remotely interested in us. Except us. I'll ring you later. Promise.'

He gave her a smile and turned back towards the house. A minute later he glanced back. She had gone.

His mind was racing. What had he got himself into? What if he refused and something happened to her? What if he agreed and something happened to him? This was supposed to be a chilled weekend with mates, some drinks, some laughs, that was it. Then it had to get complicated. And he couldn't blame anyone but himself, either. He'd leave it a couple of hours and tell her no. It was too much. Or was it? She was leaving the country for good. Whatever happened, he was not going to mention it to the others.

Back in the garden Matt had passed out on a patch of grass in the sun with his hat over his face. Paul was now reading a book. He glanced up as Thom strode past him and into the house where Jack was making a cup of tea.

'Nice walk?'

'Fine. Just going to put my head down for an hour.'

His feet felt heavy climbing the stairs. He flopped on the bed and stared at the ceiling. His brain danced around The Karen Conundrum but he couldn't bring himself to make a decision. Instead he fell into a light doze. 'Time yet for a hundred indecisions,' he muttered.

Chapter Sixteen

Weapon of Choice

The pigeonhole in the office stood bare. Damon shook his head and sighed loudly. He had made his way back home via one of his regular maildrop points at the campsite to check whether the powder had arrived, but there was no sign of a delivery.

A woman came in and picked up an envelope, glancing at him. He'd seen her before and that made him uncomfortable. It might be time to ditch this location but it was very convenient.

He drove home and sat down at the kitchen table to examine his new toy. He took the gun from its holster and lined the shells up in front of him, found a cloth, spat on it and began to polish the brass. Karen froze as she came through the back door. She was wearing a yellow T-shirt with the word 'Lifeguard' on it.

'What the hell is that?' she demanded with a frown.

'Mark III Webley & Scott flare pistol. Bought it in that big junk shop in Rye. Beautiful piece, innit? Brass body, rounded wooden handles, leather holster. Don't think Billy realised what he'd got hold of. I had it off him for a ton and a half before he could think about it too much.'

'But why?'

'Why? It's a fucking collector's item. Imagine the history! It could have been carried by a naval officer in the First or

Second World War. Might have been at Dunkirk or on a destroyer in the Atlantic sweeping for U-Boats. Best of all, it's got four cartridges. Maybe I'll have a proper firework display with it.'

She looked him in the eye. 'Don't you dare, Damon. If you start firing that thing around here people will notice and you don't want to draw attention to yourself, do you?'

'We'll see,' said Damon. He snapped the barrel back up and pointed it at her.

Karen flinched.

'It's empty you soft cow, you saw me cleaning it,' he laughed.

'I thought your firearms training would have made you a bit more sensible with weapons,' she snapped.

'Fuck the military,' snapped Damon. 'And fuck their rules.'

She didn't reply. There was nothing to be gained from antagonising him. She went to a cupboard, pulled out a pot noodle and put the kettle on to boil.

'Save anyone today, then?' asked Damon, slipping the pistol in and out of the holster smoothly.

'No, thankfully. It was quiet. Just had to remind a few kids on lilos about the currents.'

'Shame, you'd be such a hero.'

'I'd rather not be. I'd rather everyone was safe and happy and I was bored out of my head as usual.'

'That's your problem. I offered you the chance to work for me. You could be a lot better off, but no, you have to come over all moral.'

'It's not right, Damon. It's dangerous and it's not legal.'

'Do I look in danger to you? I'm helping people get fit. We've got an obesity epidemic out there, in case you haven't noticed.'

A shell overbalanced. He stood it upright again.

Karen gave him a look of disbelief. She filled the pot with hot water and stirred it with a fork. Drogba wandered in and began to drink from his water bowl, lapping loudly with a huge pink tongue.

'What are you doing tonight? Entertaining again?' sneered Damon.

'Staying in. Not that it's any of your business.'

'Sure? You could earn some good money putting it about with that lot. Why do it for free?'

'Don't be so bloody crude, Damon,' she shouted.

Damon snatched the pistol out of the holster and pointed it at her head.

'You've got to ask yourself one question: do I feel lucky?' It was a poor impression.

'Pack it up, Damon, you're turning into a psycho!'

Damon slammed the pistol down and jumped to his feet making her flinch. Veins bulged from his head.

'What are you going to do, throttle me again?' she demanded. He stood there visibly shaking with anger. She brushed past him and stomped upstairs.

In her room she put the Pot Noodle on her bedside table, climbed into bed and sat in fury. Then she stood up, reached on top of the wardrobe, pulled down her suitcase, threw it on the bed and began to empty her chest of drawers into it.

Along the corridor, the door to the Roid Room clicked shut.

Chapter Seventeen

Ice on the Wing

The power shower droned into life. Water ricocheted off Ed's shoulders in a fine spray. He was trying to wash away the hangover as much as clean up.

He began to ponder what was in store that evening. It was going to be an odd one. Highlight, 'Dead Mate's Quiz', a Netflix special in which a group of middle-aged soaks get together following a friend's early death. 'Life affirming and hilarious', 'Darkly witty and deeply moving', or 'Tedious and downbeat' and 'Overlong and pretentious'?

He pictured Will in his head. It was sick Will, not the guy they were at school with or the ambitious young man in his twenties, nor the handsome middle-aged chap. Why did that happen? Why were you stuck with the wrong pictures? It didn't seem right.

Ed had gone to see Will a couple of weeks before Christmas. Will was sitting at his desk making notes when Annie let him in. He had glanced up, removed his reading glasses and waved him in.

'Hey?'

'How you doing?'

'Fine, just don't wish me a happy new year.'

'Maybe we can sing a chorus of "Auld Lang Syne" instead then?' suggested Ed.

'Made any resolutions? I thought I might give up the ghost.'

'You'll never keep it up. Try something else,' suggested Ed.

'Give up being a git perhaps? Impossible. Give up being rude? Never going to happen. Give up work? What are you doing anyway?'

'I wasn't working, though I still do bits and pieces. Keeps me busy. No, I was writing...'

'Ooh, is it a cancer blog?' asked Ed, feigning excitement.

'No one needs another fucking cancer blog. Or, worse, a vlog. Starring in your own little tragedy. 'Week one: chemotherapy, bluuurggggh! Week two: bluuuuuurrggh!' Knowing my luck though it would get picked up by Amazon Prime after I'd flown the coop and win an award for best documentary.'

'A bucket list then?'

'Bit fucking late for that. I did consider it when I went into remission but I honestly thought I was out of the woods so I didn't put any of it into action. Then when it came back it was too late.'

Ed sneezed and reached for a paper handkerchief on the desk. He waved a hand as he put it to his nose and blew. Will put a hand over his face.

'It's OK I'm not ill, it's just dust. What was on the list? Swimming with dolphins? Going to see Mickey in Disneyland?'

Will laughed. 'And Santa Claus in Lapland. No I wanted to go heli-skiing in Alaska. And hike in the Andes, too, somewhere wild and spectacular. But 'twas not to be.'

'I'm sure they're overrated,' shrugged Ed. 'Wandsworth is so much more dramatic – the common, the prison, the err, town hall.'

'I can't even get that far. It's more like the hospital, my study and the loo. Oh yes, I've ticked 'em all off.'

Ed's phone pinged. He pulled it out of his pocket and glanced at the screen.

'Not distracting you am I?'

'Sorry it's fucking work. It's a shitstorm at the moment. Total mess. I spend all my time firefighting.'

'Nothing serious I hope, Ed.'

'Nah, nothing I can't fix.'

They chatted on about this and that. Football. West Ham were struggling again. Normally Ed, a Spurs fan, would have ribbed Will about it but it felt unnecessary. And it was the least of his worries. Instead, ever the movie buff, he recommended a few films he'd been to see and a new Netflix crime series.

'It sounds great but I don't think I'll bother. I might not get to the end of season one,' said Will dismissively.

They began to run out of things to say. Will brought the conversation to an end, complaining he was tired.

Ed bade him goodbye, popped up to see Annie and gave her a hug. After that Will refused to entertain visitors. They spoke on the phone but it was the last time he ever saw him alive. If he'd have known he'd have told him so much more but he was clinging on to hope. They all were. Waiting on a miracle.

He closed the hot water flow right down so it ran as cold as possible. He turned his face to the showerhead and let it blast him a moment, then switched it off with a shiver and stepped out of the cubicle. He wiped steam off the mirror and stared at his face. Another night's drinking lay ahead.

Paul and Jack were watching the news on the television when Matt staggered unsteadily back indoors. His shirt was creased, blades of grass clung to it. A few strands stuck in his hair, too. He looked bleary-eyed, like he'd been stunned.

'Nice snooze?'

'Mmm, must have passed out.'

He paused at the sink to drain a glass of water. At that moment Ed wandered into the room, carrying the aroma of soap with him.

'Sorry, must have passed out.'

'It's contagious, old age, isn't it?' said Jack, flaking into a chair and yawning.

Ed slumped heavily into a couch and gave a sigh. Silence descended on the room.

Matt surveyed the scene of lethargy. Intervention was needed.

'What we need is a livener.'

He dashed upstairs and came back down with the wrap in his hand. He wiped off the island and poured a pile of white powder onto it, fished out a credit card and chopped out five lines.

'Right, come on. One toot each, let's get this party started,' he said rolling a tenner and holding it out.

They all looked at each other, doubtfully. No one took up the offer.

'Come on, it's on me and it's good stuff.'

Jack stood up and walked over to examine the narcotics dubiously. He looked at Matt who smiled and held the tenner towards him.

'It must be twenty years since I did Charlie.'

'I only did it a few times and I think it was you who was responsible on each occasion then, too, Matt,' said Ed, also standing up to eye the brittle white crystals suspiciously.

At that moment Thom wandered into the room and stopped in his tracks.

'Right you're nicked, the lot of you! Failure to act your age.'

'A little Bolivian tonic for the troops,' explained Matt. 'Everyone's feeling a bit flat. Think of it like using the starting handle on an old classic.'

'Count me out,' said Paul, bluntly. 'Cocaine ruins lives. It's not a bit of fun, it's a ruthless trade created by vicious criminal cartels that peddle misery. It's also, by the way, absolute shit.'

'This is good shit though,' corrected Matt, pointing at the pile with the rolled tenner.

'No, it's not, it's probably cut. Gak is the perfect name for it. You don't know what's in it. It's almost certainly toxic and it's extremely unwise to be doing it at your age, too.'

'OK Paul, point taken, you're right,' declared Matt holding his hands up in surrender. 'But these days all you ever get is finger wagging from the establishment. Don't do this, don't do that. Do as I say, not as I do. One fag will take six months off your life, a pint is poison. So now, if we're careful, we can all live to be ninety. I mean, fucking great! What a bonus – another ten years in a fucking nursing home having your arse wiped, all respect gone. Well, fuck that, actually.'

'Will might have a different point of view if he was here,' said Paul seriously. 'I think he'd like the option.'

'This has got fuck all to do with Will! I'm sure he'd be absolutely chipper if he found himself here with us, who wouldn't fail to be in the circumstances? But I'm not talking about dying at forty or fifty, I just don't see the appeal of ending up like a basket case for years. What's the point of keeping people alive longer if they can't enjoy it? You're broke and broken at seventy. You should get more time when you're young, it's no good having it when you're a fucking dribbling senile cunt in a nappy.'

'Plenty of old folk who look after themselves enjoy long and active lives,' countered Paul whose parents were still going strong in their eighties.

This did not go down well with Matt whose beloved father, Stan, had gone into a slow decline and died four years previously following complications from a routine knee operation. He thought he was going to lose him but the old boy had pulled through. He spent the best part of a month in intensive care, two more in hospital and another three convalescing in a recovery unit. When he emerged, the active, independent gent of old was gone, replaced by an infirm shell of a man.

Following the death of Matt's mother, Stan had moved back to his north London roots. Father and son had season tickets at the Emirates. The old man played snooker and went for walks, discovering parts of the capital and its history, which he would describe to Matt in great detail over a pint at his local. He had gone from that to a husk of a man who sat in his armchair all day, refusing to do any exercise or take an interest in anything, even the football scores.

Matt bought him history books about London in the hope of sparking some interest but they went unread. He lectured him, he even shouted at him. Stan shouted back. Eventually the old boy had become unable to look after himself any longer and gone into care. Six months later he was dead.

'Fuck that. You sound like an advertisement for Sanatogen!' shouted Matt, exasperated. 'Well I want something a bit stronger, actually. And if I end up like my dad I will demand the right to go out on my own fucking terms. In fact I will expect one of you to buy me a revolver.'

With that he bent forward and vacuumed an entire line in one smooth hit.

'Ahhhhh!' he exhaled loudly, 'Get. In!'

He stood upright and extended the note to Thom. Paul sat down and snapped open his paper in fury.

Thom hesitated for a moment and glanced warily at Paul before accepting the challenge.

'Since Matt is determined to measure out his life in coke spoons I feel it's my duty to support him.'

He leant over the powder and did the second line, straightened up and sniffed deeply, wiping his nostrils reflexively.

'No, I'm Spartacus!' declared Jack. He snatched the note from Thom bent over and snorted but stopped halfway and, very deliberately, changed nostrils.

'Come on!' he yelled over dramatically, waving the note at Ed.

Ed hesitated. Matt gave him a fierce look. He was fully aware he was too old for this nonsense but Matt's expression and the sheer force of his speech made it impossible to back down. However, he reached into his pocket, pulled out his wallet and very deliberately took out a fifty and tossed the tenner back at Matt.

'If you don't mind,'

'You are such a flash bastard!' smiled Matt.

Ed then hoovered up the penultimate line.

'God damn!' he gasped, performing his best Uma Thurman impression.

Matt rerolled his tenner and snorted Paul's line without asking.

'Woah! Don't judge me!' he screwed up the note and threw it away, jogged up and down on the spot and saluted, prompting everyone but Paul to dissolve into fits of laughter.

Ed blinked hard. Chemicals trickled down the back of his throat. His heart rate was accelerating like the M3 on a clear stretch of motorway.

'All right, have some of this then!'

He rushed to the kitchen and pulled five tumblers from the cupboard and banged them onto the countertop. Then he went to the fridge and extracted a bag of green herbs and put a handful into each glass, along with a big pinch of sugar.

'What is our resident mixologist alchemising now?' inquired Jack, raising an eyebrow.

Lost in concentration, Ed sliced a couple of limes into quarters and mashed each glass in turn with the end of wooden kitchen stirrer and threw in ice. He then reached into his cardboard box for a bottle and splashed liberal measures of a clear spirit over each glass and added a sprig of mint to finish.

'Mojitos, *señors*! One hundred per cent legal and guaranteed to improve the mood of the righteously affronted,' he said, proffering one of the glasses to Paul. Paul hunkered deeper into his paper. Ed walked over and stuck it under his nose. Paul twisted away like a child. Ed set it down on the arm of the chair.

'*Arriba, abajo, al centro y adentro*!' he announced, swilling his glass and taking a sip.

'Hey, citrus. Hey liquor, I love it when we come together,' sang Matt, serenading his glass.

'Mmmm, that is very, very moreish,' agreed Jack.

'No it's very, very Cuban actually,' corrected Thom.

'What say you, Paul?' asked Ed, cajoling him.

Paul gave him a hard look. They waited in silence. He sighed, put down the paper and picked up the glass and took a sip.

'Fine. Lovely in fact, but have you noticed how everything we do together revolves around alcohol?'

'Here we go again,' sighed Matt, slumping to the floor histrionically.

'It's a constant. We never do anything that doesn't involve drink. Most of the time we meet in pubs, occasionally we meet at a party. There's never not booze.'

'It's a social lubricant,' protested Matt.

'We shouldn't need one after forty years.'

'We don't. We just choose to. And we go to see bands sometimes.'

'Which involves going to the pub first and afterwards and trips to the bar during the songs no one likes,' said Paul.

'God, you can be a wet blanket, Paul,' sighed Matt, still prone.

Paul was not to be deflected, though nor did he put his tumbler to one side.

'If we all stopped drinking, where and how would we meet up?' he demanded.

'Alcoholics Anonymous meetings?' suggested Jack.

'If alcohol is the glue and we don't use it, will we come unstuck? That's the point he's making,' said Thom, interpreting helpfully.

'Precisely.'

'Well you can come to the Arsenal,' said Matt. 'Oh, but you don't like football.'

'Would it involve going for a pint before and after the match?' asked Paul.

'It might.'

'We could go walking, then,' said Ed.

'Lots of pubs,' said Thom flatly.

'And frankly, fuck walking anyway,' added Matt.

'It seems to me the bond is permanent after forty years. How we choose to socialise can't change that,' said Jack. 'So we're wasting drinking time trying to find a healthy solution.'

Paul sighed. 'I give up.'

'Good,' said Ed. 'Can I offer you a top-up?'

'Let's play a game, instead,' announced Paul, standing up energetically. 'What about charades?'

'Parlour games? Taking the evening to a whole new level!' laughed Jack, mock affronted.

'Go on then,' said Ed, indulging him to ease him out of his mood.

'You first then, Paul,' said Thom, taking a pull from his glass and swilling it around like mouthwash.

Paul signalled 'song' and held up one finger. Then he moved to the side of the room and started stroking the wall with a wide-eyed expression on his face.

'Ecstasy!' declared Matt.

'Crack,' suggested Ed.

Paul frowned at them and shook his head. Then returned to the object of his worship.

'Fascination!' shouted Jack triumphantly. 'Human League!'

Paul shook his head and banged the plaster with the flat of his hand.

'"Wonderwall!"' yelled Matt.

Paul put his finger on his nose.

Matt jumped up and signed 'movie', two words, 'whole thing'. Then he grabbed his crotch and ran around the room as if it was dragging him.

'Cock! Knob! Penis!' yelled Paul.

'You're going to have to get that Tourette's seen to,' admonished Matt.

'Moby Dick,' shouted Ed.

'Nice try, but no.'

Matt continued to let himself be dragged around the room by his genitals. He pointed at them helpfully with his other hand.

'*Free Willy*!' declared Jack.

'Yes!' said Matt.

Jack showed no inclination to take his turn.

'What about something else? How about we do a puzzle?' he suggested. 'Or maybe there's some baskets we can weave?'

'Twenty questions?' suggested Paul helpfully. 'First question, why is Jack such a total cock?'

'If we were post-millennials we could all sit slack-jawed and play computer games for the rest of the night with only fizzy drinks and snacks to sustain us,' said Ed, who did spend the occasional evening playing computer games, and found the idea not unappealing.

'That's why they're a lost generation,' sneered Paul. 'Everything they do undermines them, even their leisure habits. In the past you'd run around playing football – not that I especially approve of that – or, I don't know, vandalising things. Now you just lock yourself away and shout at a screen or troll each other.'

'Here we go,' sighed Ed, spitting out small flakes of nut husks from a handful of nuts. Ice rattled around his empty glass.

'It's fucking true. That generation is being raped. I can see it, you can see it, but they're going to wake up too late and then it's all going to go off.'

'He's right,' said Matt. 'We could be the last generation of homeowners proper. Half of us are leveraging their wealth to rent to people poorer than them, the other half are just clinging on. If you're under forty and you're not getting a big fat bonus from the City, you're fucked. Our generation is literally enslaving the one behind.'

'So much for being young, eh?' said Paul finding double top.

Thom could feel the drink and the drugs rushing through his system now. He semi stumbled to the back door, surveyed the now deserted beach and took a few deep breaths. The light was beginning to fade and the sea was still barely visible. It was as if a large plug had been pulled somewhere mid-Channel. Acres of dark brown sand and minor lakes of trapped seawater stretched before him. He felt like going for a walk but didn't dare in case the hellhound and its handler were abroad. Damon was attaining mythic properties.

He stepped into the garden. Gusts of ozone-saturated air

hit him. He took a few more deep breaths and felt himself revive a little. The weekend was taking its toll. He resolved not to drink much for the rest of the night. He had a decision to make about Karen and he'd been putting it off. He owed it to her to at least make one.

'Let's do the quiz,' announced Matt, breaking the silence they'd all fallen into.

'Let's not,' said Jack.

'Too early,' agreed Ed. 'Why ruin things? We could order food, though.'

'You only ever think about your stomach,' said Matt, shaking his head.

Thom found a flyer for a curry house and they rang through an order. Jack opened a bottle of wine and sloshed it into a few glasses. He tasted it carefully and shrugged. Ed took a glass and went off to examine the DVDs in the cupboard.

'Jesus it's like the rack of a local charity shop: *Beaches* – girls movie, *The Water Boy* – one funny scene, *Meet the Fockers* – no funny scenes, *The 40-Year-Old Virgin* – the waxing scene's OK, ooh, *Fifty Shades of Grey* – one for Thom.'

'Bit tame,' muttered Thom from the patio.

'What about *The Girl with the Dragon Tattoo*?' Ed held up the cover. 'Did you rate her, Thom?'

Thom stepped back inside.

'She was quite hot in a fucked up way. Carrying a bit of baggage, though. I can do without that.'

'You wouldn't want to get on the wrong side of her, would you?' agreed Jack. 'Like tell her not to get another tramp stamp. She'd cut your balls off and make you eat them on toast.'

Ed continued to leaf through the collection. '*O Brother, Where Art Thou*? Not bad actually. *Gladiator*, yes! Come on.

Let's watch it while we wait for the food. You can't go wrong with Maximus Decimus unleashing hell.'

'OK but let's cut to the amphitheatre and get on with the meaty stuff,' said Paul.

Ed switched on the TV and a blew dust off the DVD player. He wiped the disc and inserted it, then spent several minutes working out which remote control worked the machine.

'Come on, do you need a manual?' prompted Jack impatiently.

'Very kind of you to offer,' said Ed, pressing a button and hoping. Credits appeared on the screen. He fast-forwarded to the first battle and they whooped as Maximus slashed his way through bearded opponents.

'Break 'em off a piece, Max!' shouted Ed in a Bronx accent.

'Bloody Barbarians. Can't appreciate a good fresco or a bit of Ovid,' agreed Paul.

Everyone settled down and began to concentrate on the movie. Matt stood up to pour himself another glass of wine and sat down again. Ed worked his way through a bowl of pistachios using the remote to fast forward to the fight scene.

'I'd watch it all, actually. It's one of those movies that sucks you in,' he said as Maximus began dismembering semi-naked figures brandishing chains and tridents.

'That's you Matt preparing to fight Conan down the road,' said Ed as the paralysed-with-fear slave urinated all over Maximus's best sandals.

'It's all of us, I'd say after the way we behaved in the pub last night. I recall we couldn't get out of there quick enough,' observed Paul.

Thom made his way upstairs, sat on his bed, took out his phone and dialled a number.

'Hi Karen? It's Thom.'

'Oh, hi Thom.' The voice on the line was barely up a whisper. She sounded hesitant.

'Hey. Listen, I was thinking, you can stay at mine, OK? No room on the bike so why not come up Monday evening when I've recovered a bit from the weekend's festivities?'

'Oh, thanks, thanks, that's brilliant, Thom. I won't be any trouble, promise,' she brightened up.

'Is everything OK?'

'Yeah, yeah, it's fine,' her voice was still faint.

'OK, see you Monday then, bye,' he rang off.

It was nothing really. He didn't know why he had spent so long dithering.

He checked through his emails and used the toilet. When he came down Maximus was mortally wounded and headed for Elysium. The room was silent as he collapsed and began to slip towards the other side. Lush fields of blue-filtered grass beckoned.

'I always feel oddly moved by this bit,' announced Ed.

'*Bambi* out-sads it,' countered Jack.

'Mmm, what about Wilson, Tom Hanks's best mate in *Castaway*, floating off into the distance? No man ever loved a ball more,' suggested Paul.

'Do you reckon Will saw anything?' said Matt.

'A bright white light at the end of a long tunnel?' sneered Jack.

'The final score at the London Stadium? A three-nil defeat,' suggested Ed.

'We're going to have to face him shortly. I just wondered. He fought for so long but I could see he'd had enough by the end,' said Matt.

'Death is hardly a surprise, is it?' said Thom. 'It's inevitable, the bullet you can't dodge and all that.'

'But it's still a mystery and it's unique to everyone,' said Paul.

'Not road crash victims,' said Jack, shooting him down.

The doorbell rang.

'Thank the good Lord for that, another minute and I'd have topped myself,' said Ed running to answer it. He came back laden with carrier bags filled with takeaway. They sat at the table and started decanting the food onto the plates.

'Will was such a curry connoisseur, not sure he'd be impressed with this,' said Jack, examining his rogan josh doubtfully.

'Whenever we decided to eat out, it was always, "Let's get a curry", his default position was curry,' agreed Thom.

'Are we ever going to be the same without him?' asked Matt, swilling red wine round his glass melancholically. 'He was always such a provocative fucker, you couldn't fail to be energised when he was around.'

'I think of us as a band that's lost its frontman,' said Paul, philosophically. 'For some groups like The Doors it's the end... beautiful friend. No one can replace a Jim Morrison. But then there's your New Orders or your AC/DCs. The ones that move to another level.'

'We're more New Order,' observed Jack. 'We're not replacing Ian Curtis, we're soldiering on without him. This is our melancholic dance phase.'

'There's nothing worse than those bands lumbering on until they drop because they don't know what else to do. Like fucking Queen,' said Paul. 'Cranking out jukebox hits to people who wish they were at Live Aid.'

'Hearing Aid now,' corrected Ed. 'Benefit for ageing rock fans.'

'It's fair to say we peaked a while ago. We haven't made a good album in years,' said Jack.

'Plateaued, more like,' corrected Thom.

'Turned round with the summit in sight and went back to base camp for a nap,' agreed Jack.

'Some of us are soldiering on determined to get to the top, actually. I'm not quitting on anything; us, or my ambition,' said Ed sticking a fork into a piece of lamb on Jack's plate.

'That's the spirit, Ed. Now why don't we just go down the pub, not the mentalist's one, the other one, and do The Brainmelter another time,' suggested Jack. 'You know, when it's all a bit less raw.'

'There's something in that,' agreed Ed.

'Is there, fuck!' declared Matt, banging down his glass. 'How often are we all in the same place at the same time with the opportunity to sit and watch this video together? Answer: never. There's always illness, working late, babysitter issues, parent-teacher evenings, school plays, couples therapy sessions...'

He stood up with a little wobble and left the room abruptly. Ed raised an eyebrow at the others and used his last piece of naan to wipe round Matt's plate, carefully absorbing all the sauce. Jack refilled his glass then Ed's and offered the bottle to Paul who waved him away and went to the kitchen for ale.

Matt came back down a few minutes later with a laptop under one arm.

'Right,' he said, wiping his nose with his free hand. He picked up Ed's half-empty bottle of rum as he passed the island and placed it on a side table, then returned for a wooden chair, setting it down in front of the TV and placing the laptop on its seat.

'Let's get quizzical.'

Chapter Eighteen

Killer Parties

The room went silent. Everyone looked at Matt, then they looked at each other.

'Right, prepare to be humiliated though,' said Jack decisively. He stood up and wiped his hands on his jeans. Ed exhaled through pursed lips. Paul chewed his lip. Thom closed his eyes. They refilled glasses and moved to the seating area.

Matt produced a pad and some pens and handed them out like a schoolteacher before a test. Thom examined his with a smile. Its transparent top contained a mermaid that drifted back and forth when you tipped it up and down. He sat there rotating it watching her navigate her way from one end to the other.

'Put your name and answers down on your paper. All mobile phones on the coffee table where we can see them, please. And no conferring. Everybody ready?'

'I'm that pissed I can barely remember my name,' said Jack.

'It's "Twat", write it down now so you don't forget it again.'

Jack duly wrote it out in capitals. Then he tore off a spare sheet of paper and wrote 'cokehead' in capitals and handed it to Matt.

'There you go. In case you forget yours.'

'Thank you,' Matt took the paper and set it down on his chair. He squatted down and flipped up the laptop lid. The screen flickered into life. He gave the battery an anxious look. It still registered less than half charged.

'The suspense is killing me,' said Ed. He lifted a cheek and farted loudly.

'I smell your tension,' said Thom wafting his hand vigorously.

Will's image sprang to life on the screen, the ghost in the machine.

'Ladies and gentlemen, I give you the one, the only Brainmelter, may the best old man win,' declared Matt, sitting down.

'Oh shit, look at him. Poor bugger,' muttered Paul.

Jack swallowed hard, Ed licked his lip.

'This reminds me of one of those made-for-TV movies where a family assembles at a solicitor's office to watch a video of the patriarch as he passes on his worldly goods, enraging everyone by leaving everything to his illegitimate lovechild,' said Thom.

'So it's a... Will reading! Geddit?' declared Jack, triumphantly.

'Or one of those sci-fi movies with a ghost ship floating in space where a boarding party discovers the final message from the doomed captain telling everyone to please God stay away,' suggested Ed.

'Shhhh!' Matt admonished, pointing a little white remote to start the video.

The room fell expectantly silent. Will sat with a wad of prompt cards stacked between both hands. He tapped them on his desk ostentatiously and looked at the camera.

'Hello wankers. Welcome to The Brainmelter, quiz of quizzes. This will be the last in the series due to the cancellation of its creator.'

'He's not going to make this easy, is he?' muttered Jack.

'Please bear with me,' Will went on, as if answering him. 'I realise this is all a bit uncomfortable but it's my way of wrapping things up. I know I saw each of you towards the end and if I'd had my way we'd all have gone on the lash one last time and I'd simply have ascended into the sky at the end of the evening. So, first up, a toast,' he raised a small plastic cup. 'The Boys!' He swigged it down in one and tossed it over his shoulder.

'The Boys!' they extended their glasses towards the screen and drank.

'Did you try the dose you swiped Matt?' asked Will, suddenly. 'How was it?'

'You didn't?!' gasped Paul. 'You took the man's medicine?'

'No, OK yes, but he had plenty. He was never going to run out,' said Matt, pausing the video with a little remote on the chair arm. 'I just wondered what it was like.'

'And what was it like, Matt?' asked Thom, giving him a pitying look.

'I drank about half at home. It tasted like strong bitter Calpol or a treacly negroni but very swiftly I felt… euphoric. I closed my eyes and I could see a deep blueness enveloping me. It felt like I was lying in a warm bath, incredibly chilled out and blissful. I didn't want to move or do anything. In fact I don't think I did anything for hours except sit there. You can see the attraction. The comedown was a bit grim, mind.'

'Jesus smacked out Christ, Matt,' said Paul, shaking his head. 'You need to see someone.'

'It was a one-off, an experiment. Altered states, and all that. And I really don't need another lecture.'

'Come on, let's get going, we're keeping the man waiting,' said Jack.

Matt pointed and, as if responding to his command, Will jumped back into life.

'I'm assuming that you're all here. Sorry I couldn't join you this year. You may be wondering how I feel about not being able to make it?'

'Christ almighty,' muttered Paul, shaking his head. Ed stood up as if about to leave. Matt gave him a pleading look and he sat back down.

'What it feels like is I've had to leave the party early. It's not the best party but the music's OK because Matt is in charge, Jack is dancing, encouraging others to join in. I can see Paul and Ed having a laugh, probably at Jack's expense. Thom is chatting up the best looking woman in the room. I just know he's going to pull. How does he still do it? Anyway, for some unspecified reason, I have to go. I resent it bitterly, but at the same time I know from experience if there's one thing worse than leaving early, it's being the last to leave. That's the worst thing of all.

'I read a news story a few years back about an old man who flew back from Pakistan, took a train north from London, walked up Saddleworth Moor and lay down to die. The sheer mystery of his final journey really caught my imagination. The magnetic pull of his final resting place might have been exerting itself his entire life. I imagined him admiring the view before lying back to watch the blue sky fade and the stars bloom before he closed his eyes for the last time. It's like you spend your entire life travelling to the place you're going to die. Unfortunately I'm stuck in my office. Oh well, we can't all go like Scott or Mallory, I suppose.

'I was genuinely looking forward to us all ageing together and being the coolest pensioners ever, maybe living in one of those retirement homes where I had the best room, Thom goosed the nurses, Matt got in trouble for turning off the muzak, and Jack upset all the other residents who had him kicked out.

'You never know what's round the corner in life. You don't expect your dad to drop dead from a heart attack, you don't expect to find yourself caught up in a global terrorist attack. Things never work out how you expect them to, that happens to other people. Other people live successful lives before slipping away in their sleep surrounded by their tearful wives, their devoted children and grandchildren. I won't even know if Charlotte has passed her A levels. Not, obviously, that any of that shit matters. Don't tell her I said that, though.'

Ed swallowed his wine nervously. Jack wiped away a small tear, hoping no one would notice. Paul pulled a face, reached for his ale and knocked it over. Beer splashed across the pale carpet.

'You really are a clumsy git, Paul,' said Jack, relieved to have someone to focus his anger on. Matt pressed pause again with a snort of frustration as Jack ran off to the kitchen and came back with a couple of tea-towels. He and Paul scrubbed the floor vigorously. Jack snatched the cloth from Paul tossed both aside and sat back down.

'Can I restart?' asked Matt, in the voice of a beleaguered school teacher.

'Fuck it, let's not. Let's go down the pub and pretend we finished it. He'll never know,' said Ed.

'But we will,' replied Jack. 'Get on with it.'

Matt pressed 'play' again.

'The world keeps on spinning without you. Fancy that. First shall be last and last shall be first. Or whatever it says in The Bible. I can't say I turned to it, even in my darkest hour, so I can't be sure. No deathbed conversion for me. If there's something on the other side I'll give you a heads up. In fact I'll fucking well haunt you on the Boys' Weekend.

'Moving on because I don't want to keep Matt up any longer than necessary. I recall he is usually asleep on the couch by the time I get to the current affairs round. So without more ado, papers at the ready, no conferring, no surreptitiously sliding off to the loo to google answers, Ed, and no copying, Jack. I'm betting on Ed to win but Paul will push him hard. Matt will take the wooden spoon again, despite acing the music questions while he can still function.

So round one. Music. Question one, easy one to kick off with: Which of these musicians didn't die of cancer? David Bowie, Bob Marley, Lemmy or Curtis Mayfield?'

'Oh, for fuck's sake!' shouted Ed. 'Do we have to do this?'

'Don't bite!' hushed Matt. 'He's just winding us up, as usual. Plus I know the answer.' He put pen to paper, finishing with an emphatic full stop that made the pen leap from his fingers.

'Sorry about that one; naughty. Question two: Who links David Bowie, Duran Duran and The Thompson Twins?'

'The Thompson Twins?' frowned Jack. Paul chewed his pen.

Matt scribbled eagerly. 'I might have to play my joker, early,' he grinned.

* * *

At the far end of the road, Karen was struggling to answer a pressing question of her own. Where was her passport? She had spent an hour packing, overfilling a large blue suitcase before steadily reducing the amount until it was possible to close it.

A large pile of clothes and shoes now lay in one corner of the room. Some things like her wet suit were indispensable. It was bulky and though she'd probably be given one, it had been expensive and fitted perfectly. On top she laid a single pair of heels, a pair of trainers and two pairs of sandals, skirts and a navy dress for dates – hopefully. In the top sleeve she slid some photographs of Dad and Mum and one of herself following a wreck dive wearing a huge smile on her face.

When the front door slammed shut, signalling Damon's departure to the pub, she went down to the kitchen for a jar of Marmite. Did they stock it in supermarkets there? No way was she having Vegemite. Could you even take Marmite on a plane?

She turned her attention to the backpack. A pair of sunglasses, a novel, diving certificates, her ageing MacBook and its charger. But when she'd gone to her bedside cabinet for the passport, there was no sign of it. She did a double take, then checked the other drawers, frowning. With increasing agitation she searched under the bed before eventually combing the entire room from top to bottom. But it was in the drawer because she'd needed it to buy the plane ticket and she had then carefully put it back under her diary. The diary was still there but not the passport.

'You bastard! she yelled, throwing a plastic hairbrush at the door. It broke in two. 'Bastard, bastard, bastard!'

She stomped across the landing to his room and searched it carefully, sifting through training kit, his washing pile and under the mattress. She tested bits of carpet to see if they were loose and stood on a chair to examine the top of wardrobe. She worked through the wardrobe going through his pockets and found a set of keys in a leather jacket. She examined them for a moment and made her way over to the Roid Room, put the larger key in the lock and turned. The latch clicked. She opened the door slowly and peered inside, half expecting to see Damon there. Entering the temple of temples was forbidden.

She scanned the room for a moment. It had to be in here somewhere. She took a deep breath and began with the filing cabinet, starting with the top drawer. She worked her way through the files, then pulled them out and checked the bottom of the drawer before working her way down. The bottom drawer contained the flare pistol. She slammed it shut in frustration and turned her attention to the rest of the room.

The workbench was neatly arranged with a laptop, printer, a burner phone, scales and some lab equipment. She turned round and took in the other side of the room. The hamster cage stood at one end of the bench, the spider tank, the other. She leafed carefully through a shelf above it, checking inside DVD boxes and lever arch files. She glanced involuntarily down at the spider tank. There, lying on the bottom in one corner by the spider she could clearly see the cover of a maroon passport.

She recoiled.

'No! You fucking bastard, no, no, no!'

She slumped to the floor, sobbing.

* * *

Up the road, everyone had settled in to tackling The Brainmelter. Now they had become accustomed to the figure on the screen it almost felt like a live link. The music round had reached its conclusion.

'Well I reckon I can dip out of the next round in the knowledge I'm well ahead,' said Matt, jumping to his feet and disappearing from the room.

'I doubt you're that far ahead,' Jack shouted after him. He reached for the remote and paused the video. Will froze, his mouth hung open.

'How did you fare there, Paul?' asked Jack.

'Bit too much dad-rock but I handled it all right, I think.'

He leant over and uncapped another bottle of ale. Matt almost jogged back into the room.

'Right. Let's kick on,' said Ed. Jack pressed play.

'Moving on to round two,' continued Will. 'The film round. Ed, the resident movie buff has an advantage here so could take the lead as Matt zonks out thanks to a huge spliff.'

Matt threw a peanut at the laptop. It bounced off the screen.

'Question one: movie cocktails. What is the favourite tipple of The Dude in *The Big Lebowski*, Jake and Elwood in *The Blues Brothers* and Rick Blaine in *Casablanca*?'

'Mmmm,' said Ed, scribbling swiftly. Jack pretended to look over his arm. Ed covered his paper and shuffled across.

'Come on Ed, let me have a squint. I'll buy you a fun pack of Mars bars.'

'Fuck off Barratt, you're not getting a sniff. I bailed you out over your homework too often and then we both got caught.'

'Jack, do I have to disqualify you?' said Matt.

'Question two: remakes. Name the original star and his remake replacement. One, *The Night of the Hunter*. Two, *Willy Wonka & the Chocolate Factory*. Three: *The Fly*. Four, *The Manchurian Candidate*.'

'Ha, piece of piss,' sneered Ed. 'Jack, look!' he waggled his paper violently in Jack's face and snatched it away.

'I don't need your help as it happens,' said Jack, writing down answers in neat script. He stopped the video abruptly and made a sudden lunge for Ed's paper. There was a scuffle.

'Fuck off, Barratt!' yelled Ed as his paper tore.

'He's spoilt his paper, miss!' declared Jack. He held a corner in one hand. Ed smoothed out the rest carefully, then sighed and began to rewrite the answers on a fresh sheet. He folded the old one over and slid it in his trouser pocket.

'This is your final warning, Jack,' said Matt, wagging a finger with a grin. His paper fell to the floor between his feet.

He reached down and attempted to retrieve it, fumbling it a couple of times. Jack pressed play.

'Question three,' began Will. 'Screen deaths...'

Ed groaned, stood up and walked off. Jack paused the video.

'Ed, where are you going?'

'Home,' he shouted back. 'I've had enough.'

An uncomfortable silence arose. Everyone was listening for the door.

'Is he serious?' asked Jack.

* * *

Back inside the Roid Room, Karen had managed to compose herself with the aid of a quarter bottle of supermarket vodka she kept in her make-up drawer. There was no way that eight-legged monster was going to defeat her. She was not leaving without that passport.

She put her phone down by the spider's terrarium and took a few deep breaths, centring herself. Then she put her hands on the lid, closed her eyes for a moment and very slowly lifted it off. The tarantula sat there, as if unaware of her presence. She picked up the phone and selected the torch app and shone it at full brightness onto the arachnid. It seemed to tense but remained where it was.

She moved the beam as close as she dare. It flinched imperceptibly but remained rooted to its spot. She shone the light on it for a while but gave up eventually. She turned around and examined the room for some kind of implement. Spying a spatula by the scales she took it, cradled it in one hand for a moment then slid it gently under the tarantula.

'I don't want to damage you JT but either you get off my passport or you're going to end up in bits,' she muttered. It took all her courage to even touch it with the utensil.

JT dug in, resisting her attempts to prise him from his position, as if Damon had ordered him to stand guard over the document.

Karen stiffened her resolve. With a deep breath she shunted it firmly towards the far end of the tank. The spider squirmed away and climbed on to a small wooden log. Karen gagged but steeled herself, shuffled the passport as far away from it as possible like a croupier and flipped it onto its edge. Then she reached in swiftly and fished it out.

'Yes! In your face!' she yelled with relief.

She leafed it open to examine her photograph. Who else's would it be? Still, it was reassuring to see her face. She leant across to pick up the lid but as she did so the spider threw a hairy, chequered leg over the lip of the tank. She watched aghast as JT began hauling himself slowly out. Moving swiftly, she attempted to block it with the spatula but it ignored her efforts and slid onto the worktop in one smooth movement.

'Oh, shit,' she gasped. 'Oh, fuck, fuck, fuck!' She glanced around in panic. Could she catch it with something else? She ran to her room and slid the passport inside her backpack then sprinted down the stairs to the kitchen in search of something that could be used to capture an escaped tarantula.

* * *

'Round three: history and politics in our times,' declared Will, restacking his prompt cards on the desk. He stopped to take a long draught of water and wiped his mouth.

'This is where Paul comes into his own. Jack might pick up a few. Ed should hold his ground and, hello, Matt, are you still awake?' he said, raising his voice.

'Yes I fucking am, you dick,' muttered Matt. His paper

had floated to the floor again. There appeared to be a lot of question marks and gaps by the numbers.

'Let us proceed then. Fifty years ago, question one: What major controversy rocked the 1968 Olympics? Five points for any of the protagonists' names. Question Two: Just four teams featured in the 1968 European Championship. England, surprisingly was one of them. Of course we were world champions but that didn't stop us losing our key game, the semi. Who did we lose to?'

'Sport. Great,' muttered Paul. 'I was too young to give a shit about it then and I give even less of one now.'

'Can we repeat that?' asked Matt, looking confused. Jack wound back and reran the question.

'Hang on I'm getting a signal,' declared Paul. 'Was it Germany?'

'East or West?' countered Ed.

* * *

Karen remounted the stairs swiftly holding a large Tupperware box in a pair of gardening gloves. She tiptoed into the room slowly, checking the ceiling above the door, half expecting to see the beast hanging there, waiting to pounce on her. She gave the door a push with her foot. It swung open slowly. The tank sat empty. Her eyes scanned the room. JT was nowhere to be seen. Where was it? The thought of it loose in the house chilled her to the bone.

She was desperate to return the insect back to its terrarium, that way Damon might not notice she'd retrieved the passport for a day or two. Then, suddenly, she spotted it. JT had worked his way across the workbench and was now clamped on top of the hamster tank.

She gasped in horror but approached the spider slowly

and prodded it gently with the spatula. It waved its front legs back defiantly. She nearly passed out. She glanced at the dwarf hamsters in their tank. They appeared to be frozen with fear. She considered hitting it hard with something heavier but the idea of splattering it also repulsed her. Damon would be apoplectic, too.

She stood there looking at it desperately but enough was enough. She wasn't equipped to handle a giant arachnid intent on a live snack. If Damon hadn't stolen her passport this would never have happened. He could deal with it. She intended to be long gone by the time he came home.

She pulled the phone from her pocket, skimmed through the short list of people who lived locally that she might stay with, and dialled Ayesha, her friend and the assistant manager at the swimming baths.

* * *

'So that wraps up round three,' said Will. He was still wearing the same hat but he'd exchanged his shirt for a polo neck jumper following a cutaway at the end of the previous round, suggesting he had taken a break from recording.

'Moving to the final round, "Our Lives and Times". Expect a few bombshells. Now I trust everyone's still with me? Matt? Matt?' he sang the name.

Matt had indeed fallen into a slumber.

'Matt wake up the house is on fire!' shouted Thom. Matt failed to stir. Jack stood up and kicked him in the shin.

'Ow! What the fuck?'

'You dozed off. We've reached the final round.'

'About time,' sniffed Matt.

'So, the first question. Who wrote the word "fucker" on the school field in bleach? It caused uproar. Despite a search for the chemicals and mass questioning, the culprit was never identified.'

'The great, unsolved incident of our school years,' smiled Jack. 'The Phantom Gardener.'

'I was off sick. Wasn't me!' said Paul.

'So you claimed. But you had the scientific knowledge and the motive,' said Jack suspiciously.

'What motive?' asked Paul.

'You hated sport.'

'Dislike is not motive,' said Paul. 'Plenty of other people didn't like sport.'

'You're not going to pretend you didn't do it again are you?' asked Ed. 'You could have sneaked in at night.'

'I did. Not. Do it,' said Paul flatly. 'If I had, I'd say so because I was properly amused.'

'I'm still putting you down,' said Ed.

'Me too,' agreed Jack.

'Question two,' Will continued, as Jack pressed play again. 'We went to a few all-night movies at the Scala back in the mid-eighties. There was a riot at the last one we attended, which was why we never went back. What song did I put on the jukebox that kicked it all off?'

'Oh yes, I thought about that only the other day. Utter madness,' laughed Matt. 'I remember exactly what it was. Will was at the jukebox in a break between Scorsese films.

'It definitely wasn't Madness,' said Jack.

'I remember the night all right. I got a black eye but I haven't got a clue what the song was,' mused Paul. 'I had just come back from the loo and the place erupted. I could see Will in the middle. I waded in and someone punched me in the face and that was that.'

'Ed legged it for the toilets,' said Jack. 'So he won't know.'

'You joined me if I recall,' said Ed, affronted. 'In the same fucking cubicle!'

'Question three,' Will went on. 'Which one of you owed

me £40,000 and, almost certainly, still does?'

'What's he on about?' asked Thom taken aback by the sudden switch in Will's line of questioning.

At that moment the screen of the laptop went black.

'Shit, the battery's gone!' said Matt with a groan. 'I knew this would happen. What are we going to do?'

'There's nothing we can do,' said Ed. 'You forgot the charger, Matt. Where are we going to find one at eleven o'clock on a Saturday night in Camber? The all-night laptop shop? The twenty-four-hour charger store?'

'If you got your shit together this wouldn't have happened,' said Jack. 'Never mind. It's been fun. We can work out the answers so far between us.'

'What about the last question?' asked Thom. 'What about that one? Who owes Will forty grand?'

There was silence.

'I don't think he was with it any more,' said Jack eventually. 'Maybe it was the medication. He's dressed differently. Perhaps he had a break and took more.'

'Bollocks he did,' said Thom. 'He looked a bit tired last round but he seems absolutely fine there.'

'We really should find out what he was on about,' agreed Matt.

'We'll just have to watch it when we get home. You can come round mine,' said Jack. 'It's not like I've got anything else to do at the moment.'

'Thom what about that woman you were with last night? Do you think she might have one?' asked Matt.

'How should I know?' replied Thom. 'Oddly it didn't come up in conversation.'

'There wasn't any in fact. Conversation that is,' said Paul.

'Ring her,' said Matt. 'You never know.'

'It's such a long shot,' complained Thom.

'Go on,' said Matt.

Thom sighed, picked up his phone and dialled. It rang for a while. He was just about to give up when it was answered.

'Hello?'

'Um, hi, Karen. How are you doing?'

'I've had better evenings.'

'Odd question I know, but do you by any chance have a power charger for a MacBook?'

'I might have. Why?'

Thom gave everyone a thumbs up.

'Yes!' said Matt fist pumping the air.

'Do you mind if we borrow it?'

'OK, but I need a favour back.'

'Sure. Can we meet halfway or something? Because of you know who…?'

'He's not here and I could do with a hand.'

'You're sure he's not there?'

'No, he's down the pub but he'll probably be back in the next half-hour.'

'OK, I'll be straight over.'

'It's the shabby house at the end of the road.'

Thom rang off and put the phone in his pocket.

'We're in luck. I'll be back in a minute,' he said. He pulled on his jacket and slid out of the back door. Matt splashed rum into his glass and sat in silence. Jack tossed him a cigarette then lit one of his own. Paul and Ed wandered off.

Thom made his way quickly along the track towards Karen's house. The temperature had dropped and the wind had picked up. He went through the gate and knocked gently on the front door. It opened swiftly, making him jump. Karen stood there. She glanced over his shoulder up the road.

'What's up?'

'He knows I'm leaving. He stole my passport and hid it in

the spider tank. I managed to get it out but the thing escaped. I need to get out of here right now but I can't get hold of any of my friends to stay with.'

'OK, OK, we'll sort it,' said Thom, stepping inside cautiously.

Karen took him upstairs to the Roid Room and tried to explain the bizarre chain of events that had led to an exotic tarantula breaking loose in Camber.

'Fuck! The size of it!' said Thom. 'Is he feeding it the steroids?' He stared at the spider resting on the hamster tank.

'I wouldn't put it past him,' said Karen.

'I can't even begin to imagine how we might recapture it.'

'Me neither.'

'So leave it, and let's get you out of here, I don't want to be around when he gets back, it's throwing-out time soon.'

Karen went to her room, picked up her rucksack and handed Thom the charger. He hauled the suitcase off her bed and they left following another swift check to see if the coast was clear.

'Just a minute,' Karen stopped by the shed.

'What is it?' Thom asked, nervously eyeing the street.

'Carry on, I'll catch you up,' she said. 'I deserve some compensation.'

She pulled out her phone and scanned the torch beam around the bottom of the shed until she saw what she was looking for. A brick supporting the base. She pulled it out, reached inside and withdrew a cash box. She'd seen Damon visit the spot enough times. She tried the second key on the ring she'd found in his pocket. With a small thrill she felt the lock turn and flipped open the lid. Thom had hesitated but now span on his heel.

'Do hurry!'

The box contained at least a dozen plastic cash bags. She

counted the contents of one, shakily. They were separated into sleeves, each containing five hundred pounds. She took two and closed the tin. Then she opened it again and took two more.

'Now we're quits,' she muttered.

She stuffed the money in her hoodie pocket and hurried after Thom.

Thom walked through the door to find Matt and Jack talking.

'I got the power!' he sang triumphantly, holding up the charger.

'You look like you've just come back from holiday. Been anywhere nice?' asked Matt, eyeing the suitcase. Thom hefted it past them and put it in the hall. A moment later Karen put her head through the back door.

'Hello everybody.'

Chapter Nineteen

Bullet with Butterfly Wings

The door almost came off its hinges as Damon slammed it behind him. He took the lead off Drogba who sidled off and sat quietly on his bed.

His mood, bad when he had left the house, had turned fearsome, a pure distillation of rage and self-loathing. He'd gone to The Camber Castle following the incident with Karen. Alcohol was an unwise choice when you were on a diet of anabolics but he needed a drink. At some point during his fourth pint, he'd received a text update from Treggers' mum saying he'd suffered kidney damage and would probably require dialysis for the rest of his life. Damon re-read the text, put the phone back in his pocket and switched to depth charges.

Now he was home and primed for confrontation. A kitchen cupboard hung open. He swatted it shut with the side of his hand.

'Karen? Karen?!' he yelled. He listened for an answer but the house was silent. Silly bitch was probably sulking up in her bedroom. Or maybe she had slipped out with that old pervert again. He went upstairs to check but before he reached the landing he could see the door of the Roid Room was hanging open. He frowned. He always shut up shop.

'You what?' he jogged up the last few steps and into the

room. Where had she found the key? The spare set was hidden outside. Then he remembered misplacing the regulars a couple of weeks ago and using the spares. He must have left them in a pocket.

'Fucking idiot!' he shouted, slapping himself on the cheek. His eyes fell on the empty terrarium and the lid on the floor.

'You are fucking kidding!'

There was absolutely no way she would have been able to do that on her own. She could barely even look at JT. And where was he? His eyes skipped around the room until they came to rest on the hamster tank.

'Oh, you stupid fucking bitch! You better not be here because if you are, I'm going to put that spider down your top when I get hold of it.'

He stepped forward and examined the arachnid. Somehow it had shifted the lid of the hamster tank slightly.

'Now come on JT, you know that's out of order. It's not a food cabinet.'

He placed a hand gently round the spider's abdomen and lifted carefully. It clung on, limpet-like and began urticating hairs.

'Come on you eight-legged fucker,' he muttered, bringing more force to bear. Furious at being parted from its supper, the beast sank its fangs into Damon's thumb. He howled and snatched his hand back, flinging the spider across the room in the process. It crunched against the wall, flopped down onto the workbench and curled up.

'You little shit!' yelled Damon, examining his thumb. It felt like it had been punctured with a hot needle. Two angry, red pinholes throbbed visibly. A small pang of fear shot through him. Could he have a reaction? Was he going to start foaming at the mouth? He was aware that its venom was mild compared to Old World species like the Baboon but you never knew. He sucked on the digit and spat on the floor a few times.

He looked across at the spider. It lay inert. He peered at it closely, then he picked up a pen and prodded it. It remained curled up, displaying no sign of life.

'Right! You are fucking dead, bitch!' he yelled.

He strode into her room and saw the pile of discarded clothes. He yanked open the doors of the empty wardrobe, grabbed the empty bottle of vodka on the chest of drawers and hurled it into the make-up table mirror, shattering it into pieces. Then he swept her ornaments off the windowsill onto the floor.

'I'm coming after you! And that old fart! No way did you do that on your own!'

He spun round and went back to the Roid Room, opened the bottom drawer of the filing cabinet, took out the flare pistol and the shells then headed down the stairs at a gallop.

'Come on Drogs, it's showtime!'

Chapter Twenty

You Want It Darker

'Ah! The owner of the suitcase,' said Jack as Karen emerged from the garden into the living room. 'Are you two eloping? That's so sweet.'

'Hello Jack, how are you?' Karen smiled, nervously.

'Never better,' said Jack. 'Nice to meet you again.'

'You've saved the day, Karen,' said Matt.

Thom went off to round up Paul and Ed while Jack poured Karen a glass of wine.

'Sorry if I was rude the other night,' Jack said. 'I was a bit pissed. Not that I'm not pissed now.'

'Don't worry. I was pretty rude myself. I get very sarky when I'm on the defensive. I don't know why I didn't go straight home. Actually I should never have gone out in the first place in retrospect.'

'It is what it is,' replied Jack philosophically. 'And you'd never have had the pleasure of meeting us.'

'Nor you me.'

Thom came back down, followed, somewhat reluctantly, by Ed and Paul.

'Karen, why don't you pop upstairs and chill out,' suggested Thom. 'You can use the room we were in the other night till we sort out sleeping arrangements.'

'Oh great, no wonder you wanted me back down,' said Ed.

'I'll be sleeping down here, Ed,' said Thom. 'You can have my bed.'

Karen left the room carrying her backpack. Thom followed her with the suitcase, before rejoining them. Jack picked up the remote as they all attempted to settle and focus on the screen again.

'Remind me, why are we doing this?' asked Paul.

'Will asks the questions, remember?' said Matt stabbing a finger at him.

Jack hit the remote and the face on the screen jumped back into life. There was a dramatic pause.

'Next question: Who, apart from me, is leaving?'

They looked at each other blankly.

'Next: which one of us needs to come out of the closet?'

'For fuck's sake! See? I knew he'd lost it,' said Ed, throwing his arms into the air.

Jack paused the video again.

'Put it back on Jack,' said Matt forcefully. 'Let's get to the end or all we'll be left with is question marks. It's too late to stop now.'

Jack took a deep breath and pressed the button.

'Final question. Which one of the Boys was screwing my wife while I was dying?'

'Woah! That's it! I'm out!' said Ed, appalled. He stood up.

'You didn't!' said Jack, looking at Thom, eyes wide.

'Whaaatt? You're kidding, right?' said Thom, taken aback.

'Come on Thom, you can't keep it in your pants,' said Jack accusingly.

'Shut up Jack, or I swear I will deck you!' said Thom, jumping to his feet, fists balled.

'Woah! Wait a minute. Calm down, calm down, this is ridiculous,' Paul leaped up and stood between them, hands outstretched.

'I really am going. I said this was a bad idea from the start,' said Ed. 'Completely macabre. I don't know what we were thinking, but I'm off.' He then wobbled and fell back in his seat.

'Ed, breaking news, you're completely pissed. You're not going anywhere. If you attempt to leave, I will stop you,' said Paul bluntly. Mild mannered, patient to a fault, Paul might have laid down the law possibly three or four times ever in their entire lifetimes but when he did no one disagreed.

'He's right. This was a bad idea,' said Matt. 'Let's leave it. The poor guy was heavily medicated, we should have realised.'

'No fucking way! I want the answer now!' shouted Thom, raging. 'I'm not having people thinking I did something like that. I know where the line is and I didn't cross it. So come on, let's have it.'

'I think Thom's right,' nodded Paul, sadly. 'I don't think we can leave this hanging with people accusing each other and questions left hanging in the air. I'd rather not have heard any of this to be honest but now it's out there we need proper answers.'

'Ed?' asked Thom.

'Whatever.'

He sat down and folded his arms defensively. Matt muttered something to himself.

'Give me the remote.' Thom snatched the box from Jack's hand and pressed play.

'So, there you have it. Pretty testing, wasn't it?' said Will, continuing. 'I did say there were a few bombshells in there. Now I imagine you want some answers rather urgently. Actually I don't have all of them but perhaps you can help me out.'

'Great. What's the point? Pure fuckery?' asked Matt, scowling.

'Shall I start with the music round and build to the big reveal?' said Will. 'Actually we should probably cut to the nitty gritty and work backwards. I imagine that teaser about Marvin Gaye's tragic demise isn't the one that needs answering the most urgently?'

'You could say that, you shitbag,' hissed Jack, shaking his head.

'He's toying with us,' said Ed, disgusted.

'Let's begin with round four and work up to the million, no trillion, dollar questions. One. I wrote "fucker" on the school playing field one night with two large bottles of Domestos. Harrison shouldn't have dropped me from the first eleven for swearing at the opposition school's clearly bent ref. No Will, no game.'

'Told you it wasn't me,' said Paul, finally exonerated.

'Question two, the song was The Specials' "Racist Friend", not the wisest choice when the Scala was full of retro greasers and rockabillies who objected to anything not recorded by rednecks thirty years previously. I was warned not to put 'anything shit' on by a quiffhead but that was a red rag. Sorry about that, though, I should add that I did get not one, but two black eyes as a result.'

'Forgiven. It was a great tune,' nodded Paul. 'And as relevant today as it was all those years ago.'

Matt muttered something incomprehensible.

'Moving on. Question three: Who borrowed forty grand from me promising, no, swearing to repay it within six months? Answer...' he left a dramatic pause. 'Ed.'

Thom clicked the remote control. Everyone looked at Ed. 'Why?'

'What did you need forty grand for?' asked Jack. 'You're loaded.'

Ed shut his eyes.

'Well?' demanded Jack more insistently.

'I never wanted to do this fucking stupid quiz in the first place,' said Ed.

'No wonder. Answer the fucking question!' said Jack fiercely.

'OK. Yes I did borrow the money and I am absolutely going to pay it back soon, I swear.'

'He said you swore,' piped up Matt. 'But you haven't, have you? Annie needs that money.'

'Do you think I don't know that?' said Ed, his voice tight. 'It's not that easy. Everything has gone to shit. Our payment system got hacked, so we spent a lot of money rebuilding our e-commerce site with a specialist company. A month later we had a ransomware breach, which we had no choice but to pay. Then we lost a key member of staff, partly over that and found ourselves in a legal dispute. It was a perfect storm. I needed money to keep us afloat. I had creditors to pay. I also had to lay staff off, which was horrible.'

'You're driving a shiny new M3, Ed,' said Jack. 'Maybe you should have left it in the showroom?'

'It's leased! Christ, what do you think I am? And my house is remortgaged. Do you know why I wasn't at Will's funeral? I was in the States trying to secure some investment. I had a deal set up for a financial injection with this guy, then he turned around at the eleventh hour and demanded a majority equity. I don't have any other options so I'm about to lose the company I founded and become an employee of it. I will be able to pay back Will, sorry, Annie, and I will clear some, but not all of my debts. Basically, I'm broke.'

The room fell silent for a moment. Ed crouched forward and stared at the carpet.

Thom was first to speak. 'I'm so sorry, Ed. I know how hard you've worked. You should have said something.'

'It was embarrassing. I'm the thriving entrepreneur, remember? I ended up trying to save face. You don't want to tell everyone you're struggling. I'm the successful one, that's my role, the one I constructed. I built it up over years. Now I'm a fucking loser.'

'Join the rest of us, Ed,' said Jack. 'It's not so bad.'

'Why do you think Will felt the need to say that?' asked Thom.

'Insurance I suppose,' said Paul. 'If we all know, then Ed has to pay the money back.'

'It's been constantly on my mind since it all started unravelling,' said Ed quietly. 'It's all I think about. In between my daughter's breakdown and my son's efforts to screw up his life. It all piles up.'

'I'm sorry, Ed. We didn't realise,' said Paul, standing up and putting a hand on his shoulder.

'No one was meant to, that was the point,' whispered Ed. 'You want everyone to buy your dream.'

'I'm sorry Ed, I didn't mean to doubt your honesty,' said Thom.

'If we can help somehow...' suggested Jack.

'Unless you've got a spare half a mil I doubt it, Jack. It's something I have to sort myself. Even if we have to sell the house I'll get Annie the money.'

'Understood. We should move on, agreed?' said Thom.

They all nodded and Thom restarted the video.

'Question four: Who's leaving? Paul. Are you still going through with it Paul? Betraying confidences here but I wanted to say you should go for it in case you're having second thoughts. It's important to follow your heart. We'll miss you... well I won't.'

'What's he talking about Paul?' asked Jack, confused.

'I'm emigrating. It's something I've been thinking about for

213

a while,' announced Paul, standing up as if he were addressing a larger audience. 'I've wanted to quit for a couple of years and do something useful. The uni has been looking at a way to drop my course from the syllabus and they've found it. I'm going to be made redundant so I have the opportunity. I can rent out my place. Ollie is grown up and working abroad and Francisca is up for it. I've taken a role with a water charity in Kenya in the autumn. After that I might teach. Not sure. I won't miss this nasty little country but obviously I will miss you. It's the only thing that's been holding me back, to be honest.'

'And digging wells for poor Africans will make you happier, Doctor Livingstone?' asked Matt sourly.

'I think doing something altruistic will help. It will certainly help my mental health. We're all so utterly self-absorbed in this day and age, it's pathetic,' said Paul. 'I don't want to stay here doing the same thing till I keel over. I want to try something new, have new experiences. I want a second life and I'm going to have it. Will told me he wished he'd done something different.'

'You could get ill, murdered, kidnapped,' protested Jack.

'It's Kenya not Syria, Jack,' said Paul.

'Boys' Weekend in Nairobi next year, it is then,' suggested Thom.

'I'd be honoured to organise it. I'll book a fuck-off lodge,' smiled Paul.

'The wildlife will probably be tamer than Camber,' added Jack.

'You're the mzungu!' proclaimed Ed.

'Then there were four,' said Jack, rather sadly. 'I'm haemorrhaging mates.'

'I'm not dying Jack, I'm just emigrating for a while,' explained Paul. 'Come and see me.'

'Moving on swiftly,' Thom clicked again with a sense of urgency.

'Question five: which member of the Boys needs to come out? I thought long and hard about this one because I don't want anyone to think I disapprove or I'm being sensationalist but the fact is I believe someone has been hiding his sexuality for years. I always had a suspicion but it was only when his wife phoned me that the truth came out...'

Will paused for a moment, as if to let the idea sink in.

'Jack, why didn't you tell us?' he said eventually.

Jack snorted. 'This is ridiculous. I am not gay. I don't know what the fuck he's on about.'

Thom clicked the remote.

'Why would he say that then? I mean, I don't give a shit, but he must have had a reason?'

'I've no idea,' said Jack flatly. 'And we can't ask him, can we?'

'Let's find out,' said Thom clicking.

'Let's not,' said Jack. 'Enough of his shit!'

He leapt from his seat and grabbed the laptop, flipped its lid shut, yanked the power cable out and put it under his arm.

'Hey, what do you think you're doing?' said Thom, intercepting him.

'I'm putting an end to this nonsense. I'm going to bed and I'm taking this with me. It's destroying us. Ed would have sorted his life out in private, Paul would have told us when he was good and ready. Will's playing God.'

'Jack, it's not your decision to make, I'm accused of something appalling and I have the right to be exonerated. It's not all about you. Give it back and sit down.'

Ed and Paul stood up, cutting off Jack's exit route. Matt groaned.

'Come on Jack, just hand it over and calm down please,' he said quietly.

Jack put the laptop behind his back.

'Jack. Please. I know you're upset but so's everyone else. Come on, it can't be that bad.'

Thom put his hand out.

'Please?'

'Oh, for fuck's sake!' spat Jack.

He thrust the computer into Thom's hand, sat down and crossed his arms tightly.

Thom replaced the laptop on the chair, plugged in the cable and opened the lid where Will was waiting, patiently. He tapped the keyboard.

'It's not like we're a bunch of homophobes,' Will continued. 'I mean we would have been surprised, shocked even. Perhaps it might have been a bit awkward for a while, I don't know… but you've kept this quiet our entire lives.

'I had my suspicions when we were younger but it was a long time ago. I forgot all about it. When we were at uni we lived in different halls of residence and each of us had our own scene. I had my football club mates, you ran the uni social soc putting on gigs and club nights. One of your crew was Jason, a gay bloke from Edinburgh. He was cool, dressed immaculately, was into all the right bands and was outrageously funny.

'I turned up at your room unexpectedly one Sunday morning, barged through the door and you were both in bed together. You went bright red and claimed he'd got paralytic, barged into your room and crashed there. Another time I saw you go into The Bridge Inn with him. The Bridge was a gay pub in town. Bit odd, I thought, but I didn't mention it. Not long after that he was beaten up by a bunch of townies and badly injured. They cracked his skull and broke his leg, I recall. Pretty shocking. He had to take a year off to convalesce and I forgot about him because it was our final year.'

'Is any of this true, Jack?' asked Ed.

Jack ignored the question.

'You also started going out with that Geordie girl, Sarah. You were a happy, boring couple. Jason was forgotten. I didn't think about it again. Not, that is, until your wife rang me out of the blue and told me you were sleeping with another man. Why she rang me, I have no idea. I mean we got on OK but we weren't that close. I have a theory that being terminally ill makes you a convenient confessional. You can offload in the knowledge that whatever's said is literally going to the grave. Or maybe she just told me so I'd tell the rest of you. Which I am but I didn't, if you see what I mean.

'So Janice rings me a few weeks ago. She's in tears and I try to calm her down. I ask what's up and she says, "Jack's having an affair". I tell her that sounds unlikely. She is adamant it's true. I say it's news to me, none of us had a clue but I'm sorry to hear it. Then she announces, it's not another woman, it's a man. I tell her not to be daft but she insists it's true. Apparently you started coming home in the early hours and working weekends. You told her it was a big project but she was suspicious. She looks at your phone and discovers lots of messages from someone called Luke she knows is gay because she's met him. They're pretty unambiguous and just in case, there's a very revealing picture of you both, too. Jack, is there something you want to tell us?'

Thom pressed pause again. Everyone looked at Jack.

Jack laughed. 'This is ridiculous!'

No one said anything.

'Jack you're prepared to believe any old shit about my sex life,' said Thom. 'Why shouldn't I believe this about yours?'

Jack gave him a hard look. Paul cracked his fingers nervously. The noise sounded like a firecracker in the excruciating silence.

'OK, maybe I'll ring Janice, myself. She can explain what she meant,' said Thom, pulling out his phone.

Jack said nothing. Thom scrolled through his contacts and put the phone on speaker. It began to ring.

'OK, OK, stop, stop!' said Jack desperately. Thom cut the phone off.

'I am not gay. I'm bisexual,' said Jack, eventually. 'I can hear you all thinking, "He's trying to say he's gay but he can't quite admit it". If you want to be distrusted by straight people and gay people just say you're bi because it polarises both sides. Straight people think you're gay, gay people think you're straight. The irony of being bi and supposedly having everything is that you often end up with nothing. No one trusts you. It is not easy to be out and you're never quite in.'

'Why did you marry Janice then?' asked Paul.

'Because I was in love with her! There was no fakery involved,' said Jack, jumping up and prowling back and forth.

'I wasn't in denial, although, if I'm honest, I also didn't know myself then. I thought I'd dabbled a bit, bohemian student stuff I'd grown out of and this was the real thing, you know? I assumed you couldn't like both sexes. You were either one or the other.

'The story about Jason is true. We did sleep together that night. It was my first time and I was shocked and ashamed but I was also aware that I didn't hate the experience either. It was confusing but it was exciting, too. And I had to admit that I was attracted to him.

'At the same time I didn't want to be queer or even bi, it didn't square with who I thought I was. We did sleep together a few times after that but he was pretty casual about his sex life and I didn't like that. I also didn't want the truth to get out either, which he considered hypocritical. I knew if Will found out he'd tell everyone, including you lot, and I couldn't bear that. And of course my parents would find out eventually, too.

'I kept in touch with Jason after he left. I went to see him a couple of times in Edinburgh later that summer. He'd lost his spleen and was still using a stick to walk. He died a couple of years later. Not from his injuries, from AIDS. We slept together the last time I saw him and I was terrified when I found out he was dying. I actually went for a test. It was negative obviously, he got it long after that but it put me off sex with men. Women were safer. To my eternal shame I never went to see him when he was dying in hospital. I regret that bitterly. I was a coward.

'Anyway, a few years later I met Jan at work and we fell for each other. I was pleased to find I was attracted to her, too. And I genuinely loved her, by the way, it wasn't a marriage of convenience. Everything was fine for years but she had her issues, too, you know. I'm not going to go into detail but after Simon came along, sex was switched on and off without warning for months at a time. I could deal with that but then a couple of years ago it stopped completely. I never knew if I would ever make love again. I was unhappy. If you're not having it with one you start to fantasise about the other. I genuinely thought my sex life was over. And if I brought the issue up it was closed down straight away.

About a year ago this guy Luke started working in the office. He's a few years younger and gay and I suddenly realised I found him quite attractive. I'd closed that side of me down. We went out after work one night, got pissed and it just happened. I was really embarrassed. And yet I realised that I wasn't being honest with myself. But I didn't want to hurt Jan and I knew it would mean divorce. I tried to keep it quiet.'

'This is unbelievable. Are you saying you're having an affair with another bloke?' said Ed, wide-eyed.

'Yes, Ed,' said Jack, looking him in the eye. 'Do you have a problem with it?'

'I'm just struggling to process it. I didn't see this coming.'

'Nor did I.'

Why didn't you tell us?' said Paul, beseechingly. 'It's not like we'd have judged you.'

'Really? I thought about it. But if I can't tell my wife, I can hardly tell you, can I? Anyone who tells you where their head is at when they're twenty is a liar. I thought all the stuff about guys would go away once I was dating a woman. And it did. You think, "Yeah I just needed straightening out", and then years later you realise that you were in denial. You could like both but not admit it. I knew there was no way she would accept that and I was right. But you start resenting yourself for living a lie and everyone for not letting you be yourself. I'm genuinely monogamous but imagine your sex life was over at fifty? Imagine never being touched again. And imagine someone else you fancied, fancied you. I'm not saying what I did to her was right but it happens every day. And you don't know how difficult this is. My kids are going to find out. It will crucify Simon. I don't know how I'm going to handle it.'

'You will though. And I don't think they'll judge you as badly as you think. We're here, you know that,' said Matt, who had been listening intently.

'And you're out now,' shrugged Paul. 'And my opinion hasn't changed. You're still the same smartarse gobshite you always were.'

'No bringing him along to Boys' Weekends, Jack,' said Thom. 'You know the rules.'

'Ed?' Jack looked at him. Ed looked away.

'See?' said Jack to the others.

'Have you ever fancied one of us?' Ed asked bluntly.

'That's exactly the sort of question I was dreading. Thanks.'

'It's the obvious one.'

'The answer is, you must be fucking kidding.'

'Look we need to move on. We can come back to this,' said Thom. He pointed the remote at the screen.

'Last question, who was screwing my wife while I was dying,' said Will. He swallowed hard and took a deep breath. There was another tense silence. Thom found he was gripping the remote so hard it hurt.

All eyes were fixed on the screen.

'Matt,' said Will. His voice came out as a whisper.

'No!' shouted Matt, jumping to his feet.

'You bastard!' yelled Thom. 'You screwed his missus and you were prepared to let me take the blame?'

'I didn't, it's not true!' pleaded Matt.

'Why would he say that then?' said Ed. 'We're agreed he was compos mentis, sharp as a surgeon's blade when it came to this quiz, so why on earth would he say something as shocking as that?'

'You're disgusting,' shouted Thom, heading for Matt, fists balled.

'Back off Thom! Listen to him,' said Paul getting between them again. Ed joined him. Together they separated the pair.

'It wasn't like that,' said Matt. 'She was in bits.'

'Oh, it was a comfort fuck?' shouted Thom.

'No. Nothing happened. But yes, I did stay the night the last time I was there.'

'Here we go,' snorted Thom.

'Shut the fuck up, right?' snarled Matt. 'I popped in to say goodbye and she was in a state. It had all got too much to deal with. I calmed her down, got her a drink.'

'Plied her with alcohol.'

'Shut up, you arsehole!' Matt lurched at him but Ed and Paul shoved him back. 'We drank a bottle of Scotch and talked about anything and everything. I cuddled her and she fell asleep in my arms, so I carried her up to bed and put her in it. Fully clothed. I found a blanket and slept in the armchair in case she was sick. She was, so I cleared it up. I left really early the following morning before anyone was up.'

'Have you seen her since?' asked Ed.

'Why are you asking me that?' replied Matt.

'Answer the man,' snapped Thom.

'A few times, just to see how she was coping. Her husband died, not sure if you remember?'

'Have you slept with her?' asked Thom.

'Fuck off and mind your own business!' hissed Matt.

'So yes.'

'No! But I'll tell you something, right,' said Matt, raging now. 'I'll tell you something. I went out with Annie first, remember? We were a couple and everything was great. And then I went and ruined it. It was my fault we split up because I had a thing for that little music PR. I knew I was being shallow but I liked hanging with the bands she looked after.

'Will and I were out one night and we bumped into Annie in a bar by complete accident. It was a bit awkward for both of us but I introduced them. Next thing they're an item. A year later they're engaged. Whoosh. I'd realised by then I was still in love with her. When they announced they were getting married I was stunned because I knew then, right, I'd made the biggest mistake of my life. I was twenty-eight and I'd ruined it. I got pissed one night shortly before their wedding and rang her. Begged her not to go through with it, told her I'd made a terrible mistake, pleaded with her. We both ended up in tears but she said she was sorry and everything, she was still very fond of me but she was going to marry Will. But I held on to the idea all these years that maybe he wasn't the one.'

'So you waited till the guy was on the way out and you made your move?' said Thom, shaking his head in disbelief.

'You have no idea. No. Fucking. Idea!' screamed Matt, pointing his finger at Thom. 'Good old Matt, the party animal! The cartoon *bon viveur*! I've been trying to keep my head above water all this time. I haven't been able to hold down a relationship because all I want is her.

'But I behaved impeccably. I sucked it up. While I was firing blanks I had to watch her have kids with him. I even became a godparent to one. I went to their christenings, the birthday parties, the summer gatherings, the Christmas dos, and all the time I was thinking, "You had your chance mate, and you blew it!" You have no idea what that feels like!

'So yes, I've seen her a few times since Will died. I've tried to be there for her because she has no one. Her folks are both dead, in case you didn't know. Which you didn't. Will's mum is not much support, they've never got on.

'And where have you lot been? What have you done for her? She told me no one had so much as rung her since the funeral. She feels like she's been forgotten. Like his death severed all links with her. Your best mate's mate,' Matt stabbed a finger at them.

Paul bit his lip and looked at Ed. It was true. None of them had called her.

'So I'm there for her and maybe something will happen, maybe it won't. She knows how I feel but I'm very, very careful to behave properly. Will was my friend, too, remember? I didn't want him to die. I wasn't secretly hoping, "Maybe he'll get some terminal disease and I can get in there". I'd rather he was here because I accepted it was my mistake a long time ago and I loved him like a brother. I had my chance and I blew it but I can't give up on her now either. And if you don't like it, you can all fuck off!'

With that Matt lurched out of the back door and into the night.

Chapter Twenty-One

Swim Until You Can't See Land

Snorting in fury, Damon strode down the garden path to the gate and yanked it open. Then something made him stop. He returned to the shed, knelt down and pulled the cash box from beneath it. It was unlocked. A swift check was enough to confirm it was also half empty.

'You thieving bitch!' He slammed the lid shut. Then he locked the box, shoved it firmly under the shed and replaced the brick.

'Come on,' he urged the dog, which was sitting patiently by the gate. 'Someone's been very, very stupid and now they're going to be very, very sorry.'

He marched along the path towards the holiday home. The dog charged back and forth, barking in anticipation. A few bedroom lights threw out a little illumination onto the empty beach, otherwise it was pitch dark with the moon concealed behind cloud. The only sound was the wind gusting testily and the breaking waves on the shore.

* * *

The back gate swung shut behind Matt as he stumbled onto the beach. He began pulling off his clothes as he walked, tossing them aside. He walked purposefully towards the water.

Damon caught sight of a figure ahead, illuminated by the light from the back of the house. He sped up as it began stripping off.

'Seek Drogs, seek!'

The dog sprinted off, barking furiously. Matt froze as it stopped a few feet away from him growling. Damon jogged up.

'Well, well. I said you were a bunch of sex cases. Going around exposing yourself like a perv.'

Matt put both hands round his genitals. 'I was going for a swim.'

He was crying.

'Go on then.' Damon nodded his head towards the water.

'I've changed my mind.'

'Don't worry, death often comes as a relief. I know people who are alive who wish they weren't. Now off you go so I can deal with the rest of the gang.' He pointed the flare pistol at Matt's head.

Matt flinched, but stood his ground.

'I'm going to count to five then I'm going to set the dog on you. He will have your balls for breakfast. When those jaws come down it's like a bear trap slamming shut. They'll come straight off in one tasty bite. Now, one...'

Matt whimpered.

'Two...'

* * *

'Something's going on outside!' Karen came running down the stairs. She had heard the argument as it raged downstairs but remained upstairs, reasoning it was none of her business. But the barking sounded familiar. Peering out of the top window she made out two figures and a dog on the beach.

Thom went to the downstairs window.

'It's your brother and Matt,' he said squinting. 'And Matt appears to be stark naked.'

'Shit!' gasped Ed. He shot Paul a look of panic.

'Now what do we do?' asked Jack, jumping to his feet anxiously.

Thom stepped out of the back door and went to the garden gate. Karen followed him.

* * *

Matt had begun to sprint shortly after 'two'. Damon held the dog back, then, when Matt had a decent head start, he let it go. Matt heard it roar and sped up. He could hear its snarls as it chased him down. He made the shoreline and carried on running, hurdling breaking waves, ignoring the shock of the cold water as it sprayed over him. It was shallow initially and Drogba kept coming but soon Matt was up to his waist. He began to swim hard, thrashing at the water urgently. The dog stopped in its tracks and backed out of the surf to bark at him from the water's edge.

After a few minutes, Matt stopped and turned round to look back, sensing he was beyond its pursuit. He trod water, gasping for air.

'One down. Stay,' Damon commanded the dog and turned back towards the house. He opened the Very pistol, which had been empty when he had aimed it at Matt, inserted a cartridge into the muzzle, snapped it shut and strode towards the house. Halfway there he stopped, pointed the pistol in the air and pulled the trigger.

A flare fizzed out of the barrel and streaked into the night sky, leaving a thin trail of smoke. For a moment, time slowed down, then the shell ignited, throwing out a white, phosphorescent light, transforming the beach into a vast film negative as if a switch had been flicked in the heavens. It reminded Damon of the coils of magnesium he used to steal from school, sputtering luminescently on the beach as he sat there, lighter in hand. He whooped.

'Let there be light!'

Matt's eyes followed the flare as it fishtailed skywards before bursting incandescently in the darkness, a mirrorball for Damon's death disco. It was then he noticed he was drifting away from shore. He tried to swim back, only to discover he could make no progress. A quiver of panic went through him. He fought harder against the current.

* * *

'I can see Matt,' said Karen. 'He's in the sea. He's not going to last long in there and he might not be able to swim back. There're rips.' She went out of the gate on to the beach.

'Wait Karen, your brother's lost it,' said Thom, putting a hand on her shoulder.

'Don't worry, I'll deal with him,' she said without looking back.

'Well, look who it isn't?' shouted Damon as she strode towards him. 'My thieving fucking sister.'

'Put it down Damon!' she snapped, too angry to be scared. 'Don't you think the coastguard will have seen the flare? Everyone is going to wonder what's happening. Curtains are twitching, meaning you're drawing attention to yourself, which is the last thing you want to do, isn't it?'

'Too late now,' snapped Damon, putting his face right in hers. She stood her ground.

'Damon, please, stop and think about what you're doing. What would Mum say?'

Damon hesitated for a moment. Then he reloaded the pistol and spat on the ground.

Suddenly Karen sprinted past him towards the water. He trained the flare gun at her back.

'Don't you dare!' Thom yelled as he started out of the back gate. Damon spun round.

'Ah, the old shagger himself! Mr Viagra.' He pointed the pistol at Thom who turned tail instantly and ran back inside. Damon laughed hysterically.

'Come out, come out or I'll burn your house down!'

He spun back round but Karen was too far away for an accurate shot. She was headed for the water, which meant she was going to have to return at some point. Returning his attention to the house, he aimed the flare pistol at the bedroom window and pulled the trigger. The hammer fell with a click.

'Bollocks! Reload!'

He ejected the dud shell, fumbled in his pocket and shoved another into the breach.

Thom ducked back inside the house.

'I've phoned the police and the ambulance!' said Paul, sliding the glass door shut and locking it.

Thom raced past him, through the house and straight out of the front door.

'Where are you going?' shouted Ed as it slammed shut.

Damon advanced closer to the rear gate and pointed the gun at the house again.

'I want my money, bring it out and we're square. If not I'll burn the place down with you in it.'

There was no reply.

'I'll count to five, then you're going to get it. Five, four...'

'What's he on about?' asked Jack frantically, unable to catch what he was saying.

'Something about money,' said Paul, frowning.

Damon was still counting, 'Two, one!'

He pulled the trigger. The hammer snapped down again. Silence.

'Billy, I'm going to do you! You thieving shit!'

He flipped out the shell, slammed the last one in and pointed the gun at the rear window again.

* * *

Karen had raced past Drogba and was now swimming towards Matt, sensing the rip carrying her swiftly as she cut through the water with powerful strokes.

She had taken part in numerous lifesaving exercises but this was different. No buoyancy aid and they'd both been drinking. Alcohol and water were a bad combination. She swam hard and reached Matt just as he was beginning to go under. She came round behind him swiftly as he began to sink.

'OK, calm down, Matt. I've got you, I've got you,' she shouted. He was choking and confused.

'Where's Will?' he spluttered.

She rolled them both on their backs so she was underneath, then she began to kick hard in the water, swiftly manoeuvring the pair of them parallel to the shore and out of the rip channel using all her strength. She doubted she possessed the energy to make it back carrying him.

'The mermaid…' he mumbled.

Back on shore, Damon was in no mood for further debate. 'Fire in the hole!'

A red distress flare streaked out of the barrel and speared towards the upper rear window of the house, leaving a thin trail of smoke in its wake. It hit the pane dead centre and crashed into the bedroom. There was no detonation but a bright red light began to glow inside the room.

'A hit!' shouted Damon, punching the air. Meanwhile, the light from the star shell was fading as it began to burn out. Gradually the beach was returning to darkness as if an unseen hand was working a dimmer switch. In the distance the strains of a siren could now be heard.

* * *

Jack, Ed and Paul jumped as the flare crashed through the upstairs window.

'It'll burn the house down! Get out!' shouted Ed, panicking.

'Maybe we can put it out!' said Jack, making for the stairs.

'Be careful!' Ed called after him as he reached the landing. Behind him, Paul suddenly began to rummage through a hall cupboard. Tentatively, Jack pushed the bedroom door open. The room was full of smoke but not yet seriously ablaze. The ageing shell, sputtered, burning poorly. Nevertheless flames were beginning to lick across the carpet. They had moments to put it out before it took hold.

Paul suddenly joined him. He had in his hand a small fire extinguisher. Pulling the pin out swiftly, he squeezed the lever, spraying the neon bonfire with furious, white jets of CO_2. The smouldering subsided rapidly. Jack stepped past him and threw a bucket of water from the bathroom onto the embers.

They fell back out of the room, coughing loudly, leaving a sodden black hole in the floor.

'Thank God for the fire extinguisher. How did you know there was one?' asked Ed joining them.

'All holiday lets have to have them, by law. I found it in the cupboard with the vacuum,' shrugged Paul.

'I don't care what anyone says about you,' said Ed, hugging him.

'Matt!' said Jack urgently, dashing back down the stairs.

* * *

Thom had raced out the front door and made his way back onto the beach via the dunes. He scooted towards the water, keeping low and downwind from the dog, which had returned to its master. Damon was too preoccupied with the house to notice him.

He scanned the water anxiously. It was still difficult to see anything, despite the illumination from the flare. He was looking towards the point where Karen had run into the water but what if she'd been carried further along? He readjusted his point of view until he was staring straight ahead. Then he caught sight of two heads sixty or seventy metres out. He kicked off his trainers, sprinted through the shallows and dived into the water, hacking his way through the waves towards the spot he had seen them floating, concentrating on being as economical as possible. The chill of the water speared deep into his core. Both would be suffering from hypothermia pretty soon, if they weren't already.

'Karen, hang on, I'm coming!' he yelled as he approached them, taking in a mouthful of seawater and gagging. Finally, he saw them and called her name louder.

'Thom, thank God,' stammered Karen, her teeth chattering. 'I thought I was hearing things!'

She was struggling to support Matt, barely treading water. Matt was silent.

'You need to get him out. I don't have the strength.'

'What about you?' asked Thom, hauling Matt off her, making sure to keep his head out of the water.

'I'll be OK now I don't have him. Just get going and I'll follow. We need to do CPR as soon as he's on the beach.'

Thom didn't bother arguing. He turned away and began to kick hard, using his free arm to backstroke. He concentrated all his effort into repeating the action and getting some kind of rhythm going but the cold was already leaching away his energy.

The shore was still some way off and Matt was like an anchor but he kept kicking. After what felt like an age he twisted round to check his progress. He was barely halfway. Redoubling his effort he ploughed on but his energy was ebbing and soon he had no choice but to stop. He dared put a foot down and was relieved to touch the seabed. They were in about four feet of water. He put both feet down and propelled Matt a little further, then he began to drag his ragdoll body through the surf, panting with effort. He hoisted him over his shoulder, staggered to the shoreline and dropped him onto wet sand just beyond the breaking waves. He lay there gasping for a few moments, then sat astride Matt and began pumping his chest.

'Come on Matt!' he yelled, pummelling him. He paused to think for a moment. What did you do for CPR again? He tilted Matt's head back and placed his mouth on Matt's sandy lips and blew air in. Paul was always giving out slobbery kisses but this was taking it to another level. He spat, wiped his mouth and repeated the action three more times, then recommenced pumping his chest.

'Come on Matt! I'm sorry I said all that stuff. We can sort it! Come on mate! Please!'

* * *

Karen was floating on her back staring up at the heavens. Dark clouds rolled overhead. She had made a little headway but her energy was drained. She was just taking a breather, she told herself, though she knew she had to keep going. The sea lapped gently around her. House lights bobbed up and down on the shore, still a way off.

Don't panic, don't panic, she kept telling herself, but the cold was crippling.

'It's OK, it's OK,' she panted aloud. 'Just… a… little… rest.'

She gave it a minute then swam a few more metres but she was now running on empty. She stopped again and trod water weakly. There was nothing left in her arms and legs. She tried to compose herself but her consciousness was drifting. She thought of her dad and her mum. For some reason she brought to mind a trip to the London Aquarium when she was a little girl. The thrill it gave her at the time was better than anything she had seen at the cinema; the elegance of the sharks in the tank as they ghosted effortlessly through the water and the rays hovering serenely above them. She closed her eyes for a moment. She could do this.

When she reopened them, a bright blue spot was pulsing directly beneath her with millions of silver bubbles pouring from it. She blinked hard but it was definitely there and the water felt warmer. She dropped down towards it. It was a little deeper than it looked but she knew she could hold her breath for ages because she used to sit and time herself for fun. She descended, fluttering her feet and performing long, wide strokes with her arms.

The bubbles rushed past, tickling her face as she entered blissfully warm, aquamarine water. She could feel herself recharging. A reef flickered into view. A shoal of blue damselfish hung above it, motionless. She smiled and paused to admire them. A lone clownfish skipped over pink coral. It was so peaceful down here. She should have come ages ago.

Sunlight glowed beyond the centre of the water. She twisted and kicked hard towards it.

* * *

On the shoreline Thom heard the flare crash through the window and Damon whoop. He twisted round and saw the orange glow ignite the bedroom. He shut his eyes for a moment. The Boys would surely get out safely but was that lunatic going to come back for him now?

The sound of sirens snapped Damon out of his rampage. He spun round to face the darkness of the sea. Karen hadn't emerged yet, or had he missed her in all the excitement? Time stretches in a firefight. He wondered what to do. What did the army teach you? Regardless of the seriousness of the situation, put on the face and move forward.

She could swim, swim for England could Karen. But a sense of dread rippled through him. He sprinted down to the water's edge and began to scan the darkness. If only he had another star shell. If he had, he would have seen Thom less than a hundred metres away kneeling over Matt.

'Kaz! Sis! Come out, it's over!' he yelled. He began to wade into the surf till he was up to his waist. He could feel the pull of the tide.

'Kaz! Kaz! I'm sorry. Come out, we can sort this. I don't care about the money!'

His words were greeted by the roar of the surf and then, closer now, sirens.

'Shit!' Damon slapped the water in frustration, then he turned back to shore, wading hard. She was obviously out already. He found Drogba trotting anxiously back and forth and the pair sprinted for home.

Still pumping at Matt's chest, Thom glanced round at the sea. Why hadn't Karen had made it out before him? Waves broke rhythmically on the beach but there was no sign of her. She'd have come to help, surely?

Matt spasmed beneath him suddenly, his body twisted and he coughed up a jet of foaming sea water. Then he began to gag and retch.

'Yes mate! Yes!' shouted Thom, banging him on the back as he heaved violently.

'Thom, Thom!' Jack ran down the beach towards him. Behind him, Ed and Paul followed with two paramedics.

Jack knelt down next to him as Matt belched and heaved for air.

'Is he OK? I thought you'd both had it!'

'I'm not sure,' said Thom, standing up to let the paramedics take charge. He turned to stare at the water anxiously but there was still no sign of Karen and he began to wade back in.

'Woah! Where are you going?' shouted Jack, rushing after him and putting a hand on his shoulder.

'Karen's still out there, I brought Matt back in and she was behind me but I can't see her anymore,' said Thom desperately. He paddled slowly into the water.

'You can't go in again Thom, you were lucky to make it back!' pleaded Jack. Thom pressed on. The three of them began yelling at him not to go back in. Jack ran in front of him and put a hand on his chest. Ed and Paul threw their arms round him. Thom didn't have the strength to throw them off. The adrenaline had subsided and he was completely exhausted. He stared over Jack's shoulder shivering and called her name weakly.

'They've called the lifeboat out, that'll be it over there,' said Jack. 'They'll find her.'

He indicated a bright beam of light heading swiftly across the water. Behind them the paramedics had already placed an oxygen mask on Matt and secured him to the stretcher. Jack and Paul helped them carry him back to the ambulance and watched it leave. Ed used the torch from his phone to help the small Y-class lifeboat locate them. He strode into the waves to offer a swift explanation of the situation and the boat motored rapidly back out to sea to commence a search. Down the road, a police car pulled up outside Damon's house but the Roid Room stood empty and the Mercedes was gone.

Thom stood there, his arms clenched around him as the boat began a sweep of the waters, hoping desperately that its searchlight would locate her. Shivering violently, he was eventually persuaded to return to the house. There, he peeled off his wet clothes, took a swift hot shower to restore some circulation then stood at the back gate wrapped in a blanket, holding a mug of tea. After a while, he came back in with a shake of the head and they all sat in silence. A helicopter droned overhead, its raking searchlight played across the water making it glitter like acres of hematite.

'Do you think Matt will be OK?' asked Jack eventually.

'I don't know. There could be complications,' said Thom. 'There can be issues… lungs, heart. At least he came to and could tell the paramedics his name.'

'I'm amazed he survived out there for more than a few minutes given his fitness, or lack of it,' said Paul, shaking his head.

'He wouldn't have done if Karen hadn't got to him,' said Thom quietly. 'She saved his life.'

He looked anxiously at his watch. How long since the search began now? Fifteen minutes? Twenty?

'Why do you think he did it?' asked Ed.

'Conan?'

'No. Will.'

'God knows. He always had to be the centre of attention. And he could be a right stirrer, we knew that.' said Jack. 'Maybe he just wanted to sweep all the pieces off the board if he couldn't play anymore.'

'I'm not sure it was malicious. He once advised me to throw everything in the air and see how it came down,' suggested Paul. 'Said he wished he'd done it himself. Maybe he tried it out on us instead. He clearly couldn't have foreseen it unravelling like it did or he would have done things differently, I'm sure.'

Jack nodded. There was no way he would have wanted to tear his friends apart.

'What about all the stuff about Matt and Annie, though?' asked Ed. 'That was shocking. Did he know Matt still had a thing for her?'

'Possibly. I mean he was obviously aware they'd dated for a while before he met her. We all were,' said Paul. 'Was he jealous at the thought of Matt rekindling things with her when he was gone? Possibly. His mind must have been playing horrible tricks on him at the end.'

'Poor Matt. All those years pretending, maintaining face. He must have been in agony. And the guilt, too. His friend is dying, yet he still can't help loving his wife. I should have let him explain himself. Instead I pushed him over the edge,' said Thom bitterly. 'What a mate.'

He put his head in his hands and began to sob. Jack got up, put an arm on his shoulder and gripped it. Thom stood up and put his face into his shoulder. Jack cradled his head while he cried.

'She's dead,' he choked.

No one protested. It had been too long.

The police returned, took statements and left. They all

dozed downstairs in the chairs, keeping each other company. The noise of the helicopter had long since receded. The boat had also gone, its search abandoned. Finally, dawn broke and Thom woke with a start. For a moment it felt like he'd had a nightmare, but the scene around him brought the grim reality straight back like a slap. He felt sadness saturate him.

His neck ached from the angle he'd slept, although he couldn't have been out for more than thirty minutes. He stood up, massaged it and went upstairs for another shower. Then he changed and rang the hospital. Matt was out of intensive care and under observation. He sighed with relief.

He checked in Ed's room. Wind blew through the shattered window, flapping a newspaper on a chest of drawers. Shards of glass lay everywhere and the sharp smell of chemicals hung in the air despite the draught. An ugly burn disfigured the carpet on the far side of the room. The ceiling directly above was scorched red and black.

Karen's suitcase stood near the window. He opened it. There were a handful of photos in the top sleeve. The top one captured her in a wetsuit. She smiled back at him, positive, confident. He felt a lump in his throat. He barely knew her and yet he felt her loss deeply. A tear ran down his cheek and he sat heavily on the edge of the bed. She wanted out of there so badly but her dream had been washed away. She deserved a second life, too.

'I'm sorry Karen, I'm so sorry,' he whispered.

He shut his eyes a moment. A picture of her as a mermaid formed in his mind. She was somewhere far out to sea, cresting the waves, flanked by a pod of dolphins. It was a bit Disney, but at the same time it felt comforting and he resolved to hang on to the image.

'"I have heard the mermaids singing, each to each, I do not think that they sing to me,"' he muttered, standing stiffly.

He looked around for the backpack. No point in letting the authorities have the cash when he could give it to the RNLI. But for some reason he couldn't find it. Maybe one of the others had taken it out when the fire started.

He jogged back down the stairs.

'Good news! Matt's out of intensive care. I'm off to the hospital to keep him company. I'll report back as soon as I know more,' he said excitedly.

'Yes! Brilliant!' Jack's face broke into a wide smile. Paul closed his eyes in a silent prayer of thanks. Ed breathed a loud sigh of relief.

'Maybe we should all go?' suggested Jack.

'I don't think they'll let that many of us in. We're not family, well not as far as they're concerned,' explained Thom.

He opened his arms and the four stepped into a group hug.

'What about his laptop?' asked Paul, looking at the computer suspiciously.

'I'll take it with me, he might want it, I suppose. Can you take the rest of his stuff Ed?' asked Thom. Ed nodded.

'Do you think Will had anything else to say? He hadn't finished, had he?' asked Jack.

'I don't really care if he did,' said Thom, heading for the door.

'Don't suppose any of you have seen Karen's backpack, have you?' he said, pausing in the doorway.

They looked at each other and shook their heads.

'Why?' asked Paul.

'No reason.'

'Delete that bloody video,' said Ed. Thom nodded.

'I feel like we've all been stress tested,' said Jack. He looked worried. 'I don't know what you all think of me anymore.'

'I don't care, you big queer,' said Ed.

Paul's eyes widened, he glanced at Jack.

Ed laughed and planted a big kiss on Jack's cheek.

'Thanks Ed,' said Jack, wiping away the wet patch with the back of his hand.

'No matter how much you think you know someone, you rarely ever do,' reflected Paul, sitting down. 'Everyone has their secret inner world. And they should be allowed to have it. Knowing everything about someone isn't necessarily a good thing.'

'Unless they're a kiddie fiddler,' added Jack, puncturing his philosophising.

'Do you think we'll ever do one of these weekends again?' asked Ed, doubtfully.

'After what just happened? No,' said Thom, shaking his head. 'I couldn't sit around in a swish place by the sea saying things like, "Hope it's more fun than last year!" as if Karen never existed. Poor woman. She was that close. I let her down.'

'No, her crazy brother let her down. He's responsible for what happened,' said Paul. 'Do not blame yourself. You did everything right.'

'It's not the end of us though, is it?' said Ed, looking at them anxiously.

'Course not,' said Thom, zipping up his jacket and heading for the door. 'Friends die, friendship never dies. And it's a bit late to find replacement mates now anyway.'

The door slammed behind him.

Epilogue

I Can't Give Everything Away

Matt lay on the couch with the MacBook on his lap as it groaned into life. He'd not opened it since the tumultuous final night of the Boys' Weekend six weeks ago. Time had drifted past in a haze since his release from hospital.

A consultant had informed him he had come close to death from complications, something loosely referred to as secondary drowning, a thing he didn't even know was possible. You could drown in your own bed, who knew that? All those dangers lurking just beneath the surface.

Thom had imparted the awful news about Karen the day after he regained consciousness. He could recall little of what had happened after he'd been carried out to sea by the rip. Once he realised he didn't have the ability to reach shore he had expected to drown and, after the initial stab of fear, he had discovered he didn't care. He had a vague image of her swimming to him and gathering him in her arms but everything that happened subsequently was a blank.

He had survived, but his rescuer had not. He still couldn't process that. Those sort of things didn't happen to people you knew or people you barely knew. It was a horrible tragedy and it was one more example of life's random cruelty as far as he was concerned. There was no order to anything, you were just flotsam and jetsam tossed around in a violent sea.

He would have gladly switched places with Karen at the time but had come to the conclusion that it would be a betrayal to continue to think like that. She had shown no concern for her own life when she swam out to save him and for that reason he owed it to her to show some for his.

To that end, he had resolved to sort himself out. He had quit drinking and smoking and it had proved easier than expected. He no longer felt the urge to anaesthetise himself all the time. He had a different outlook on life. He was going to do whatever it took to enrich it from now on. He would still take photographs but photographs that mattered. He had reached out to the RNLI with his story and a proposal themed around the work of its volunteers, reuniting them with people they had rescued.

Karen's body had never been found, presumably carried out to sea and lost among the currents. Damon was still at large, apparently. The Mercedes had been found abandoned in a multi-storey car park in Dover.

As for the others, Ed was attempting to rebuild his business. Another buyer had come forward at the last minute thanks to the efforts of his wife while he was away and they had been able to retain a significant stake in the company. All the money outstanding to Annie had been repaid, although it transpired she was unaware it had ever been loaned in the first place because there was no mention of it in the will. Meanwhile, Jack had moved in with his new partner and Paul was preparing to rent out his home so he could leave in the next couple of months.

Last week Thom had rung Matt excitedly. He had just received a call from his ex in which she had explained that his son had had a serious falling out with his stepdad and it was causing a lot of friction in their relationship. The boy was coming to stay with him for the summer.

The previous weekend Matt had caught an early train to Rye from where he had taken a cab to Winchelsea. Carrying his camera over one shoulder he walked down the opposite bank of the River Rother to the one the Boys had taken on their hike.

The weather was unpredictable, alternating between dazzling sunshine and fierce showers. Few people were out risking the elements that morning. He passed the red-roofed hut and crunched across the shingle taking photos of the stark coastal landscape. A gnarled piece of tree root resembling an insect protruded from the damp sand where the tide had retreated. He crouched down and shot it from several angles, checking the exposure in his viewfinder.

He walked on to the weathered Mary Stanford Lifeboat House, the only building visible along the shore for miles. There, he read a plaque with a short graphic story, which told the tale of the 1928 disaster from the perspective of the wife of a lost crewman. It depicted how the Mary Stanford had been launched to save a stricken vessel but another lifeboat had reached it first. The station had fired recall flares but they had gone unseen in the appalling conditions and the lifeboat had capsized in heavy seas off Camber. The seventeen men who had gone to save a crew in distress with no thought for themselves had all been lost.

The story ended with two simple but poignant words from the widow: "Goodbye dear". Suddenly overwhelmed, Matt slumped down and began to sob uncontrollably. He lay back and stared up at the sky, feeling guilt consume him. A lone seagull wheeled overhead, its cry heartrending.

By the time he'd recomposed himself the weather had changed. A squall was headed towards him from the direction of Hastings. The sky cycled swiftly through the greyscale as it bore down on him until it was almost dark. He stood there working the shutter until the rain came down in silver sheets, then he sprinted to an old pillbox with the camera under his jacket and waited there, dripping in silence until it passed. Back home, when he downloaded the images, it was clear they were the best pictures he'd taken in years.

Annie rang the hospital the day after he had regained consciousness and had come to see him the weekend following his release. They sat drinking tea in his resolutely bachelor living room. A shelf to one side held a sound-system crowned by an expensive Linn turntable. Beneath it lay racks of alphabetically-arranged vinyl. The sleeve for Ólafur Arnalds' *...And They Have Escaped the Weight of Darkness*, one of the records he'd bought in Rye, lay on the turntable lid. He'd played it once and found it unbearably sad.

Annie was looking rather careworn, he thought, as soon as he opened the door to her. But then he was looking none too chipper himself, he reflected.

The good news was that Steven had accepted his invitation to come to the forthcoming England match at Wembley. However, the conversation had flowed less easily as Annie attempted to piece together the events that led to Matt floating naked in the English Channel supported by the sister of a volatile local steroid dealer while he embarked upon a destructive rampage. Matt explained how Thom had met her and how they had become entangled with Damon who needed little provocation. He omitted to mention the confrontational questions posed by her late husband, which catalysed the night's catastrophic events.

'That poor girl,' she said, shaking her head sadly. 'What a terrible thing to have happened to her. Her own brother, too.'

'I know. Life's not fair, is it?' He nodded. 'All she wanted to do was move on and start again. I understand that feeling.'

He glanced at her and then away. He wanted to say more,

to explain everything. In the new-found spirit of carpe diem he wanted to declare his love for her right there and then, but still he didn't dare. Even now he couldn't bear the idea that it might burn the only bridge between them. It was his final remaining hope of inner peace.

She pulled a strand of hair from between her lips.

'Matt, I can't have anything happen to you. I couldn't bear it, not after everything else,' she said, softly. 'Please be more careful.'

'Trust me, no more midnight swims,' he joked weakly.

'And the rest. Burning the candle at both ends. We're not kids any more. I need you around.'

'I'm a reformed character. Promise,' he held up a hand, as if taking the pledge.

They stood and hugged. He held on as long as possible then she kissed him quickly on the lips and hurried off to pick up Steven from training.

Another lost opportunity. How many was he going to let slip by? And yet he sensed it was still too soon. If it felt wrong, it was wrong.

The laptop was up and running now. Thom had told him he'd deleted the quiz file but Matt opened the wastebasket and there it was. He extracted it, put it on the desktop and stared at it for a while, wondering what he was doing. But he had to hear what Will was going to say. He took a deep breath, clicked on the file and felt the tension rise as he waited for it to open. Through the living room window, the setting sun was beginning to turn the sky amber.

Will's face materialised once more, freed from the zeroes and ones. There he was, back in his study holding cue cards, as if in limbo. Matt dragged the cursor and sped forward until he was at the place when Will had sent the evening into meltdown.

'Matt!' announced Will abruptly, staring hard out of the screen.

'Wrong,' said Matt.

There was a pause, then Will tossed the cue cards to one side.

'I knew you stayed that night because I heard you go up the stairs after your visit and you didn't come back down. Neither of my children were home that night so I was absolutely sure. I assumed you'd gone up to say goodbye but when you didn't come back down I began to wonder. I could hear voices. Floorboards creaked. After an hour I was concerned and, as the night went on, it was all I could think of. My best mate and my wife. Could he? Could she? Surely not. But it started to eat away at me. I was going to come up the stairs several times but I didn't have the energy and I was frightened of what I might discover. I was still awake when I heard you leave early the following morning.'

'Sorry Will, I just didn't think,' Matt whispered to the screen.

'I know you've always held a candle for her,' continued Will. 'Probably never got over her, in truth. She never spoke about your relationship but I knew it was a big thing in her life. But she was mine, I won her fair and square. And now I've lost her. So maybe you now have a second chance. Not often you get that in life, Matt.

'I've given this a lot of thought. I won't ever know what went on that night so I'm throwing down a challenge. Given everything I just said, I don't think you'd do that. Would you? Just tell me. Them.'

'Course bloody not, you complete idiot!' shouted Matt, leaning into the screen.

'God knows, I've played this through in my head again and again but you're my mate and she's my mate. She needs someone. Deserves someone. I can't expect her to remain a widow for the rest of her life like my mum. If my kids are going to have another father I'd rather it was you than anyone else. You might be a massive lush but at least you have the best record collection of anyone I know. You're also a lovely bloke. Even if you do support Arsenal.'

Tears were rolling down Will's cheek now. They began to roll down Matt's, too. He wiped them away but they kept coming.

'Best of luck, Matt. I hope you have a second life. And goodbye to you, my oldest, bestest, most trusted friends.'

Will fired off a salute at the camera, then the screen went blank.

About the Author

Mike Pattenden is a freelance journalist with thirty years' experience in newspapers and magazines. A former music writer, he is also author of *Last Orders At The Liars' Bar*, the official biography of Paul Heaton and The Beautiful South. He is married with two grown-up children and lives in Hertfordshire.